Praise for
NINA KIRIKI HOFFMAN

"A Nina Hoffman story is, by definition,
a thing of high quality and mesmeric appeal."
—**Roger Zelazny**

"Nina Kiriki Hoffman is a magician. Her words create worlds no
one has seen before. Her characters are charming, her prose lyrical.
She is one of the fantasy field's greatest talents."
—**Kristine Kathryn Rusch**

"Most writers show and tell. Nina Hoffman sings."
—**Algis Budrys**

"There is absolutely no other voice
in contemporary fantasy like Hoffman's."
—**Ed Bryant**

"Nina Kiriki Hoffman is enormously talented."
—**Kate Wilhelm**

"Is Nina Hoffman a genius? Oh, yes. Yes, indeed."
—*The Magazine of Fantasy & Science Fiction*

"[Nina Kiriki Hoffman's] stories are like fire—some are
sparks that shoot in the night and catch you sideways when
you're not looking, others glow like red hot coals that
make you all toasty on one side and sensitive
to the cold around you."
—*Rave Reviews*

A RED HEART OF MEMORIES

Nina Kiriki Hoffman

ACE BOOKS, NEW YORK

This is a work of fiction. Names, characters, places, and incidents are either the product of the author's imagination or are used fictitiously, and any resemblance to actual persons, living or dead, business establishments, events, or locales is entirely coincidental.

A RED HEART OF MEMORIES

An Ace Book / published by arrangement with the author

Ace hardcover edition / October 1999
Ace trade paperback edition / December 2000

The Penguin Putnam Inc. World Wide Web site address is
http://www.penguinputnam.com

Check out the ACE Science Fiction & Fantasy newsletter and much more at Club PPI!

ISBN: 0-441-00768-6

ACE®
Ace Books are published by
The Berkley Publishing Group, a division of Penguin Putnam Inc.,
375 Hudson Street, New York, New York 10014.
ACE and the "A" design are trademarks belonging to Penguin Putnam Inc.

10 9 8 7 6 5 4 3 2

Dedication

. . . . .

This book is for:
Jenny, and Nancy E.,
M. J. Engh, owlwoman,
and the Poetry Lunch crowd:
Holly Arrow, Martha Bayless,
Bruce Holland Rogers,
Ray Vukcevich, and Leslie What
and for Lois Tilton, who asked for more about Matt

Chapter One

· · · · ·

MATT Black met the moss man on Christmas Eve.

She was sitting on a stone bench in a pioneer cemetery, with a wall of ivy-covered brick at her back and a brown paper bag full of past-their-expiration-date plastic-wrapped sandwiches beside her. The short cool daylight faded. Mist bred in the low spots and spread. The damp in the air smelled like winter, dead leaves, iced water, chill and no comfort. Matt was glad of her thick olive-drab army jacket.

She liked the look of the old mossy gravestones in the brushy grass, some tilted and some broken, but all mute against the wet shrubs and vanishing distance. The people who had come here to commune with the dead had all died, too; no fresh dreams troubled the stillness. This was as close to nature as she liked to get, a tamed wilderness only a short walk away from a town where she could go to find warmth and comfort after she had had her supper. Here, there were still plenty of human-made things she could talk with if she wanted conversation, but she could see a forest too, gauzed in mist and twilight.

She unwrapped one of the sandwiches and sniffed it. Roast beef and yellow cheese. It smelled fine. She took a sample bite, waited to see if her stomach would tell her anything, and then ate the rest of the sandwich. The bread was dry and the edges of the cheese hard, but it was better than a lot of other things she had eaten.

Her stomach thanked her. She opened another sandwich, ham and Swiss, tested it, and ate it.

She was sitting and feeling her own comfort when she noticed there was some dreaming going on to her left, a quiet swirl of leafy images emerging from the layers-thick ivy on the wall. She wondered if she were seeing the dream of a plant. She had never seen a plant dream before, though she could see what people dreamed, and what things shaped by people dreamed. This seemed like a strange time to start understanding plants.

She turned to get a better look at the dream, and it changed. The leaves wove together into green skin, the skin smoothed and formed a man, and then a man all green stepped away from the wall, shaking his head slowly.

Some texture in the sound and smell of him told her he was no dream at all.

Matt grabbed the loose plastic wrap on the bench beside her and asked it if it would cover the man's face if she threw it. It said yes. If he came at her . . . she touched the bench she was sitting on. It was too old and sleepy to mobilize. She put her feet on the ground and tensed to run.

The man blinked. His face looked like a mannequin's, no real expression, no movement of the tiny muscles, a polished and unreal perfection to the features. He turned and stared at her.

"Who are you?" she asked after the silence had stretched.

"Edmund," he said.

"What do you want?"

"Nothing," he said.

"Nothing? Why'd you move if you don't want anything? You could of just stayed in the wall." She had never met anybody who wanted nothing.

"It was time to move," he said. Something was happening to his skin in the waning light; the green faded, left tan behind. His clothes and curly hair stayed green. She hadn't noticed the clothes until the rest of him changed. T-shirt, pants—green, mossy even; tan arms and face, hands and feet. It was freezing, but he didn't seem to feel the cold.

"Want a sandwich?" she said.

He stretched and yawned. He came closer. She had thought his expression was wooden, but now she saw it was more like ice, frozen . . . though thaw was coming. He blinked. He finally smiled. It changed her image of him completely: he looked friendly and almost goofy.

Still gripping the plastic wrap just in case, she scooted over, leaving room on the bench. He sat down.

She peered into the brown paper bag. "Looks like I got a tuna and a ham-and-cheese left. The tuna might be bad. Fish goes bad faster than cured meat."

"I'll try the ham-and-cheese," he said. "Thanks."

She gave him the sandwich. He struggled with the plastic wrap. His fingers didn't bend right yet. She grabbed the sandwich and unwrapped it for him. "How long you been part of a wall, anyway?"

"I don't know," he said. "I wonder if my car will run." He bit the sandwich and chewed, abstracted, as though he were listening to his mouth. "Hmm."

"It's Christmas Eve," Matt said when he had finished the sandwich and sat watching her, smiling faintly.

"Huh," he said. "Been a wall a couple months then, I guess."

She opened dream-eyes and peeked at his mental landscape. A forest clearing, with a single tree rising from the center, sunlight stroking one side of its trunk. Wind blew and the tree leaned into it as though its bark were skin, its core supple. The leaves wavered and flickered, winking diamonds of light.

Not threatening, but not clear, either. "What were you doing in the wall?"

"Standing still."

"How come?"

"That's how the spirit moved me."

"Huh?"

He shrugged. "I just wander around until something tells me to act. I happened to stop here a while back, and the wall spoke to me."

Matt felt a stir inside. She traveled far and often and had been talking with human-made things all over the country for years. She'd never met anyone else who talked with them. "What did it say?"

" 'Come here.' "

She glanced back at the wall under its cloak of ivy. —Did you say "come here" to this guy?— she asked it.

—Yes,— said the wall.

—Why?—

—I wanted him.—

Nothing ever seemed to want Matt, though lots of things enjoyed meeting her, and most of them were nice to her. —Why?—

—He's a certain kind of brick. He's hot. He makes everything fit better.—

Matt looked at Edmund. His eyebrows rose.

"You're a brick?" she said.

"A brick," he repeated, with a question in it.

"Wall says you're a brick. A hot brick."

"What?" He glanced at the wall. He reached out and placed his palm flat against it.

Seemed like he hadn't heard her conversation, then. Matt felt better. She had been talking to everything for a long time without other human beings hearing her. She didn't want to be overheard.

Edmund's arm stained brick red.

—What's he doing?— Matt asked the wall.

—Connecting,— the wall said. —Are you talking to me?— Its voice had changed slightly.

—Am I?— Matt looked at Edmund. His mouth opened slightly, and his eyebrows stayed up.

—Yes,— said the wall. "Yes," said Edmund.

Matt swallowed. —This is so strange.—

—Yes.—

Slowly he pulled his hand away from the wall. His skin faded to tan again. He held his hand out to Matt. She stared at it without touching it.

"What do you want?" he asked her. "What do you need?"

"Me? I don't need anything," she said.

"I'm here for you."

"What?"

He dropped his hand to his thigh. "I follow as the spirit leads me," he said. "It led me to you. Let me know when you figure out what you want."

"I take care of myself," she said.

"Yes," he said.

"I don't need anything else."

"All right."

"What do you want?" she asked him again.

He smiled wide. "Nothing," he said again. "Guess that makes us a match."

"I don't turn into a brick," said Matt, unnerved. She hadn't realized until this moment how much she valued being different and special, even if no one else knew just how special. She knew, and that had been enough. She didn't want this man to be anything like her.

He said, "Would you like to be a brick? I like it. It's nice being part of something so solid."

"No." Matt shook her head. "No, no."

"Okay," he said. He pulled his legs up, bent knees against his chest, and gripped his feet.

She watched him for a while. His feet and hands started to gray to match the stone bench, and then the dark grew too heavy for her to make out details.

"Uh," she said. "I'm going back to town now. Nice to meet you."

"I'll come with you."

"I'd rather you didn't."

"Oh. All right. Thanks for the sandwich."

"You're welcome." She stood and walked away, chasing mist whenever she could.

She found a newspaper in a phone booth and scanned the page of church services, picked an early one. She liked churches on Christmas Eve, the pageantry, the carols, the candles and greenery, the warmth, the smells of hot wax and pine and incense and perfume and even mothballs from some of the fancy clothes people wore. She liked the idea that a kid born in a cave could be important.

She settled in a back pew and watched everything with interest. Children thought about presents, those opened and those still waiting, full of promises. Some of the grown-ups did too. Some people were thinking about the service, and some were thinking about going to sleep. Some were remembering their dinners. Some were worried because they hadn't finished wrapping things or they hadn't found the right presents, and others were happy because they had done what they could.

A woman in front of Matt kept thinking about washing a mountain of dishes. She would sigh, and start the task in her mind again, go through it dish by dish, each spoon and fork and knife; and sigh, and start again.

Matt tuned her out and focused on a child who was watching the candles and listening to the singing and thinking about the words of the songs and making the flames go in and out of focus, flames, flat disks of light, flames.

A child in another place looked at every scrap of red clothing, hoping to glimpse Santa Claus.

A man cradled a sleeping child. When he looked down at her he saw his arms full of golden light.

Another child looked at the priest and saw angels behind him. Matt wondered if the angels were really there. They had beautiful smiles and kind eyes.

The church was full. It lived and breathed, a big organism full of different cells and tissues, everything cooperating.

Matt kept an eye out for the moss man. What did he want from her? He wasn't a normal human. She couldn't guess which way he'd jump.

She didn't see him again until she left the church. She was walking through a quiet neighborhood talking to houses she passed, asking if any of them would like some extra company tonight, and listening to their stories about the festivities they had hosted, the lighted trees they held inside, the way their humans had dressed them in jewelry of lights, when an old rust-blotched brown Volvo station wagon pulled up beside her, its engine surprisingly quiet considering its exterior, and Edmund leaned along the seat and said out the rolled-down passenger-side window, "Want a ride?"

"What?" she said.

"Want a ride?"

"No," she said. She wondered if she should run.

He pulled the car over to the curb and turned off the engine. "Want company?" he said, and got out. He had on hiking boots and a dark jacket now.

—What's with this guy?— she asked the car.

—He won't hurt you,— the car said. Its voice was gentle and warm and somehow feminine.

—Do you know what hurts?—

—Yes,— said the car. —At least I know some of the things that hurt people. Edmund won't hurt you.—

"What do you want?" Matt asked Edmund for the third time.

He rounded the front of the car and stood near her. "I want to walk around with you. I want to take your hand. I want to make sure you're warm enough tonight, and safe."

"Why?"

"Because that's where spirit is leading me."

She reached out her gloved hand and he took it, his own warm through the leather of her glove, his grip firm without threatening. "Thank you," he said.

"I don't get it," she muttered.

"That's okay." He moved to stand beside her, still holding her hand, and said, "Would you like to walk?"

"All right."

They walked without speaking for a while. Matt watched the way their breaths misted in front of them, and the way the mist globed the orange streetlights, as though fires floated on air, or small clumsy stars dipped low. He was tall beside her, his hand warm in hers, his footsteps almost silent. It took a while for her defenses to gentle down, and then she realized that it felt good to walk with another person. She couldn't remember the last time she had done it like this—if ever.

"Sometimes I feel like I might just float away," he said presently. "I have a sister. I visit her once in a while. It keeps my feet on the ground."

"I saw my sister last spring." Matt had talked to her sister last Christmas for the first time in years. In the spring Matt had hitchhiked across the top of the country from Ohio to Seattle, catching rides sometimes from people and sometimes from friendly trucks, who opened their back doors to her at truckstops and let her out at other truckstops when they were about to turn away from her route.

Seeing Pam had been strange and difficult. Matt and her sister had started out from the same place and gone such different directions that they had almost no common ground left. Pam and her husband had offered Matt a room to stay in, and help finding a job. Matt had fixed a broken dishwasher and repaired a reluctant vacuum cleaner and a tired clothes dryer, and then she had hugged Pam and left.

"Mostly I just wander from one place to the next," said Edmund, "waiting to be needed for something, then trying to figure out what it is."

Matt wandered too, always looking at things. Sometimes she helped people, but she didn't go around looking for people to help. "What about what you want?"

"I don't know," he said. They walked farther. "I used to do what I wanted, and then one time I did what I wanted and it was the wrong thing. Scared me. I wasn't the person I wanted to be. So I decided to be the opposite."

"And things want you?"

He nodded. "Sometimes it's nothing urgent. The cemetery wall had been falling to pieces for ages, and it could have gone on disintegrating without disturbing the integrity of the local space-time continuum." She looked up at him. He smiled. "I know, I can't believe I talk like that either. Especially when I'm not used to talking at all. The wall wanted to be pulled back together. I wasn't busy, so I melted in and helped the wall collect itself and strengthen its bonds with its pieces. Then just as I finished, there you were."

"What makes you think I'm your next project?"

"That's the way spirit works. I finish one task and then comes another."

"So what are you supposed to do about me?"

He shook his head and smiled. "Maybe nothing. I know you don't need me or anybody."

She stopped in the darkness between streetlights and stared across the street at a house draped with colored blinking lights, realizing that the lights blurred because her eyes had heated with tears. Something inside her tremored, small shakes at first, which worked their way outward to her edges and turned into big shakes.

"What is it?" he murmured.

"I—" She gripped his hand harder.

He stood beside her as she shook, and then he stepped closer and slid his arms around her. She held onto him, pressed her face into his chest, smelled his strange wood-smoke and spring skies scent, and felt the choke of sobs welling up in her throat. She fought them back down, wanting not to cry in front of this stranger or against this stranger or anywhere near this stranger. She held it all in. She had not cried in a thousand years. Especially not where anyone else could hear.

He stroked her back, a gentle rub up and down of his hand over her shoulder blade. He was warm and smelled like wool and fire.

—What? What are you doing to me?— she cried without voice.

—Just waiting,— he said.

—Stop pushing!— she screamed.

He stood quiet; his arms embraced her without force. She knew she could free herself with a step backward. He did not move except for the slow exhalations and inhalations she could feel and hear beneath her cheek and ear, and the faint bumping of his heart.

—Just waiting,— he said.

Something was pushing. Something inside her. It pushed up from her chest into her throat. It hurt! Her head felt fever-hot. Then a sob broke out of her, and another, and then they were coming out, wave after wave, and the hot heavy pushing thing eased. She shook and cried, loud gulping embarrassing sobs, her nose running, her throat bobbing open and shut, and he stood quiet and just held her.

Once she stopped trying to stop herself from crying, she felt much better; she just let the sobs and tears come out however they seemed to want to. Inside her crying, she lost track of everything else, another luxury she hadn't had in all these recent years of hyperawareness of everything around her. She worried because she didn't know how to stop crying, but somehow she let that worry rise and fade like the others.

When at last the sobs died away and all her impulse to cry was gone, she couldn't understand where she was. She was warm straight through, and lying on something hard but not flat, more bumpy and falling away at the sides. She felt as limp as an overcooked noodle. She lifted her head. There wasn't much light, but she could make out a face below her, peaceful, sleeping, smooth as a statue's face. Arms around her. A blanket over her? She wasn't sure about that part.

She listened to their breathing and realized they were some-place small.

Her arms were down at her sides. She sneaked them up until she could push away from what she was lying on. The arms around her fell away. She looked down into the face, and realized it was that guy, Edmund, realized that yes, she was lying on him, on top of a guy, something she hadn't done on purpose since the zoned years. His eyes opened. He looked at her, his face serene.

"You okay?" he asked.

She rubbed her nose on her sleeve. "I don't know. What happened? Where are we?" She looked around. They were in a small, enclosed space, but she could see windows now. Car windows, all steamed over.

"We're in my car. I have a futon in the back where I sleep sometimes. It seemed like a better place for crying than the middle of the sidewalk on a freezing night."

"Let me out." She scrambled off him and crawled over to one of the doors, frantically searching for a handle, finding one, pressing, pulling, twisting. Trapped. Everything in her screamed panic.

He was beside her. He edged his hand under hers and opened the door, and she fell out into the street. She jumped up and ran.

A block. She turned a corner. She scanned for a hiding place, saw a low fence and a dense tree, jumped the fence, hid inside the shadow the tree's branches cast. She slowed her breath and tried to catch up to herself.

Nothing followed her.

Usually she found a refuge for the night in something human-built that welcomed her, someplace warm, but tonight she curled up on the cool, damp ground in the treeshadow, stilled her mind, and searched for sleep.

She lay hugging her knees to her chest for a long while, her knit cap pulled down over her ears. Her neck was cold, and her ear, with only a layer of cloth to protect it from the earth, was freezing. Cold air inched up her pantlegs past her thick socks. Usually she could shut those sensations off one by one and feel comfortable and safe, and then she could sleep.

Tonight she felt strange. Her head felt floaty. Lightness was all through her, as though she had taken an unfamiliar drug. The cold, which she knew from experience wasn't enough to kill her, kept telling her it was there. She put her gloved hands up around her neck. The smooth outsides of her gloves were cold against her bare skin, and woke her more than cold air had.

She sighed and sat up. She did her best to take good care of herself. She loved her life, even though some of it was difficult. She wanted to be warm.

She remembered how warm she had been inside Edmund's car, and how strange that warmth had felt. His arms around her, not tight, but enough to let her know she was being held. She thought of being his project and didn't like that at all. Who was his spirit to decide that he should work on her? She knew that everything had spirit—she talked to the spirit in many things—but she had never felt spirit was ordering her around, making her decisions for her. Maybe Edmund was deluded. Maybe his spirit only applied to him.

Even if he was deluded, he had been nice to her.

She stretched and edged out from under the sheltering branches. She crossed the lawn, hopped the fence, and knelt on the sidewalk. Then she pulled off her glove and touched the cold cement. —Edmund?— she asked it. —Moss man?—

—No,— said the sidewalk.

—Do you know the one I'm talking about? Do you know where he is?—

—I'll ask.—

The thread of question rippled out around her. She sat down, waiting while cold seeped through the seat of her jeans. She had asked long-distance questions before, and gotten answers. She wasn't sure how the sidewalk would recognize Edmund when it found him, though.

The mist made the night seem quiet, almost dead. Porch lights and Christmas lights and streetlights blurred and hazed only a short way from her. She reached out and touched the fence beside her to make sure it was still there.

She didn't even hear his steps, but she saw him come out of the mist. He knelt in front of her and smiled gently. "Hi."

She opened her arms and he edged forward and scooped her up, then rose to his feet. Carrying her, he walked for a while. She clung to him, for a moment trying to remember the last time she had been carried, had reached for the one carrying her, had leaned against his warmth and felt so safe and strange. Her mind blanked.

He stopped and loosed one of his arms to reach for the backdoor of his car. It opened without sound. He leaned forward and set her on the mattress. It was warm. The inside of his car smelled like mountain pine and desert sagebrush. She crawled into the shadowy hollow and he came in after her, pulling the door shut behind him.

She crept up toward the front of the car and leaned against

the back of the passenger seat, tucked hat and gloves into her pockets, and waited for the warmth to thaw her edges.

"Thirsty?" he asked after a little while.

"Guess I am."

He opened what looked like a dark box and pulled out an oblong something that gurgled, then edged closer to her and held it out.

"What is it?"

"Water."

She reached out. Her hand touched his. "You're so warm," she whispered. "How do you stay so warm?"

"Spirit," he said. He shifted the bottle until she got a grip on it. It was plastic and cool.

She screwed the cap off and sipped cool fresh water. "Thanks."

"You're welcome. I'm glad you called."

"Why?" She drank more water, then capped the bottle and handed it back to him.

"I wanted to see you again."

"Why?"

"I don't know." He sounded frustrated. "I don't know. I need—I don't know what it is, but I need something."

"You need something from me? I thought spirit gave you everything."

"I thought it did too, until you left." He was quiet for a while. "There's an ache inside me now that wasn't there before."

"Oh, no. No." She remembered the void that opened within her sometimes when she left behind people she had liked. Often they invited her to stay. They showed her how she could live and be with them. She found comfort and friendship and warmth and a future, soil ripe for roots. The instant she thought of staying anyplace longer than four or five weeks, though, panic burned through her. The bottoms of her feet itched until she moved on. Distant roads called and carried her away.

Once the miles were behind her, she remembered how nice the places and people had been. She yearned for them. She mourned lost moments: orange marmalade on English muffins on someone's back porch on a summer morning; an old man reciting Robert Service poetry beside a crackling fire late one winter night; rubbing shoulders with a pack of wild dirty kids as they all hid in a hayloft together and watched confused grown-ups running below; sitting alone on grass and watching people's dreams during a concert of classical music in a park; stadium fireworks with an older couple one Fourth of July. Losing them hurt. But she never went back.

"You say no, but the ache is still there," Edmund murmured.

"I'm sorry." She reached for his hand. Held it. His fingers were warm, and gripped hers back.

"You feel it."

"Yeah," she whispered. "But I don't know what to do about it."

He slid closer to her, let go of her hand and put his arm around her shoulders. Feeling strange, she leaned against his chest. She pushed her hand down between the futon and the side of the car. —What does he want? What does he need?— she asked the car, since Edmund had never given her a straight answer.

—He needs four flat tires and no spare,— the car said.

"What!" A laugh startled out of her.

"What?" Edmund asked.

"Car says you need four flats and no spare."

He didn't say anything for a little while. Finally, he said, "Maybe I do. Do you ever feel like that's what you need?"

She shook her head. "No. No. I'd go crazy if I was stuck in one place."

"Are you sure?"

Yes. "No."

"I don't know," he said. "Maybe it's time I stopped following spirit around. Spirit's all over the place anyway. Maybe I'll stay here for a while."

"Here? A little old town in the middle of nowhere?"

"Why'd you come here if you thought that?"

"Because there's always something new and interesting everywhere I go."

"Yes," he said. "Here there's a wildlife preserve that needs some preserving. I saw it this evening after we split up. Earth that needs revitalizing, water that wants unpoisoning, plants that need encouragement, animals that need better cover and more things to eat. I could work on that." He paused, then said, "You could help me."

"I don't do stuff like that." There was nothing she could talk to in a landscape like that, except maybe Edmund. She got along fine with appliances and machines; plants and animals were total mysteries.

"What do *you* want to do?"

"Right now, or tomorrow?"

"Right now."

"Go to sleep, I guess."

He laughed; she could feel it and hear it. "Merry Christmas," he said. He gripped her shoulders gently and edged her over, then eased her down onto the mattress so she was lying on her back, and she let him do it. He leaned and reached for something toward the back of the car, pulled it up over them—it was a quilt—and lay down beside her.

"Merry Christmas," she whispered.

During the zoned years she had awakened next to strange men as often as not, her head full of hangover, her body marked with bruises she couldn't remember how she had gotten, her psyche battered with scratches and aches that she would drink away before the next night fell. That was before things talked to her. Back then, even when people talked to her she mostly didn't care or understand what they were talking about. The important thing was to get as close to drowning as she could, because that was where oblivion lay. Everything else hurt too much.

This was the first time in the unzoned years that she opened her eyes from sleep to morning light and looked into a man's face so near hers. His eyes were closed. His breathing was slow and deep and smelled like mint.

It was also the first time she had gotten a really good look at his face. He looked . . . beautiful.

Pretty much everything looked beautiful if you studied it long enough, but he looked beautiful at first glance: clear tanned skin over clean planes of cheek and jawbone, straight narrow nose, heavy domed eyelids fringed with dark lashes, neat dark arched brows, a high clean forehead, brown curls touched with gold. His mouth smiled in his sleep.

One eye opened, the other squinting shut. His eye was green. "Hi."

"Hi," she said, and looked away. He was warm and near, but not touching.

"Did you dream?"

"I don't remember. Did you?"

"Yeah. I dreamed about when I was a kid."

"A different life," said Matt. Her mother had taken her shopping for dresses for the junior prom. "Try this one, Matilda." Matt had tried a lot of them, and every one produced a stranger in the mirror, a young woman with wavy waist-length brown hair and shaved legs and armpits, and sparkles down her front. She had looked at herself and wondered what her future would be. Would there be a prince? Would there be a glamorous job? College? Parties? Adventures?

Never in a million years had she imagined this future.

"Yes. How did you know?" Edmund sat up and stretched, his hands flattening against the roof of the car. Matt sat up, too, and turned to sit cross-legged, facing him. He said, "Before this happened to me and I had to figure out what to do about it, I had these friends. We did stuff every afternoon after school, dumb stuff like going over to someone's house and watching cartoons and eating sugar cereal straight out of the box, or riding our bikes fast down hills, just for the rush of wondering whether we'd be able to brake before hitting something at the bottom. We spent whole afternoons gluing little model airplane parts into planes. I wonder who my friends turned into. I haven't thought of them in a long time."

"You probably wouldn't know them now."

He smiled. "I think I'd know them. We were really good friends."

"Would they know you?" Matt remembered knocking on her

sister's door in Seattle, having a man answer. His face had shuttered over right away. Matt had understood. It had been three states since she had been to a laundromat, but only a few miles from the barber where she had gotten her head shaved; her last ride had been in the back of an onion truck. She had a black plastic garbage bag containing her belongings over her shoulder. Her army jacket was a map of her encounters with various kinds of dirt and grease. There were holes in her shoes.

"What is it?" the man had said in an almost kind voice.

"Is Pam home?"

"Just a minute." He closed the door. It had opened a few minutes later to reveal a heavy, long-haired woman who wore blue-rimmed glasses, and a long green dress that made her look like a queen.

"Pam?" Matt had said.

"Mattie? Is that you? Oh, Mattie!" Her sister swept her up into an embrace . . . just the way Edmund had picked her up last night. Warmth, comfort, and safety. With Pammy it had only lasted a little while. There had been too many questions afterward.

"I don't know if they'd know me," said Edmund. His smile widened. "Might be fun to find out."

"What about your preserve?"

"Maybe it's time to take a break from spirit work." A moment after he said that, his eyes widened, and he looked around at his car, at her, at the ceiling, as if waiting for a sign or a blow. Nothing happened.

"It would be hard to stop being a priest and then start again," Matt said. "Wouldn't it?"

"I don't want to stop." He sat still for a moment, staring

beyond her shoulder, a worry dent between his brows. "I would try to stay in that state where I'm sensitive to signs of what needs or wants doing. But I would pick my path for a change, instead of drifting. I would ask questions because I want to know the answers, instead of to find out what I should do next. Is that all right?" He looked at the roof, at the steamed-over and frosted windows, toward the front of the car—Matt glanced forward too, and saw that the dashboard of the car was covered with dried leaves, curved driftwood, feathers, moss, acorns and seed pods, seashells, eggshells from wild birds, a sand dollar, a twisted silver gum wrapper, a religious medal, small rocks, some smooth and some sharp-edged, the shed skin of a snake . . .

The shed skin of a snake rose into the air.

Matt hugged herself. People had accused her of doing magic before, because when she talked to inanimate objects, they could animate themselves. She didn't consider that magic: it was a door's choice whether to unlock itself, a spoon's choice whether to stir itself in a cup of coffee. All Matt did was let things know they had those choices.

But this snakeskin wasn't moving itself. Something else moved it, something Matt didn't understand or recognize.

The skin drifted over the front seats and came to wind itself around Edmund's wrist, clinging for a moment before dropping off.

"Thanks," he said, picking up the skin and pressing it against his cheek.

"That's a yes?" asked Matt.

He smiled. "Change and growth. Merry Christmas."

"So you're going to go find your friends?"

"Yeah."

What if he found them and they didn't recognize or remember him? What if he found them and they didn't like him? What if he had changed so much they were scared of him? When she looked at him and thought of him stepping out of the wall of ivy, it was hard to connect him with a boy who watched cartoons and ate sugar cereal. What if he and his friends had no places where their edges met anymore? What if he were heading for disappointment, all on a bright winter's morning?

He was a grown man and a magician or a priest or something. He'd been on his own for years, the same way she had. He could take care of himself.

She thought of how the crying had pushed up out of her last night, a lost river from somewhere inside, dammed for who knew how long, and how Edmund had waited by the waterfall, not asking questions or making demands or talking or judging or anything.

What if he had a river like that inside him? Had he ever had someone to stand by while he let it out? Maybe his spirit took care of things like that, but maybe not. A spirit that sent you a snakeskin wasn't the same as somebody's arms around you when you were cold and sad.

"Can I come?" she said.

His smile widened. "That would be great."

That would be crazy. She'd never asked a question like that before. What did she think, she could help him?

Maybe she could.

Chapter Two

· · · · ·

"READY to meet one of my best friends from when I was a kid?" Edmund asked Matt.

"Yep," said Matt.

They were walking the streets of a small sea wind–scoured Oregon coast town named Guthrie, wrapped now in mist and evening. The air smelled of salt and fish and rain, and kissed Matt's face with chill. This was the place where Edmund had grown up.

It had taken them two days in Edmund's battered brown station wagon to get here from where they had met.

Edmund parked the car on a side street. He and Matt ambled along the coast highway, looked into darkened shop windows still decorated for the Christmas just past, then stopped at an all-night bakery and bought six assorted doughnuts to go, and coffee in lidded cups. Matt loaded her coffee with cream and sugar. Edmund smiled at the large woman behind the counter and she smiled back without recognition.

"Did you know her?" Matt asked after they pushed out of the bread-fragrant warmth into the cool of the night street again.

"Uh-huh. Mrs. Danvers." He finished a doughnut and licked his fingers.

Matt offered him the open-mouthed bag of doughnuts, but he shook his head. She rolled the bag closed and shoved it into a deep pocket of her army jacket. She sipped hot coffee, held its sweet smooth bitterness on her tongue a moment, then swallowed and said, "She didn't know you at all."

He shoved his hands into his navy pea jacket pockets, hunched his shoulders. "I guess I must look different. I don't know. In the mirror I look the same as I did when I left here—I was eighteen. My sister ages and I don't. That might be a side effect of spirit work, arresting my physical development, though I don't know why. Or maybe I just can't see my real self in mirrors."

"Weird," said Matt. "Why wouldn't that woman know you, if you look just the same?"

"Baffling," Edmund said.

Matt ate a glazed old-fashioned doughnut. She didn't usually buy food; cheaper to find it in the trash, and not too difficult, since the trash helped her look. Edmund had some money. Sometimes people paid him for odd jobs, he had told her, and his needs were so simple—spirit took care of most of them—that he hadn't had anything to spend money on except gas. Matt rarely tasted anything as good as this fresh doughnut. She wanted to make it last, but she was too hungry. "How long has it been since you were here?"

"I think it's been . . . ten or twelve years. How strange. Maybe even fifteen."

"How can you be sure this friend of yours is still around?" They hadn't checked the phone book to see if his friends were still listed. She hadn't seen him question spirit, either.

How would his childhood friends feel about an old friend who had turned into a missionary or a priest or whatever he was? She always felt suspicious of people who wanted to change her for her own good. Edmund wasn't a very pushy missionary, though. He didn't try to convert you. He just tried to help you.

Edmund said, "Because he's one of the few people I know who can't leave his house except under special circumstances. He's a ghost."

"A ghost!" Matt had seen dreams and talked to buildings with long memories and to cars and household appliances and doors unnumbered. Sometimes she had seen ghosts in the memories of people who mourned, waking phantoms of very sad dreams; but she had never found these dreams interactive. She couldn't remember meeting a ghost outside someone else's head. She wondered if she would be able to see this one.

"I'm a witch. You talk to cars and walls and sidewalks. A ghost surprises you?" Edmund asked.

"Yep," she said.

"Come on. He haunts a house at the north end of town." He quickened his pace. She walked faster to keep up with his long strides.

"How does the town look to you?" she asked.

"Pretty much the same, at least this part of it," he said. They walked past a restaurant. Wonderful seafood smells came out the door as it opened to let out a family. "This place is new," he said, "and one of my old family favorites is closed. Turned from a restaurant into a realty office." He pointed across the street at a sign that said Tidewater Realty. "Those billboards we passed coming over the mountains advertised things that weren't here when I lived here. Factory outlet stores. A casino. A wax museum. That big convention hotel. But you can't see any of those from this part of the highway. This store has been here forever." They glanced in the window of a store that sold tourist trinkets: mugs from Taiwan that said "Oregon Coast," cement seagulls, crabs made of seashells not native to these waters. "So has some of the junk inside." He smiled.

"So a lot of it looks the same," she said. "And you already saw one person you knew, and she didn't know you back." Matt had gone back to her hometown after a long absence, and it had disturbed her. When she had first left the town years earlier, she had not gained her dream-eyes yet. On her return, she could see a lot of things she hadn't known or understood before. She had learned from her father what she needed to know: he was bowed down under the guilt he felt for violating her and her sister, but he didn't let it enter his conscious mind. Nothing she said could touch him or make him take responsibility. She had had to work it out on her own.

"Are you okay?" she asked Edmund.

Edmund stopped. Matt stopped. He cocked his head, considering.

"You're right," he said after a moment. "I don't know how I feel to be here after all this time. Mixed up."

"Your parents still live here?"

"No, they moved to Albuquerque. I haven't seen them in a

long time. My dad doesn't know what he did wrong to make me turn out so weird. I make him nervous."

"How about your mom?"

He took a big breath, let it out. "I should go see my mom. She didn't understand me either, but she wasn't so worried about it. My friends knew what happened to me, once I got it figured out, but they didn't really get it. My sister Abby was the only one who understood what happened and why. She's still my friend."

"She's the one who lives in California? The one who ages while you don't?"

"Yeah. She used to be younger than me, six years younger. Now she's married and has three kids—her oldest is six. She's a responsible adult, and I—I feel like I'm still eighteen."

"My sister got weird since I went away, too."

"Are you sure it wasn't you?"

"Good point." She knew she had become a stranger to everyone who had known her two lives ago, but there was more to it than that. Like Edmund's sister, Matt's sister had settled into another kind of being, as far from the way Matt was as it could be: Wife. Homeowner. Steady job. Deep roots. "The spirit never leads you back to your family?"

"Not so far. I mean, I see Abby every year, sometimes more often, depending on how I feel. I like her kids. I want to know them. But I never get that spirit sense while I'm with them that there's anything I need to do there."

"Is spirit telling you anything about being here?"

Edmund closed his eyes. His face stilled. She watched him listen for spirit. He looked comfortable doing it, almost like a statue, serene, expectant.

Maybe spirit talked to Edmund the way other things talked to her. She listened, too, closing her eyes.

All she noticed was that it was getting colder, and the coffee cup in her hand was Styrofoam and warm against her palm.

"Go on," said Edmund.

"Huh?" Matt opened her eyes.

"That's what it says. Go on."

"Go on? Oh yeah, to the ghost house, huh?"

He smiled at her. He did that a lot, though he almost never laughed. Sometimes she wondered if she was obligated to smile back, but she rarely did, and Edmund didn't seem to mind.

He reached for her free hand. They walked north, past closed gas stations, open video rental places, dark banks, and a lighted grocery store with red and green Christmas lights along its roofline. Presently they ran out of things to walk past besides wind-warped pines and houses huddled behind salt-scrubbed fences, and Edmund turned down a lane toward the ocean. Matt saw the water a few blocks below, pale in the night, restless and forever, disappearing into mist and distance. Its wet salt scented the air. They had walked beyond street lights. The mist caught light and held it above them.

Edmund turned right onto Lee Street, a narrow way between looming pines, its edges crowded with low dark bushes, parted only rarely by driveways to the left and right that led into the tangle and disappeared. This street was darker than the previous one. The pavement roughened. Matt stumbled in a pothole. "Shoulda brought my flashlight," she muttered. Like the rest of her things, her flashlight was back in Edmund's car, parked on the highway near the bakery.

"This is dark to you?"

"Yeah." She almost snapped at him, but then she thought, he was a witch; who knew what senses he had? Maybe he didn't notice.

"Let me see what I can do," he said, pausing in the center of the street. There was no traffic. All she could hear was the hush and tumble of waves not far beyond the screening pines.

Edmund drank the rest of his coffee and stuffed the cup in his jacket pocket, then held his left hand up. He murmured something below her range of hearing and twitched his fingers. After a little while his hand glowed with pale gray light.

"Eww," said Matt. It was the kind of glow she thought of dead things having, the light of decay.

He waited a little longer, and the glow around his hand grew brighter. She could see his face better now. Calm, intent. The light stayed gray, none of the welcome yellow of fire or lamplight in it, but it showed the road ahead of them.

"What is that?" Matt asked.

"Starlight," said Edmund, holding his hand in front of him. It cast enough light for her to make out her surroundings. "Ready?"

"I guess," said Matt.

At the very end of the dark crooked street they came to a tangle taller than the salal bushes, an upwelling of blackberry canes behind a pale weathered fence with pickets missing or sagging. The gate hung loose on its hinges, its corner dug into untracked dirt.

Matt pulled her hand free of Edmund's and reached out to touch the gate. —Hey?— she whispered to it.

—Hey! Who are you?— it said, alert, alive, excited.

—Uh, Matt,— she said. Its energy surprised her. Most things she talked to were sleepy at first.

—Hi! Who's your friend? You coming in?—

—Is it all right? This place looks deserted!—

—Well, it's supposed to,— said the gate. —Got to keep up appearances.— The gate creaked open with theatrical shrieks.

"Nice," said Edmund.

There was a narrow path through the blackberry brambles. "You go first," said Matt.

"Okay," Edmund said. He stepped past the gate, holding his lighted hand behind him so that she could see where she was walking. She expected to be snagged, but the brambles leaned away from her.

—What kind of path are you?— she whispered to the earth beneath her shoes.

—An adjustable one,— it said, —depending on who's coming. Who's this man with the glowing hand?—

—Don't you know him? He used to come here a lot.—

—He seems familiar and different. Who is he?—

"I think you should ask him," Matt said out loud.

"Ask who what?" Edmund said.

"The path wants to know who you are," Matt said.

Edmund stopped and turned back to her. Something in his face made her throat tighten. She stepped forward and hugged him. Here he is, she thought, back in the place where his other life happened, and nothing knows him. Eternal stranger. Story of my life.

He hugged her for a long moment, then released her and knelt on the path, placing his palms, one glowing, the other not, against its earth.

Matt heard a storm of whispers: the path asking itself questions and trying out answers, arguing, all in a moment. —Edmund? Edmund? *Edmund?*—

"Edmund?" The beautiful mid-range voice held equal parts surprise and delight. Edmund turned toward it, his face bright with joy.

"What on Earth have you done to yourself?" said the boy on the path ahead of them. He looked like a young teenager in weird clothes: pale dress shirt, suspenders, short pants that buckled under the knee, dark stockings, and black shoes that buttoned up to above his ankles. He glowed with gray internal light. Matt could see through his edges.

"Nathan!" Edmund said, rising. "Oh, Nathan!" Holding out his hands, he went to the phantom, and right through him, then turned back, his face startled.

"Ouch! Aren't you forgetting something?"

"Sorry!" Edmund said. He reached out slowly, trying to stroke the image of antique boy, but there was nothing solid to touch.

"Did that really hurt?" Matt asked.

"No, it didn't," said Nathan. "Come on inside, Matt, Edmund."

—How does he know my name?— she asked the path as she followed Edmund and the specter.

—You told me,— it said.

—I told the gate.—

—The gate, the path, the brambles, the house—it's all me, Nathan.—

—How . . . I don't understand.—

—That's all right. It's even more complicated than that. I'm the house, actually, and Nathan is kind of a piece of me, though he has self-will, memories, opinions, and a certain measure of independence. I'm the earth in this small place. Welcome.—

—Thank you,— Matt thought. —I really, really don't get this. Most earth I can't talk to at all.—

—I'm haunted by gruesome death. That makes me livelier than other kinds of earth.—

—Ewww!—

—At least, we thought it was gruesome at the time. Much worse things happen now and leave little trace in their earth. It's very strange.—

The house rose from the brambles, a small and once-tidy three-story Victorian. Now its shutters hung crooked; its paint was mostly gone; its downstairs windows stared, vacant of glass and light. Gaps showed like missing teeth in the fish-scale shingles that covered the various roofs. The house didn't just sit there. It loomed.

"Jeeze!" said Matt.

"Well, it's haunted," said Nathan.

"Oh, yeah. I forgot. Edmund could fix it. He likes fixing things."

"Fixing it would be a mistake," said Edmund. "It's supposed to look creepy. If it didn't, people might want to move in. Besides, it's perfectly nice inside."

"Huh," said Matt.

"Come inside and see," said Nathan. The front door creaked open, again with shrieks that sounded like someone in pain.

"How do you do that?" Matt asked.

"Practice."

"Cool," said Matt. One of the porch steps had collapsed. She stepped over it and crossed the porch, accompanied by creaks and followed by Edmund. Beyond the threshold all she could see was darkness. For a second she hesitated, not wanting to put her foot through the floor, but then she thought, here's this nice house and ghost boy talking to me, and Edmund being my friend. Nothing's going to happen. She walked in.

"Lights," said Nathan. Light bulbs in mirror-mosaic-backed sconces on the walls glowed with a dimmer, yellower light than she was used to. Matt saw a front hall, with a room to the left partly hidden by a half wall topped with slender pillars, and a big room through double doors to the right. Everything looked dusty and decrepit. Cobwebs dangled in ropes from the ceiling, made dirty lace against the walls.

She'd slept in much worse places. "Perfectly nice," she said, with only a hint of question in it.

"Well, okay, upstairs it's nice," said Edmund. "Hello, House!"

"Hello, Boy," said the house. Out loud. In a deep, feminine voice. As often as Matt had talked to things, she had never heard them speak out loud unless they were mechanized and computerized, and then they didn't speak in their own voices or words. The hair on her neck prickled.

"Furniture," said Nathan.

A runner rug, Persian, grew beneath her feet. Furniture faded into sight to the right and left: a tall carved chair with coat hooks and a mirror attached to its back on the right; in the room to the left, comfortable wing chairs, foot stools, shelves displaying knickknacks, a full-sized gilded harp, a squat rectangular piano with a scattering of sheet music on its music stand, a bright red-and-blue carpet, small tables with potted crocuses, flower arrangements, and vases on them, pictures hanging on the walls from cords attached to rosette medallions on a line of trim below the ceiling, a big portrait of a woman in a green dress above the fireplace, candlesticks and oriental fans on the mantel; in the room to the right, a dining room set, all the chair and table legs carved and ornate. The table could seat eight. The chairs had high backs like thrones. In the middle of the table was a big complicated twisting silver something, and elaborate silver candlesticks flanked it.

"Wow," said Matt.

"Wow!" said Edmund. "I forgot. You can do this without Susan now?"

"Yep."

"Can we sit on it?" Matt asked.

"I'm not sure. The stuff upstairs is solid and never goes away. I haven't tried this trick in a while."

Matt went to the hall chair and touched one of the coat hooks. It felt solid. She took off her weather-beaten army jacket and hung it up, then patted the furniture. "Thanks," she said. "This is really great."

"Glad you like it," said Nathan. "Welcome to the House."

"Thank you," she said. "What a great house."

"Toldja," said Edmund.

"Edmund?" said Nathan.

"Nathan."

"There's something very strange about you."

"Like what?" Edmund looked down at himself, spread his arms, palms up. His left hand was still glowing. "Thanks," he muttered, and shook his hand. Its light fled.

"It's difficult to pinpoint. You look the same, but you feel completely different."

"It's your fault."

"What do you mean?"

"You remember. Halloween. The curse you put on me."

"You cursed him?" Matt asked Nathan. "Your best friend put a curse on you?" Matt asked Edmund.

"Uh-huh," Edmund said. "Before the curse, me, normal. After the curse, powers. Confusing powers."

"Oh, *that* curse," said Nathan. "I thought you liked it. I would have taken it off if you had asked me to."

"I know."

"You can do that?" Matt asked Nathan. "Give people powers?"

"That was the only time I've ever done it. I turned Edmund and the twins into witches. I don't know what came over me. It's only certain nights a year I can do things like that, and I usually don't. That was pretty extreme."

"His life turned upside down," she said.

"How do you know?" Edmund asked.

"It's there." She held out her hands, fisted them. "You now," she said, and flexed one fist. "You before," she said, flexed the other, and held her fists out at opposite sides of her body, her arms stretched wide.

"I met her three days ago," Edmund said to Nathan. "I don't know how she knows what she knows about me."

Nathan raised an eyebrow. —He met you three days ago and he brings you here? He hasn't been back here in years. And he never knows how I'll treat strangers.—

—He wanted to come back, and I didn't want him to come alone. He's really mixed up.—

—The hug in the front yard. For reassurance?—

—Yeah. He's been drifting through life, following spirit guides, no direction, no goals, just doing what he thinks needs doing and moving on. That's how I live too, except no spirit guides. But then we bumped into each other. He wondered where he's going and where he came from. Retracing the path, kind of. I thought I'd come with him. What if there was no welcome?—

—You've already retraced your own path?—

—Part of it I could never find again, even if I wanted to. I did go back over the part I needed to remember and let go of. No welcomes. I did it by myself, and it needed doing, but it was hard alone.— She shrugged. —I'm still drifting. Don't know if I'll ever stop.—

—Are you happy?—

—Sometimes. Often enough to keep me warm.— On even the coldest nights she could wrap herself in good memories. —There's always something new and wonderful to see. Look at this house. I never met a ghost before.—

—Huh! Yet you speak my language?—

—I guess. Mostly I talk to houses.—

—And gates and pathways. I get it.—

"Hey," said Edmund, looking from Matt to Nathan.

"Where are my manners?" Nathan asked. "Please, come into the parlor. I wish I could offer you something to eat or drink, but I don't have any living friends stocking the kitchen at the moment." He led them into the living room, gestured at chairs.

Matt sat down in a blue velvet–upholstered armchair. A little footstool scooted close enough for her to put her feet up. "Thanks," she said. "We have doughnuts." She had left them in her coat pocket, though, and her coat was hanging in the hall.

Edmund sat down in the red chair to her left. "I didn't mean hey, let's go sit down," he said. "I meant, hey, how come you guys are staring at each other without speaking?"

"We were speaking," said Matt.

"What? Talking to walls works with Nathan?"

"Uh-huh."

"Can you teach me how you do that?"

"I don't think so. I don't know how it works. It wasn't like I was born with it. I did a lot of drugs. I got drunk a lot. I did things I can't even remember. I woke up one morning, and there it was. Things talked to me. It's probably brain damage. I don't know how you hear spirit, either. I was trying to listen when you were, and I didn't hear anything."

"Nathan?"

The ghost shook his head. "I find it inexplicable that Matt can talk to me at that remove. I've never met another living person who could." He sat in a brown chair to Matt's right.

Edmund reached into a coat pocket and brought out what Matt thought of as his portable devotions kit. It was a Chinese silk roll-up packet tied with red cord, its exterior midnight blue woven with sprays of green leaves. Unrolled, it revealed its interior, white silk with many small zipper pockets. She had seen Edmund open the kit at dawn and at dusk and sometimes in between. She couldn't tell what the stuff in its pockets was. Different kinds and colors of dust was what it looked like, each with a distinctive scent. Edmund took pinches of dust and breathed on them, or ground them between his fingers and sprinkled them, or rubbed them between his hands, or blew them in different directions. Once he mixed some with water and drank it. He had even set some on fire. He usually muttered things while he was playing with the dust.

"So what were you talking about when I couldn't hear you?" he said.

"You," said Nathan.

"Great." Edmund sounded peeved, which wasn't a tone Matt expected from him. Nothing had irritated him since she had met him, not bad traffic, bad service, bad food, or bad moods in those around him. She had found his serenity daunting.

She said, "Naw, we didn't just talk about you, Edmund. We talked about me too. We didn't talk enough about Nathan, though. Like, what kind of gruesome death?"

"You told her about gruesome death?" Edmund sounded even more irked.

"I didn't. The house did." Nathan shook his head. "I'm not telling you about gruesome death, Matt. You'll just have to imagine it."

"All right." Matt thought about ghost stories she had heard, where you could tell what ghosts had died from—Anne Boleyn with her head tucked underneath her arm, stuff like that. No clues there: Nathan looked normal, aside from being slightly transparent and dressed funny.

Edmund opened one of the pockets in his kit and took out a pinch of something. His face had gone remote. He put the dust on his palm, rubbed it between his hands, then blew it up into the air. It turned into golden sparkles and settled down around them: specks touched each of them and winked out.

"What the heck are you doing?" Nathan asked.

"Witchcraft."

"I've never seen any craft like that."

"I invented my own."

"What does it accomplish?"

"Guidance."

"Oh? What did you learn?"

Edmund sighed. "This is where I should be."

"You doubted? Never doubt your welcome, Edmund."

"I'm unnerved."

"Ah. You're thinking too hard. Are you tired?"

"Yes."

"Matt?"

"Yeah, I guess I am."

"I've got guest rooms upstairs, and bedclothes, pretty much everything you need. I think we could even manage hot baths."

"You could?" Matt said. Most unlived-in houses she had been in didn't offer anything but shelter. "Who pays your electric bills?"

"We don't get bills. We're not on most maps. House has a certain relationship with the past." Nathan glanced at one of the mirror-backed lights. "If a thing ever worked here, well . . ."

"Cool," Matt whispered.

"Want to spend the night?"

"Oh, yes," she said.

Edmund placed palm to palm and pushed his index fingers against his mouth, his thumbs supporting his chin.

"This isn't going to work for you?" Nathan asked him.

"I just—I'm so—I can't explain it."

Matt stood up. "Look. Your dust told you this is the place to be. Okay?"

Edmund looked at her. For once his gaze wasn't tranquil. Upset touched his eyes. Where was the sense in that? What had happened since they arrived that would bother him, her mystic friend who tapped into universal forces around him?

Well. Matt had talked privately to Nathan. Matt had understood things about Edmund that Edmund might not understand himself. Was that a problem?

Or maybe Nathan hadn't greeted him the way he expected to be greeted?

What was missing?

She walked to Edmund and stared into his eyes. "Listen. We're not going to get it unless you tell us. What's wrong?"

He touched his chest. "There's a war in here. Here where it's been quiet as a tomb for I don't know how many years. Conflict. Who am I?"

She opened dream-eyes and looked for his mental landscape.

She hadn't done it very much while she was with him. There was no reason for her to know more than he chose to tell her: he wasn't a threat, and he hadn't seemed to be in trouble.

When she first met him, she had looked at his mental landscape and seen a forest. Now she saw three people: a boy with a bike, looking at an older boy who glowed bright red, and standing behind the red boy like a shadow or a stain, a man, midnight blue. None of them were talking to each other. The red teenager's eyes were wide and angry, and he glared at the younger boy. Sparks flew off him, shooting everywhere. One darted toward the dark man behind him, lighting up his features. The man's face was Edmund's, utterly sad.

"Ed!" she cried, grabbing his hands. "Who's that red boy?"

"What?"

"I thought you had two lives, now and before, but there's one in between. What happened?"

"Matt," he said. "What are you talking about?"

—What *are* you talking about?— the house asked.

"The red boy, the one spitting fire, he makes you so sad, but you don't do anything about it."

Edmund blinked twice. The pictures in his thoughtscape melted into colored streaks, then swirled and reformed. Two rooms beside each other. In one, baby blue wallpaper; a floor scattered with action figures, Matchbox cars, comic books, loose-leaf notebook paper scrawled with pencil art: planes, strafing something off the page; motorcycles; submarines and sea monsters. On the back wall there were three shadows of people, and one sketched outline filled with a pale glow: Edmund's living friends and the ghost? In the other room, a wall the color of arctic ice; a waterfall, a tree-hemmed glade, the rising slope of a mountain, deer grazing, sun and rain mingled. The room seemed to go off into some dim distance without end.

Between the rooms, a red wall, pulsing with heat, like lava that breathed.

Matt thought of holding out her fists on either side of her, one his life before, the other his life after, the whole of her in between. The red wall was as big a thing as she was, compared to her fists.

She said, "How can you connect to your past life through all that fire?"

"I don't know," Edmund said.

"No wonder you keep looking the other way. What happened?"

"Matt, what are you doing?" He frowned at her. "What are you seeing, and how?"

"I, well, I'm looking at your thoughts, that's all."

"That's all?" He half smiled.

"Yeah. It's something I do. Like when you play with that dust. I don't do it all the time. Just when it seems like a good idea."

"He has a red boy in his thoughts?" Nathan asked.

"A red wall between his old life and the life now," she said. "There's no door through the fire. What happened right before you started wandering around doing whatever spirit told you to?"

His whole thoughtscape stained red, a red so burning bright it hurt her dream-eyes to look at it. She closed them.

"I don't know," he said. "I don't remember."

She thought about the room full of toys, the shadows on the wall. She sat down. "Start from the other end. You left your first life . . . the night Nathan cursed you?"

"It took a little longer, because I couldn't figure out what was going on. He told me not to come over that night, but I disobeyed him. So he cursed me, and I left. I thought it was a joke. Then things started happening around me. When I snapped my fingers, things broke. Or things appeared. Or things changed. I had no control, and no idea of what was going on. My sister Abby helped me tame that part. She figured it out before I did, from watching me, and she was so little it didn't bother her that I made impossible things happen.

"Every time I talked, people stared at me. Julio helped me figure out that part. It was a good curse. It confused me a lot."

Nathan said, "I forgot about the voice. An unexpected side effect. You don't sound like that now. What happened?"

"It was too disruptive. I toned it down."

"What did the curse do to your voice?" Matt asked.

"I never heard it," said Edmund. "People told me it was beautiful. They didn't care what I said, they just wanted me to talk. Julio said it was music. It was so compelling I couldn't communicate with it. They'd listen, but they wouldn't understand the words. It was like I had no language, and all I did was perform."

"It was lovely, Matt. He sounded like Christmas bells and angels," Nathan said.

"Huh," said Matt. "Do you ever use that voice now?"

Edmund shook his head.

"Could you if you wanted?"

"I don't know."

Matt hugged herself and thought of talents abandoned, gifts given up, tracks switched away from. She didn't pursue any of her gifts as though they were careers. She didn't use them toward an end, except survival. But she didn't lock them up either.

She shifted gears, remembering where this conversation had been heading before they talked about voices. "But you guys knew each other a while before Nathan put the curse on you? I mean, not every kid has a ghost for a friend. Things in your first life were already moving away from normal, right?"

"I knew Nathan two or three years before he turned me into a witch," said Edmund.

"They came here to meet," Nathan said.

"Who?"

"Edmund, Julio, Susan, and Deirdre."

"Those are your friends?" Matt asked Edmund.

"Yes. My best friends. Deirdre, Julio, and I knew each other since third grade. Julio knew Susan at least that long—his mom worked as a housekeeper for her family—but she went to private school; we finally all got together when we were in eighth grade. We got really tight with each other. We did everything together. We snuck into this house together that first time, and Nathan scared us . . ."

"Just doing my job."

"I knocked myself out trying to get away from him, and he revived me. That's how I met him."

"Huh," said Matt. How many times had she sneaked into abandoned houses to spend the night? More times than she could remember; nights with leaks, nights with noises, nights when she and the house talked away the dark, whole histories of families moved or dead. She had never met a ghost until now. Nothing scared her except other people. Well, and nature, a little. She wondered how she would have felt if she had come into this house and Nathan had haunted her.

—Would you have haunted me if I came here alone?—

—No,— he thought. —You talked to me before you approached. I would have assumed you were a ghost.—

—Huh. Ghosts greet each other?—

—There are certain ground rules. Most ghosts don't go wandering, but I've met a couple who did.—

—I've never met a ghost before, and I've been wandering for quite a while.—

He grinned. —Maybe you scare them.—

—Come on. I don't scare anyone.—

—Don't be so sure. Anyway, I don't haunt the way I used to before I met these kids. They changed everything.—

Matt glanced at Edmund, who was watching them again, his face bleak. —Say that out loud.—

"I don't haunt the way I used to before I met Edmund and his friends," Nathan said. "I was lonely for so long before they came. When I stopped trying to frighten them, I had a reason for existing again, which was a relief, since I am compelled to exist in this form for a while longer. They brought life here and let me pretend I was part of it."

"It was great," Edmund said. "The perfect hideout. We came here after school. We each had a room upstairs to use for what we wanted, a room no parents ever entered. We had a ghost for company. We did stuff together, and we did our own things too."

"I loved having you here. So now when company comes I wait awhile to see what their intentions are before I start all the sound and fury."

Matt wondered if her history would have been different if she had had a place like this to run away to when she really needed it. Would she have stabilized and put down roots? Well, Edmund had had this place, and he hadn't put down roots. Why not?

"This is cool and everything," she said, "but what happened? Why the curse? What happened afterward?"

"Edmund was always interested in magic," said Nathan. "When he first came here, he wanted to find out about witchcraft. He was reading books about it. He didn't know any actual witches."

"You wanted to do magic? Why?" Matt asked Edmund.

"When I was in sixth grade, our teacher had a magician give a magic show for the class. He made things disappear. He pulled a rabbit out of a hat. He poured milk and eggs into the hat and took out cookies. I'd been cruising through school fairly interested in everything, but when I saw that show, it woke me up. I just got fascinated."

"Yeah, but those were just tricks."

"I know. I went to the hobby shop and bought magic tricks and a book of card tricks, and I practiced and got pretty good at some of 'em. I started wondering about other stuff, though, magic that would really work. I wanted that sense of surprise and joy I got when I thought the magician was actually doing magic things. After I met Nathan, I believed again that real magic must exist. He could make things float, no strings, no mirrors. He could disappear and walk through walls. I couldn't find that in the witchcraft books I was reading, but I kept thinking there had to be a way."

"So," said Matt, "the curse happened how?"

"Halloween is different from every other night for me," Nathan said. "Rules relax, and powers come to me. I can leave the house and circle the world. At least, the night side of the world."

"Uh-huh."

"One year I took Julio with me," Nathan said, "and one year I took Susan. One year I just wanted to go by myself, and I told them all to stay away."

"Or else. I was going to stay away," Edmund said, "but I was riding my bike past here and I saw these strange girls heading for the house."

"You were riding your bike past here?" Matt asked, skeptical. "Is this place really on your way to anywhere else?" It had looked like the end of the road to her.

"There's a shortcut through the woods to a road that goes to the grocery store in North End. Saves a little distance."

"You weren't just hanging around thinking about disobeying his wishes?" she asked.

"Maybe a little." He smiled and shrugged. "I wouldn't have set foot inside the fence, but those girls were halfway to the porch. At that point I didn't know much about Nathan's Halloweens, but I thought he might be dangerous. So I tried to warn them. They didn't listen very well."

"They argued," Nathan said.

"I followed them in and tried to pull them back out."

"But they were too stubborn, and it was too late." Nathan frowned. "Never before or since have I done something like that." He shook his head. "It took powers I didn't know I had, and it rode emotions I don't usually have either. I felt angry and capricious. It didn't feel like me at all. I put a curse on all three of them and left, laughing my best haunting laugh."

"Spirit," said Edmund.

"Is that a joke?" asked the ghost.

Edmund's eyebrows rose. "No. Maybe you were doing spirit work and you didn't know it."

"How likely is that?" Nathan asked. "Look, I know what I'm supposed to do as long as I'm stuck here. I'm restricted in lots of ways. At that point I was pretty mad at the rules, but I didn't think there was any way for me to change people's lives except by scaring them. There was no voice coming down from above saying, 'Change these three people into witches.' There was just me and this ridiculous anger."

Edmund shrugged.

"This uncharacteristic anger," Nathan said slowly, "and this poor self-control, also uncharacteristic . . ." —House?—

—I'm not answering any questions about this,— thought the house.

"Creepy," said Matt. "Makes you feel like somebody's pulling strings. I hate that."

"Me too," Nathan said.

"Waiting for strings to be pulled, that's how I live," Edmund said. "Except I'm not trying to avoid the strings. I'm looking for them."

"You hand your life over to the nearest person who can pull your strings?" asked Matt. "How can you be sure it's a good string-puller?"

"I only respond to one puller. Spirit."

"How do you know for sure?"

Edmund stared at her a moment. His eyes widened. He slumped in his chair, sagged as if all his muscles had relaxed at once. His chin dropped to his chest. His eyelids fluttered. "No," he murmured. "No. Won't let you do that. No."

"What is it?" Matt asked.

He covered his face with his hands and moaned.

"Ed, come on. Ed." She rose, went to him, put a hand on his shoulder. His muscles went rigid under her palm. She recognized the flinch of someone who had been touched wrong too recently to know that there were okay touches. She released him. Everything had changed since a moment ago, when he had been one of the few people whose touches didn't scare her at all, whom she could touch without worry, whom she let hold her.

This flip over into Other, it was what scared her about people.

The red boy.

She said, "Ed, come back. Come back to who you are now."

He tilted his head up enough to look at her. It was another person staring out of his eyes. Fire flared in the circles of his pupils. "Don't call me that. Don't touch me. Don't tell me what to do."

"Okay. Okay," she said. She glanced at Nathan, backed to stand beside his chair. They both watched Edmund and waited.

"What are you looking at?" he said. His voice was strange to Matt: not the warm, quiet voice she had grown used to, but a sharp-edged voice with a new range of silvery overtones that made it compelling. "What do you want?"

"Nothing," she said. "What about you?"

"I want *everyone* to leave me alone."

"Okay," Matt said again, exchanging glances with Nathan. —Was he like this when you knew him before?—

—No. He wasn't like the person you brought with you either, though.—

"Stop it," said Edmund, his brows low over his narrowed eyes. He raised his hand, thumb hard against middle finger. Matt knew it was a threat, though she didn't know what it meant.

"Edmund." Nathan rose, edged in front of Matt. "You're a guest in my house. Don't abuse my hospitality."

Edmund lowered his hand slowly. "Stop talking about me as though I'm not here."

"All right."

Edmund opened his hands and rested them on his thighs. He sighed, a sound edged with heat.

"Could you hear what we said?" Matt asked, looking at Edmund over Nathan's shoulder.

"Of course."

"You couldn't before."

"Before what? Who are you, anyway?"

"I'm Matt. We've been traveling together for three days."

Edmund shook his head. He leaned forward and looked at her with his head cocked. "I don't remember," he said, "but it's true, isn't it? You believe it's true."

"Yes." She frowned. "Maybe. I mean, I came here with you, but it wasn't the same you."

He bit his lower lip. The flame in his eyes was dying down. "Nathan, what—I don't get this."

"How old are you?"

"What do you mean?"

"You know, your age in years. What is it?"

"Eighteen." Edmund looked away, then down at his hands, then up at Nathan.

"You don't come to visit me anymore, do you?"

"Are you lonely?" His voice still sounded strange to Matt, younger and unfamiliar and beautiful.

"Whether I'm lonely isn't important," Nathan said. "I understand there are tides in your life. One will pull you away from me and everything you did here. You move on. You move away. You get older. It's all right. I'm just trying to get a sense of where you are at this moment."

"As opposed to when?"

"The future."

Edmund looked at Matt, questions in his eyes. No more flames. No threats. Just confusion.

"I don't get it either," she said. "And it's not going to be easy to explain, but I met you when you're about thirty or thirty-five or something. I just asked you the wrong question and you fell into your younger self."

He squinted at her. "What's the wrong question?"

"How do you know who's pulling your strings?"

His eyes opened very wide. The flames were back. "No!"

Chapter Three

· · · · ·

"Edmund." Nathan's voice was full of ice. Matt shivered. "We're not doing it. Either of us. Do you understand?"

"What?" Edmund shook his head, blinking. "I feel sick."

"Well, no wonder," said Matt. "You're jerking around inside. You remember what we were just talking about? Do you know me?"

"No. Wait. Matt." He shook his head again, frowning in confusion. "Ouch!"

"Edmund," said Matt. "Reach into your pocket."

He patted his coat pockets, reached into the one with the devotions kit, pulled it out. "What's this?"

"It's part of your magic."

"Magic," he said.

"Yes. You're a witch, okay? Do you remember that part at all?"

He blinked. "Sort of."

"Open the kit."

He untied the string and opened the rolled silk, stared bemused at the little pockets.

—Kit,— Matt said. She stared at Edmund, then walked around Nathan and approached Edmund. "I'm going to touch this, okay?" She pointed to the silk kit in his lap.

"Touch it? Talk to it?"

"That's right. I don't want to hurt you. I just want to help you. Is it okay with you if I touch this thing?"

"I guess."

She knelt before him and touched the white silk. —Kit? We need some help here.—

—Yes,— said the kit.

—Can you help us?—

—Yes.—

—Which pocket? What should he do with the dust?—

A zipper flickered on one of the pockets. Edmund stared at it.

The kit's small, dry, precise voice said, —Place some in his palm, let him breathe it.—

"Did you get that?" Matt asked.

"Get what?"

"What the kit said?"

"I heard your questions, but I didn't hear its answers."

"This is *so* weird," Matt said. Then she explained what the kit had told her.

Edmund opened the pocket and took out a pinch of gray dust. "What is this stuff?"

"I don't know. You use all the things in here, but I don't know how or why. Just put some in your hand and snort it, okay?"

"What is it going to do?"

"The kit didn't say. Help is all I know."

"This thing wants to help me?"

"We all do."

He hesitated, looking at her, then placed the pinch of dust in his palm and sniffed it. "It smells like cemeteries," he whispered, "and dead dreams and lost hopes."

Matt sat back on her heels.

"This is supposed to help me?"

"That's what the kit said. It's your kit. I don't know why it would try to hurt you."

He sat back. He stared at her, then glanced at Nathan and all around the room. After a moment when all Matt could hear was her breathing and Edmund's, he lifted his hand to his face and breathed in the dust of defeat.

His eyes drifted shut and he leaned back against the chair, his stance limp. After a little while he opened his eyes. The serene Edmund she had first met looked at Matt. He smiled, then frowned.

Dead dreams and lost hopes?

"Can you remember the past half hour, Edmund?" Nathan asked from just behind Matt.

"Oh, my." He flipped the kit and it rolled shut. He tied its string, slid it back into his pocket, then reached out and laid his hand on Matt's head. Warmth, friendship, no fear. "I'm sorry I scared you. Never in a million years did I mean to."

"I know." She hesitated. "Are all your dreams dead?"

"Spirit will provide," he said.

"I don't think that's fair." Gently, she reached up and pulled his hand off her head. She rose. "You're walking around like a dead man. I don't think that's right."

"I'm not dead. I'm alive to possibilities."

"There's something back there you need to look at. Something big made that young you curl up and die, that turned you into that red boy, and then this you replaced him. I mean, you're not a bad person. You're a really good person. I know this about you. But what about that dead boy? Are you going to let him lie there in his grave? Don't you think he deserves a chance to get up and walk around?"

"Matt . . ." His face crumpled, grief etched into it.

She gripped his hand. It didn't move inside hers. "Maybe I'm wrong, Edmund. Maybe I don't know what I'm talking about. You're the person I met, and I like you. Love you, even. You took care of me. I don't usually let people take care of me. I never go places with other people, but I came here with you."

"Spirit," he whispered.

"No!" she said. The denial was hot inside her throat. She didn't want to be jerked around by something she couldn't see or talk to.

She stood still for a long moment. This spirit that guided and directed his actions, that talked to him, it was his reality, a place he'd been living for years. What about her reality, the way she walked through the world talking to things, befriending them, being embraced by them, when to everyone else they were inanimate and dumb? How could she be sure he was wrong? So many people didn't understand her reality. "Maybe it *is* spirit! I don't know! Spirit says for you to be here now, and look what's happening here! The red boy is trying to wake up."

"The red boy."

"The red boy in your thoughts. The person you were after you were your kid self and before you turned into a spirit follower. He was here for a couple seconds. More than once. He's really mad. He doesn't want anyone to touch him or tell him what to do. He's eighteen. Someone hurt him."

"Do you remember that, Edmund?" Nathan asked.

Edmund frowned. "What I remember is this great disruption inside. Like a huge crushing hand squeezing my lungs shut. Couldn't breathe, and I hurt. I remember you guys talking to me and me answering, but I wasn't paying attention to that. I couldn't understand how I could even talk with no air." His voice shifted as he spoke, young tones rising, seeping away. Frustration edged his words. "My head felt like it was burning up."

"I think that was the red boy dying. Who killed him?"

Edmund shook his head. He looked stubborn, another aspect of him that Matt hadn't experienced before. "It's all gone." He sighed.

Matt glanced at Nathan, who raised his eyebrows.

Matt licked her upper lip. "You want to just let it go?"

"Sure," Edmund said.

"Ask spirit. I dare you."

"Ask it what?"

"Ask it if you should just let go of the past now."

He squinted at her for a moment, then smiled. "Let's go to sleep."

"Something's going on here, Edmund. If this was one of your regular missions, you'd follow through, wouldn't you? You kept coming after me even though I told you to leave me alone."

"We've done enough for today. Aren't you tired?"

She looked at him, then glanced away. "If this is something

you don't want me to know about, I'll go away until you finish it. Don't give up."

He bit his lip. "It's not about whether I want you to know."

"What is it, then?"

"It's—I don't want to know. It hurts like death."

She leaned forward and touched his knee. "Look. You survived it the first time. Now it's years later and you've done a lot of spirit work. You're different inside, strong and good. You have powers and you know how they work. Whoever it was who did it to you is not here now, right? It wasn't Nathan, was it?"

—You don't know what it is, do you?— Matt asked Nathan as an afterthought.

—It didn't happen here or the house would remember,— Nathan thought.

—House?— Matt thought.

—It happened somewhere else. I don't think he ever came back after it happened. Eighteen was when he stopped coming here.—

"I don't think it had anything to do with Nathan," Edmund said.

—The red boy can hear us and this Edmund can't?— thought Matt.

—Peculiar,— Nathan agreed.

Matt thought for a while, paced, then said, "Here's how it works. You look at all your strengths. You're strong in your spirit. Ask spirit to stay with you and strengthen and protect you. We're your friends, and we're here to help you. Whoever hurt you is not here. You're in the future now, and that thing is not happening to you. It was years ago. Now it's safe to look at. You can let it come back. It didn't kill you last time. It can't kill you this time."

"You've done this before?" Edmund asked.

"Yep. You tell yourself it's okay to stop anytime. You can do it in little pieces if you have to." She glanced up at him. "Do you understand?"

"I'm not sure." He glanced at Nathan.

"I'm not sure I understand either," said the ghost, "but I'll help any way I can."

"Listen." Matt repeated her directions, stopping after each sentence to see if he had questions about it. "Are you too tired to work on this tonight, for real? We could sleep and start in the morning." What was she saying? He had never said he was interested in working his way back in the first place. It was all her idea. He had even said no to it, more than once. Maybe this was a mistake.

It felt like a mission, though.

Edmund sighed and pulled out his kit again, opened a different pocket, took out a pinch of dust, rolled it between finger and thumb and blew it into the air. It exploded into blue sparkles that spiraled around each other, then spun in wider arcs until they touched the walls and vanished.

"Meaning what?" asked Nathan.

"I don't know," Edmund said. "It's never done that before."

"Maybe it means you should let this whole thing rest in peace. It's up to you," Matt said. "We could just forget it." She sat down, leaned back in the blue velvet chair as tiredness ran along her muscles, making her arms and legs heavy. She could sleep, easily. "Don't do it just because I'm being pushy. It took me a long time to make my trip back. You have to want to do it for yourself."

Edmund looked at her, his hands resting on his kit. He

sighed. Then he straightened. "Let's start. Maybe with just a little piece."

"Okay. Do you know where to start?" she asked. She didn't want to ask him the question about pulling strings again. She wondered if he would like her to look at his interior landscape. She didn't want to do that again without asking him.

"I remembered part of it," he whispered. He stared at the wall for a little while, and then said, "Susan's mother died." He looked toward Nathan. "You remember that?"

"Yes," Nathan said slowly. "Susan stopped coming here when you did. She never said good-bye either. Julio told me she moved to San Francisco to live with her aunt and uncle because her mother died and something happened to her father."

Matt listened to the undertone of pain in Nathan's voice. She imagined losing two friends without farewells. Would a ghost feel the same way a living person would about that? Seemed like he did.

"Susan's mother died," Edmund said.

Nathan stared at him.

—Wait for it,— Matt thought.

After a long pause, Edmund said, "I had these powers. I was getting them under control, learning to understand them. I could snap my fingers and make neat things happen. Once I drove a car for miles after it ran out of gas. I could make things fly, make lights go on and off, move things from across the room. I could touch things and hear them talk to me. Trees. Chairs. Animals. All the studying I had done before you spelled me, the magic books I had read, they started to make a different kind of sense. Spells I had done before on faith I could do and see actual results. Sometimes I just did dumb stuff, like making a paper airplane fly really far or sliding a note to a girl who was sitting at a desk three rows ahead of me. I could make things happen."

"Yes," Matt whispered.

"Susan's mother died. Did Julio tell you how?"

Nathan shook his head. "He wouldn't talk about it."

"Did Deirdre tell you?"

"No. I lost you all for a while. Julio came back later. And Deirdre stopped in a few years afterward, with this boy she was thinking of marrying. It was a dare. I think she was testing him by bringing him here, to see what he would do if he met a ghost, but by the time she showed up, she had almost stopped believing in me herself. She had changed so much I didn't recognize her at first. I wasn't sure whether she really wanted to see me." He glanced away for a moment. "I did talk to her, eventually. We didn't have much of a conversation, but she seemed happy."

"Do you see any of them now?"

Nathan stared into the empty fireplace. "I see . . . who Julio is now once in a while. I see some other people I met later. A new family moved into a house down the street last month; a couple of their kids have been sneaking closer and closer to House. I'll meet them sometime soon." He paused. "I haven't seen you or Susan since that time, until now." His voice was quiet, with a strange stillness in it.

Edmund watched Nathan until Nathan turned back to meet his gaze. After a moment, Edmund said, "We were in high school. Susan started spending time with this guy named Scott when she was in eleventh grade. She was with him one afternoon. She went home half an hour late that day. You know how controlling her father was, how he micromanaged everything about her, but he was supposed to be at his office till five. Usually she got away with it.

"So that day she was half an hour late, and when she got home she found her mom in the kitchen, dying from a blow to the head. She called the paramedics, but there was nothing they could do."

"Her father did it?" Nathan asked.

"We thought so. We knew so." Edmund glanced at Matt. "When we first met her, Susan didn't tell us what was happening in her house. She had been taught never to tell anybody anything. Even Julio, who had known her for years, didn't really know—he wasn't allowed to visit her at home.

"We finally got Susan to trust us, though. She told us that whenever she did anything her father didn't like, her father would hurt her mother. There were a lot of things he didn't like. When we first found out what her father was doing, we told a cop, and he arrested her dad. We thought that would take care of it, but it didn't. All the evidence disappeared, and Susan's dad was set loose, and the one cop we knew and trusted was fired and blacklisted. Susan's mother wouldn't press charges or do anything in her own defense. Susan just shut up about everything again.

"This was before I was a witch. We were just kids. We couldn't figure out what to do when arresting him didn't work. Her dad was some big attorney in town, and he knew something bad about everybody important here. We started feeling like there was nothing we could do about him except help Susan be subversive.

"We didn't know how to stop him." His voice faded to a whisper.

"That's a tough one," Matt said.

"It was horrible." The younger self spoke, his tone bleak. "It was the worst. You got so you couldn't think about it after a while."

"I know how that goes."

"And then I got turned into a witch, but I wasn't thinking about what was going on at Susan's. It was already background, a constant, unchangeable. It didn't occur to me that maybe I could do something for her. It might have, eventually, once I got used to having powers. I was still growing into them and worrying about everything I did with them because I wasn't sure anything would work the way I expected it to.

"So anyway, one day Susan comes home and finds her mother near death, and she's not exactly surprised." He put his palms over his eyes, cradling his forehead in his fingers. "She thinks it's her fault, too, for staying late with a boy. Somehow the how of it gets hushed up, it's never investigated, the paper says her mother died of heart failure, Susan goes on living at home with her father."

No one said anything for a little while.

Finally Edmund looked up.

"I wish she had come here." Pain was an undertone in Nathan's voice.

"I wish we all had. I wish we had told you what was going on and asked you to help us. But that's not what happened. By that point we were growing apart, you know? Julio and I still did things together, but Susan and Deirdre had gone other directions. We all went to the funeral. Susan took me aside afterward and asked me . . ."

His face went bleak.

Nathan and Matt waited.

"Susan asked me to conduct a séance, just her and me. She wanted to talk to her mother."

"Why didn't you come here?" Nathan whispered.

"She was pretty sure you would try to talk us out of it. I tried to talk her out of it. She wouldn't listen. She said she had to know for sure what happened." Edmund shook his head. "As if there were any doubt. But then again, the way all the facts disappeared, and everybody just seemed to assume it was natural causes, that was pretty spooky . . . sometimes it was so hard to figure out what was real. She wanted to know for sure what happened. She wanted to see if her mother blamed her and if there was anything she could do to make it up to her mother. She wanted to know for sure that her mother was someplace safer."

"Death takes you someplace safer?" Matt muttered to Nathan.

"Almost always. What happened, Edmund? Did you give her her séance?"

"I'd never exactly learned how to do a séance, but I had been to some," said Edmund.

"You *had*?" Matt asked.

"Sure, I was interested in everything occult, before *and* after I turned into a witch. There were a couple of channelers here when I was a teenager, and one practicing medium. I got her to summon Nathan just to see if she was real. She was. She called him up, and I broke the circle so he could get free of the house for a night, and he took me with him."

"How'd you find a medium?" she said. How does anybody? The yellow pages? "Never mind. It's not important."

He looked at her and smiled. His smile faded and he stared

into the past again. "So three days after her mother died, Susan and I cut school at lunchtime and snuck up to her house. Her father was supposed to be at work until five and the housekeeper wasn't there that day. We went to the attic with a couple of candles and cleared a space between dusty trunks and broken furniture and sat on the floor and summoned Susan's mother."

"Did she come?" asked Matt.

"She did." He closed his eyes a moment. Opened them, glanced at Matt. "She looked so beautiful. I'd never really talked to her before. None of us were welcome at Susan's house, even though Julio's mother was their housekeeper. The two times I saw Susan's mom while she was alive, she was sitting in the kitchen doing a crossword puzzle. Once she was wearing a scarf and dark glasses, and the other time she looked all perfect, makeup and hair just right. Blonde. Gorgeous. Like Susan. But she had no spirit in her. She was flat.

"She seemed more alive as a ghost. Happy and radiant and not scared of anything. She told Susan how much she loved her. She told Susan her death wasn't Susan's fault. Susan asked her how she had died, and she said, 'It doesn't matter now. It's enough that he can't use me as a hostage against you anymore. Promise me you'll leave this house as soon as possible, my darling.'

"Susan asked where she could go—"

"Here. Anytime," Nathan said.

Edmund looked at him. "Our heads weren't working that way. I don't know if it would have been good enough, even if we had thought of it. This isn't far enough away, Nathan."

"I would not have permitted Susan's father across my threshold."

"She would have been a prisoner of the house, then. Safe inside, but no way to leave."

"But—"

"Nathan," said Matt. "Edmund can't tell you what-ifs. This isn't an argument. He needs to tell what was."

"Oh." Nathan studied her face, then nodded to Edmund. "Sorry. Go on."

"Her mom said, 'Go to San Francisco to my sister.' She told us she was fine, that nothing hurt and she was happy if she could only be sure Susan would be safe and happy. After she and Susan had said good-bye, I released her.

"Then we went downstairs to pack."

He crossed his arms and buried his hands in his armpits, hunching his shoulders. He began to shake.

"Then her dad came home," he whispered, shivering.

After several minutes slipped by, Matt asked, "Do you want help?"

"What do you mean?"

"You remember it, I'll watch it, I'll say it." She wasn't sure if that would help or hinder him on his journey through this dark place. Maybe it was better if he brought up the fire and the wounds in his own words, let her and Nathan's listening to him wash the words away.

"I don't—I don't think—I'm not sure I can go on."

"We can stop."

"Give me a minute." His teeth chattered. He sat shaking in the chair for a little while. Then he took some deep, slow breaths and his body stilled, settled. His arms came down. "Spirit be with me," he murmured. "Spirit be in me. Spirit surround me. Spirit protect me. Spirit please help me." He repeated it several times.

Then he looked at her with tranquil eyes. "All right," he said. "Let's try it your way."

Matt opened her dream-eyes. Superimposed on the Victorian living room she and Nathan and Edmund sat in was a girl's bedroom, a confection of pink and white. A pale slender girl with long straight white-blonde hair and big blue eyes stood staring at the door to the room. A pale blue Alice ribbon held her hair back off her face, and she was wearing a powder blue dress that covered her from neck to knees. She hugged an armload of clothes to her chest. A shadow person stood on the other side of the bed from her, also holding clothes and watching the door. Edmund's placeholder self? He knew he was in the room, but he didn't need to make a clear image of himself, because he was inside himself looking out.

"That's Susan?" Matt asked.

—You see Susan?— Nathan asked her. —How? Can I use your eyes?—

—I don't know. Can you?—

Cold enveloped her right hand. She closed her dream-eyes for a moment and looked to see that Nathan had put his hand through hers. "What?" she said, and jerked her hand away, leaving his behind.

—If you let me inside of you . . .—

—No! Nobody inside me, not without asking! Nobody. Nobody ever again.—

He looked at her, turned his head away. "I'm sorry," he said.

She shivered. Edmund glanced at her, eyebrows up, then at Nathan.

Matt stilled. This wasn't the thing she feared. This was something she didn't know anything about, and this was a person she liked and almost trusted. —Tell me about it,— she thought to Nathan. —What is it you want to do?—

—If I settle inside of you, use your senses, maybe I can see what you're seeing. I've joined with Julio before. It didn't bother him.—

—Possession?— Matt wondered. She hated that word. She was allergic to being owned.

—We didn't feel like that about each other,— Nathan thought. —It was two friends in a very small space together.—

—Would you get out the second I asked you to?—

—Oh, yes.—

—You promise?—

He crossed his heart.

—Okay. Let's try it again. If I scream, you get out of me, understand?—

—I will.—

"What are you talking about now?" Edmund asked.

"Nathan wants to get inside me and look through my eyes."

"Oh. Like you did with Julio?" Edmund asked Nathan.

"Right."

"We're going to try it, but if I don't like it, he's going to leave. He says he will, anyway. Will he, Edmund?"

"Sure. He almost never does things to people against their will, except when he scares them. And they usually come here looking for that."

"He cursed you into a witch against your will."

"I'm not so sure about that. I mean, that was my dream. And he did warn me."

She frowned at him, then shook her head and turned to Nathan. "Come on," she said.

He turned away and sat in her lap, except he didn't stop at her lap. Chill invaded her front to back. She watched as Nathan's arms drifted down and inside her own, translucence eclipsed by her solidity. For an instant she froze, tingling with cold, as he vanished. Then the feeling went away. She stretched, pushing her hands toward the ceiling, straightening her legs so that her combat boots lifted from the floor. —You in here?— she asked. She couldn't feel him at all.

—Uh-huh.—

—Can you see?—

—Yeah. Looks like my living room.—

She opened her dream-eyes and looked at Edmund. There was a forest around him.

—Whoa!— thought Nathan.

—You see the trees? Good.— "You're in a forest," Matt said.

"Oh. Right," said Edmund. "That's where I go when I meditate."

"Are you ready to go back to Susan's room?"

He sighed. The trees faded and the bedroom came back. Susan kindled into being like a candle unmelting, her arms full of clothes, her face tense, eyes watching the door.

—Wow,— whispered Nathan.

Matt found herself staring at Susan. Nathan's longing was strong and strange inside her, less than sexual, more than affection. A hunger for some impossible food. —Quit that,— she thought.

—Oh! Sorry. Sorry.— Nathan stopped directing the use of the dream-eyes.

Matt looked around, located the Edmund shadow, studied Susan's room. It was so clean it almost hurt, and nothing in it looked strong; spindly legs on the furniture, fragile porcelain dolls in frilly dresses on the shelves.

"You're standing there. Both of you are standing there staring at the door," Matt said, though why she should describe this when Edmund knew what he was thinking and Nathan could see it for himself now, she didn't know.

The door slammed open and a tall, pale-haired, business-suited man shrouded in darkness stood there. His mouth was open, his face wide with words. Black flame flickered off him, rose as smudgy smoke. Silver arrows shot from his mouth, plunged into Susan and Edmund's placeholder self.

Edmund gasped, and the image vanished. Red fire blazed all around Edmund, obscuring the past and the living room. The flames were so bright and big Matt almost felt her eyebrows sizzle. Everything in her told her it was a good time to panic. Her muscles tensed; her hands gripped the chair arms.

—No heat,— Nathan thought. —House isn't hurt.—

Matt sucked in a deep breath. It was cool and carried no taste of burning.

The flames shifted, solidified, darkened: retreated and turned to trees. Presently a forest stood around Edmund again, whole and green and cool.

Matt and Nathan studied it. Every tree a piece of his anger, a potential fire-home: there were a lot of trees, some of them so tall their tops melted into the mist and sky.

"I can't," Edmund whispered. "I can't go there right now. I don't remember."

"Okay," said Matt. Her breathing steadied. What had happened next? Something so big it had changed him into a different person. She licked her lips. Her throat was dry from the image of flames. "We can't go to the red boy now." All that fire! A huge burned-out place in his history. Could he be whole without it? Matt didn't think so.

Maybe Edmund didn't need to be whole. He was okay the way he was.

Dead dreams and lost hopes . . .

He's not mine. He's his own person. He gets to figure out who he wants to be.

She thought of him coming to her in the cemetery, saying spirit had moved him—that spirit always moved him. Spirit, a spiral of blue sparkles that melted into the walls. *He's his own person, but I'm with him now. I can't make him do anything. I don't want to make him do anything. I can talk to him, though.*

She said, slowly, "What about the other boy? The young one, the one you used to be? He's been in limbo a long time too. Maybe we don't have to go through the fire to find him. Maybe we can go around."

"What do you mean?" Edmund asked.

She hesitated, staring at nothing and trying to think through her impressions. Edmund could remember being that younger boy before the red boy. He was dreaming that boy, sometimes even speaking with his voice. If he built a bridge back to that boy across the burned place, that would be a start.

"Listen," she said. "This is just me talking. It's okay if you don't want to do what I say. I'm just having thoughts. No guarantee they're true thoughts."

Edmund smiled and touched her hand. "Keep talking."

"You kind of cut yourself into three pieces, and one of the pieces is all burned up." Matt frowned, pondering that. Fire seemed pretty permanent and final. There was some kind of bird that rose from ashes, though; and she had seen the red boy. Edmund hadn't killed him, exactly, just put him to sleep inside the trees.

"The second piece is who you are now. And the third piece, the younger one from before the fire, it looked pretty okay," she went on. "You could hook up with that piece again."

Edmund watched her for a while. She hunched her shoulders, relaxed again, wondering if he thought she was crazy.
—Does this make any sense to you?— she asked Nathan.

—I don't understand it,— he thought from inside her, —but there's something deeper at work here.—

Edmund said, "How?"

Matt licked her lip. —House, will you help me?—

—What is it you want to do?—

—Did you see Susan and Susan's room through Nathan's eyes, through my eyes? Do you see the forest Edmund made that's all around him now?—

—Yes. Astonishing and marvelous.—

—All this furniture that wasn't here before, you brought it from somewhere . . .—

—From the past.—

Matt frowned. —Time-traveling furniture?—

—I know the shape of it because it was here before, a part of me. I can recreate it.—

—If I could show you images of other things, could you bring them here? Make them look like solid things?—

—I don't know,— thought the house.

—Interesting!— Nathan thought.

—I saw this image of Edmund in his thoughtscape, Edmund as a kid, and I was wondering if you could make him look—make it so we could see him. I mean, he used to be here too, didn't he?—

Matt sensed a low hum under her feet, growing louder, like sleeping bees awakened by the promise of spring. The house was excited.

—I remember what he looked like,— Nathan thought, and the image of a boy formed before the fireplace, younger than Edmund though just as tall, slender and awkward in high-top tennis shoes, jeans, and a cream-colored cableknit fisherman's sweater, half-smiling, his hands shoved deep into his pockets, his shoulders hunched, his head covered with unruly brown curls.

—Can you make him so Edmund sees him?—

—What a question!— Nathan thought. —New frontiers in ghostliness! Can I make ghosts of people I've known? People still alive? What about people I invent? How about animals?—

—Of course we can make him visible,— the house said. —Solid would be harder. Visible is something we do every day.—

The air tightened around them, and the boy flickered. Suddenly he seemed more present: light from the wall sconces stopped when it came to him and bounced off, the way it behaved with real people, giving him shading, three dimensions. He had a shadow.

Real Edmund stared, his mouth half open.

"Part of you," Matt said. "Or like part of you, anyway. Can you touch him yet?"

Edmund put a hand flat on his chest above his heart, stared at the image of his younger self, breathed shallow breaths.

"Do you understand what I'm asking?"

"No," he whispered.

"He's here," she said. "All you have to do is let him in."

Edmund stared at the boy in front of the fireplace. "Oh, I don't know," he said. Wind rustled the leaves of the trees around him, blew cold out of his mental landscape and across Matt's face.

—What the hey?— thought Nathan, lifting one of her hands and sifting breeze between the fingers.

—He's a witch,— Matt thought. Nathan's being able to move her arm disturbed her. She clenched her hand into a fist and dropped it to her side.

—Sorry.—

"Your choice," Matt said. She leaned back in the blue velvet wing chair, feeling again how tired she was. "There he is, anyway. Just say no and we'll make him go away."

"I don't think that's fair," said the younger Edmund, his voice young and plain and plaintive. "You want to throw my life away?"

—Who's doing that?— Nathan thought.

"What was so wrong with it? You want to throw away summer night bonfires on the beach, and teaching Abby checkers, and daring Julio to walk on the edge of the roof, and tide pools and slide shows and field trips and fireworks, and scrambled eggs for breakfast, and s'mores for supper, and chalk dust and pollywogs and salamanders and bikes? You too spiritual for TV and Spider-man and pizza?"

—How are you—who are you—hey . . .— Nathan jumped up out of Matt and walked to the younger Edmund, stared at him.

"Amaze your friends! Confound your enemies!" Young Edmund held up six large gleaming steel rings. "Confuse the heck out of your parents . . ." He waved the rings around separately, then clanged them together and held them between his out-stretched hands, showed that they were now linked, a chain.

"How did you do that?" Nathan asked, his tone fizzy with delight and surprise.

"Magic." Young Edmund grinned and waggled his eyebrows. "Bitchin', huh?"

"I hate that word."

"Sorry. I forgot."

"It's so rude."

"You're so old-fashioned."

"Shoot me."

Young Edmund laughed and dropped the rings, separate again, and they clanged on the floor, rolled and wobbled away from him. "Hey, you!" he said to the Edmund sitting in the chair, "you ever do any magic like that, huh? Classy, flashy, babe-magnet magic?"

"Nope," said Edmund the elder.

"I could teach you."

"Could you?" Edmund whispered. He stood, took a step toward the fireplace and this second self, then another.

"Sure. Hold out your hand."

Edmund held out both his hands, and his younger self reached for them and then through them and into Edmund's chest, and then the younger self melted inside the older self. Edmund gasped and clutched his stomach, then looked up, his face pale, his eyes wide. He backed up and fell into his chair, still holding his stomach.

—Matt!— Nathan thought. —I gave you an image. Who was that inside it? Where did he come from?—

—I don't know. You, the house, maybe Edmund too.— "Are you all right?" she asked Edmund.

"I don't know." Each word came out a different pitch. He coughed, let go of his stomach, clutched his head. He laughed. "Oh, criminy. This is so confusing." He flicked his fist three times and a bouquet of colorful feather flowers appeared in his hand. "Matt?"

"Yeah?"

"Here."

She accepted the flowers from him. They were made of soft dyed chicken feathers, green ones like leaves, red, orange, yellow ones like petals, a dozen feathery flowers. She brushed them against her cheek and smelled roses in the soft caress. "Thanks," she muttered, feeling strange. No one gave her flowers. Accepting the bouquet made her feel like a woman, and she almost never felt like a woman. She stared at Edmund, wondering who he was now: strange friend? Hormonal teenager?

His eyes were warm. He looked different from the man she had met, but he didn't look scary. His face, which had been strange and beautiful and still, looked lived in now.

"It's just a trick," he said.

"Really?"

"I can make 'em disappear if you like."

She stroked the flowers. They were so soft she imagined it was like touching a cloud or a thought. "Not yet." She could live with this strange discomfort if he could live with his younger self. "You all right?" she asked again.

"I think . . . yeah. I think so." He frowned. He smiled. He shook his head. "Oh, man! This is *so* weird."

Matt yawned, surprising herself. Then she yawned again. "Sorry," she said.

Nathan smiled and vanished, then reappeared a moment later. "Guest room's all set up," he said. "Edmund, do you need anything right now?"

"Sleep might be a good idea," he said, his voice still wavering.

Matt woke in a strange place, the way she did most mornings, and reached out to touch the nearest piece of furniture, a wooden table. —Hi. Where am I, please?—

—Hi, Matt. Oregon. Guthrie. Lee Street. Inside me.—

—House! Thanks for a nice night. Thanks for everything.—

—You're entirely welcome.—

Matt sat up, sheet and featherbed bunching around her waist. She was wearing the olive-green waffle-weave top of her long johns and a pair of underpants. She glanced over at the other bed. Edmund was still asleep under his covers. His face did not look rested.

She slipped out of bed. Her other clothes were folded on a nearby chair. She grabbed them and went toward the door, which opened for her without a sound and closed behind her.

—Bathroom's this way.— A door down the hall opened.

—Thanks.— Indoor plumbing that actually worked. A luxury. She washed up, dressed, and went downstairs.

All of the furniture had gone. She sat in the dust of the old living room and picked up the feather bouquet Edmund had given her. —Where did you come from?— she asked it, brushing the feather petals against her lips.

—I've been in a lot of dark places,— said the bouquet.

—Last I knew, I was inside a magic wand. I always whisk here and there. It's nice to be able to just spread out for a change.—

She grinned at the flowers and carried them to where her coat had fallen to the hall floor. She fished out the crumpled bag of doughnuts and took coat, bouquet, and doughnuts upstairs.

In the bedroom she smoothed the covers of the bed she had slept in, making as little noise as possible. She set the bouquet on the cream-colored featherbed, then sat and watched Edmund sleep as mist-filtered morning light sneaked through the lace curtains and crept toward where he lay.

Look what she had done. Dragged half of a story out of him, pulled a piece out of him, made him look at it and take it back. Now there was that second half to the story waiting for them, with fire all through it. Matt had an itch that said they wouldn't be able to let go of it. What if Edmund was unhappy with that hanging over his head? He had always been so calm and contented before. Had she ruined his life? If this was how a mission worked, she didn't want any more of them. Hear that, Edmund's spirit?

He opened his eyes and stretched. He smiled at her. "What a dream I had," he said.

"What happened? Was it a good dream?"

"It was a great dream."

"Want a doughnut?"

He sat up. He nodded. She fished a chocolate-covered doughnut out of the sack and tossed it toward him. It slowed in midair and dropped into his outstretched hands. "Cool," she said.

He waggled his eyebrows at her and grinned.

She smiled back. Maybe he would be okay. She got a doughnut for herself, white frosting, colored sprinkles. She tasted it. Almost as good as the one yesterday; she was used to stale.

Edmund took a huge bite of doughnut, chewed little, swallowed, said, "It was a dream about swimming in the lake at night with the others. The air was warm, but we built a fire anyway. I love the color of firelight at night. We roasted hot dogs. We told ghost stories. Pretty funny when you think about it."

"Nice," she said.

"We never did that, though. Susan wasn't allowed to get wet, or stay out after dark. In the dream she was swimming too . . ."

Susan, Matt thought. What had she seen that night?

Edmund set half a doughnut on the bedside table. He stared toward invisible distance. "That dream," he said slowly. "Everything seemed so nice and normal. But last night . . ."

"Last night," Matt said when the silence had stretched.

"You know how long it's been since I was scared? Years. Spirit takes care of me everywhere I go, and I am not afraid. Last night I found a place I fear to go."

"You don't have to go there. You never have to go there. The choice is yours."

"Yes," he said. He sighed. "I do want to go there, but I'm not ready to do it without a guide. Susan was there. She knows what happened. Maybe she can tell me, even though talking isn't one of her strengths." He glanced down at his hands in his lap. "And if it scared me, who knows how she felt about it? I know how she probably dealt with it: silence. I wonder if she's all right. I think I better find her, Matt. Will you come with me?"

"Yes."

Chapter Four

· · · · ·

"Matt?"

She lifted her hand from the bedroom doorjamb, where she had been touching tiny diamond-shaped inlaid chips of ebony—so many cool things about this house!—and looked up.

Inside a nearby wall, water flowed through pipes. Edmund was running a bath. With water that came from long ago? Matt couldn't work it out; all she knew was that when she had washed her face earlier, hot water came out of the tap in the sink.

Nathan stood in the hall just beyond the doorway, hands behind his back. He looked more solid than shadow, but still untouchable.

Matt straightened, met his gaze, smiled.

"I'm really glad you came. Thank you for sharing so much with me."

"You're welcome," she said. She meant it. She had let this boy inside her, and he had respected her limits. "Thanks for having me." She had to smile again. She couldn't remember the last time she had had a conversation like this, stilted but sincere. "It's a great house."

"Mm," he said.

—But he gets lonely,— said the house.

Nathan closed his eyes a moment, opened them, offered Matt a smile. "I wasn't going to say that."

"I getcha." She knew the house was only trying to help him, even though it embarrassed him. —I never stay anywhere very long,— she told the house.

—Will you come back?—

—I never come back,— she thought. And then she thought, —But some of my nevers are changing right now, because of Edmund. So I'm not sure about anything anymore.— She laid her hand on the doorjamb again, felt its smooth strength, thought about how this house had been a refuge to Edmund and his friends not so long ago. —You're the best place to run away to I ever found,— she thought.

—Come whenever you like. Stay as long as you like.—

Matt leaned her forehead against the doorjamb and thought about Home. She had had a home once, when she was a kid, when her mother was still alive. It had disappeared, and even though she had learned to be at home almost everywhere she went, she had never found another place that felt so deeply safe.

She looked at Nathan, thought about inviting him inside herself: how he had become part of her. That didn't make sense, and yet . . .

"Home?" she said.

His smile started slow and small, then widened. "Please," he said.

"Thanks." She studied him for a long moment, letting her sense of the house grow inside her. She got a sense of its skeleton, how it cupped rooms inside itself, how air flowed through it, entering and leaving, how its heart beat long and slow in the basement, circulating magic through it. Its spirit went deep into the ground and stretched to include yard, plants, even half the sidewalk. Its power came from the sky and from underground and from the energy of being in a town. It had changed from something human-built to something more, life form and world in itself. It felt muscular and alert. Wood warmed under her palm, as if the house pressed back.

"Want a tour?" Nathan asked.

It took Matt a moment to wake from her trance. "Sure."

He stepped across the threshold, looked around the bedroom where she and Edmund had spent the night. "This used to belong to twin aunts of mine. When they disappeared, it became the guest room," he said.

"All this happened a long time ago?" she said.

"Nineteen-ten, I think."

"You don't have to tell me about way back then," she said. "Maybe a time closer to now. What was it like when Edmund came here before?"

He glanced around, frowning. "They each picked rooms. This one was Julio's, and—" He narrowed his eyes, studying the twin beds. "We moved one of those into my old room, for Susan, so—"

House energy shimmered, and the view of the room changed. One bed, a mandolin on the dresser, a music stand with sheet music on it, and some other instruments leaning against the wall below the windows—a guitar, and something small and squat and stringed that Matt didn't recognize.

"Mm," said Matt. "So what did Julio look like?"

"Huh?" Nathan stared at her, eyebrows up. "Oh, yeah. We can do that too. I forgot." He smiled. Shadows collected in the center of the room, forming a short column. They densed. Color flowed over them, separated out until the image solidified: a short, slender, caramel-skinned boy in a red shirt, with his thumbs hooked through the belt loops of his jeans. Black hair, short on the sides and long on top, flopped forward, half-obscuring his dark, shining eyes. He had a wide gamin grin.

Matt couldn't help smiling back, even though she knew this was just an image. "Nice," she said.

"He doesn't look like that anymore."

She turned, more questions in mind, but the door opened and Edmund walked in. "Hey," he said, striding forward, hand outstretched, "Julio!"

He walked through the image, which faded. The view of the room-that-was vanished, leaving it the room Matt and Edmund had awakened in this morning. Edmund whirled, confusion in his gaze. "What?"

"Sorry. Just showing Matt some of our past," Nathan said.

"Ah," said Edmund. After a moment, he went on, "This is a very neat new thing, these images."

"I like them too. Let's go try another one."

Nathan headed out the door and across the hall, past the stairs to another bedroom. "This was Deirdre's room," he said as Matt and Edmund followed him in. A bed with wooden head- and footboards, ornately carved around the edges, stood against the far wall, with matching pieces of furniture near it. Bookshelves leaned along the right wall near the window, stocked with leather-bound books whose titles gleamed in flaky gold, and a vanity with a stool in front of it bumped against the left wall.

Nathan stood with his back to them for a moment, his hands loose fists at his sides. Matt sensed energy gathering.

The image of a girl formed. She wore overalls and a yellow T-shirt and stood with feet planted firmly on the floor, hands at her hips, arms akimbo. Her brown hair was pulled back into two tight braids except for fluffy bangs above her oval face. Large brown eyes glared below definite dark eyebrows.

Nathan glanced over his shoulder at Edmund, eyebrows up.

"Pretty close," Edmund said.

"This is what she looked like when I first met her," Nathan said to Matt. "The last time I saw her . . ."

The image darkened, stretched, reformed: a taller woman of about twenty, her hair now chin-length and stylish, her lipsticked mouth smiling. She wore a yellow blouse, a light-blue denim skirt, and black slip-on shoes. Her hands rested in the skirt pockets.

"Wow," said Edmund. "I don't remember her like that at all. I wonder what happened?"

"Mm," said Nathan, and a man's image formed beside Deirdre's grownup self. It was indistinct, but he looked tall and muscular. "We weren't paying enough attention to him," Nathan said when the details didn't sort themselves out. "His name was Andrew, that much I remember."

"She brought him here?" asked Edmund.

"It was puzzling," Nathan said. "I hadn't seen any of you except Julio for a couple years. When she came to the house, she acted like a stranger. I didn't know her at first. These two strangers knocked on the front door. House opened it for them, and I wasn't sure why. It was evening. They had flashlights. They came in, and she said, 'I had some really great times here.' And he looked around at the dust and said, 'I don't get it. What's fun about this?' She said: 'It's haunted. Nathan?'

"I didn't know what to do. Haunt them or show up? I settled for something in between."

"What comes between haunting and showing up?" Matt asked.

Nathan turned to her. His image shifted from solid-looking boy to see-through; all his edges glowed foxfire green.

"Nice," she said.

Edmund stepped closer to the image of Deirdre. "I can't connect her to the kid I knew all those years," he said, walking around her, glancing at the shadowy man beside her. "This is no future I ever imagined for her."

"What did you imagine?" asked Nathan.

Deirdre's image turned and stared into Edmund's eyes. He backed up a step.

"Didn't think very hard about it, I guess," Edmund said. "Roller derby or mud-wrestling, maybe. Possibly secret agent."

Deirdre's image smiled faintly and turned from him.

Nathan said, "She met Andrew in college. She was studying veterinary medicine. He was studying chemical engineering, and she wanted him to know that science didn't answer all the questions." Nathan stared down at his hand until it lost its transparence and looked alive again. "I'm not sure we convinced him, but he seemed willing to listen. Still, it was a strange visit. She was so . . . grown up. Close to not believing in me herself."

He frowned. "As if I'm something you outgrow. I guess that's the plain truth."

Matt cocked her head. "People do outgrow lots of stuff, but not always the right stuff," she said. She thought of Edmund's childhood room. Action figures, Matchbox cars, comic books. She thought about some of the grownup mindscapes she'd seen with nothing but work and sleep and TV and dishes and laundry in them. People moved away from magic all the time, as if the world squished it out of them, stepped on its hem and the people went on walking without noticing that the magic got left behind. But it couldn't be the world doing that: everywhere Matt looked or listened, she saw and heard magic. Something about the way people looked at things changed.

Matt frowned at Deirdre's image. "She was your friend," she told Nathan. "She shouldn't be treating you like a zoo or a landmark or something."

"I take what I can get," he said, and shrugged. Deirdre's image and that of her boyfriend faded.

Nathan walked through a wall. Matt and Edmund used the door and met Nathan out in the hall. He led them to a third bedroom. It had only a dresser in it. "This room used to be mine," he said slowly. "And then Susan's."

Matt remembered his yearning toward the Susan in Edmund's memories. Susan had taken Nathan's old room.

Everything seemed to mean something.

Matt went to the window and looked out at pine trees and bramble bushes and silvery morning fog. She touched the windowsill, seeking information, but the house said nothing. Well, why should it? They had open lines of communication already.

Was Nathan going to summon Susan's image, the way he

had Julio's and Deirdre's? Matt studied Nathan and he studied her in return. She already knew what Susan looked like, at least what she had looked like to Edmund. Maybe Nathan figured that was enough.

Something else was going on.

She crossed the room and stared at a piece of wall. Something about it . . . She glanced back at Nathan, who smiled. She placed her palm flat on the wall, and it moved away from her, opening into darkness.

"The secret panel," Nathan said.

House laughed under her feet.

—How did you do that?— she asked it. —You didn't tell me about this, but I came over here anyway.—

—I tweaked you in the intuition,— said the house.

She shook her head and walked into the darkness.

"Wait," Edmund said.

She had stepped into a small square dark space, with the opening behind her, but air flowed from her left. She reached in that direction and felt wall, then stooped and felt an opening below waist height.

"He left his mortal remains in there," Edmund said. "Wait, Matt."

She sat on the floor and reached into dark space. Her hand drifted down and touched the dry, airy bars of a rib cage. Shock jolted up her arm from the contact.

She could talk with things that people had made or used or changed—trash, streets, cars, furniture, houses, clothing, dishes, all had their created lives and their subsequent lives: what they had been made for, what they actually got used for, and, finally, how they felt about it.

Human-made, used, changed: human bones. She couldn't remember touching any since she had opened dream-eyes, and probably not before then.

Nathan's life lay under her hand, and his death too, such a rush, such an upwelling of history, choices, hates, likes, loves, fears, hopes. How pale yesterday's joining had been, compared to this. Life interrupted, cut off at fourteen by his own hand, the only choice he could understand in a desperate time. Half-life stretching on afterward, growing in experience and knowledge but never aging; interested in everything, unable to touch anything; perceiving the range of adult behavior time after time, but never knowing what it was like from the inside, only guessing.

Only guessing. And getting grown out of.

She closed her eyes and tasted the infinitely sweet and endless sorrow of that.

"Matt," Nathan said from in front of her. "Stop it."

She sniffled. She lifted her hand to wipe the damp off her cheek and lost contact with the bones and their intensity. "I'm sorry," she said in a choked voice.

"It's okay," he said.

"I didn't mean to."

"I know that. It's all right."

"I would have asked first, but I didn't know—"

"Hey," he said. "Bet you're hungry."

Her stomach growled on cue.

"I don't have anything to offer you, though."

"I know," she said. As his half-life had washed over her, she had discovered more about how strongly interwoven his existence was with the house's, how much the house understood about human needs because of its connection with Nathan, who used, anyway, to have human needs. The house regretted that it had nothing to offer her and Edmund.

Nothing except magic and shelter and delight, friendship and mystery. Home. Great stuff. Not quite enough to live on.

Matt scrambled to her feet, stepped back into the bedroom where Edmund waited. Nathan came with her, and the panel closed behind them.

She stared at Nathan for a long moment, connecting his image to all she now knew about him. Edmund moved to stand just behind her and rested a hand on her shoulder. Silence stretched.

She could understand why Nathan had switched subjects, but she didn't know where to go from here. She glanced up at Edmund. His face had gone still, thoughts and feelings invisible. His hand on her shoulder felt warm, despite the distance in his eyes.

"We have to go find Susan and find out what happened to her and her dad," Matt said to Nathan. "Once we leave, we won't be back right away."

"I understand," Nathan said.

"I know you do," said Matt, then shook her head. "I'll—I'll be back." Something she hadn't said to anybody in a long, long time.

His eyes glowed. He lifted his hand and touched her lips. A faint kiss of cold. Then he vanished.

"How do you feel?" Matt asked Edmund as they retraced their way through town toward the car. Fog melted, leaving blue sky above and mist diamonds on spiderwebs and leaf edges. The air was winter cool, but absolutely clear.

"Anxious. Unsettled," he said. "These boy-thoughts keep flitting through my mind. It's not restful."

She looked up at him. She had to take two steps for every one of his, and today he wasn't paying attention to that fact. The comforting, considerate man she had met a few days ago had turned into someone else, and she had helped him do it.

She gripped his sleeve. "Slow down a little," she said.

He started, noticed her, came to a standstill. "Sorry," he said, looking like himself again.

"It's okay," she said.

He hesitated, then said, "I keep having these thoughts. I really don't like them."

"Like what?"

He smiled his most beautiful, tranquil smile and shook his head. "They're utterly embarrassing and unworthy. This is difficult."

She tucked her hand into the sleeve of her army jacket and touched the feather flowers that nestled there against the inside of her forearm. The boy had given her this bouquet, and the boy was probably the one giving him uncomfortable thoughts. She liked the boy. "Your mind is out of control?"

He sighed. "Exactly."

She stared up the street. Half a block ahead stood Captain Nemo's Coffee Shop. It looked like lots of other beat-up, run-down coffee shops she'd seen. It looked like paradise. Her stomach muttered aloud.

"Aha," said Edmund.

She swallowed. She glanced at him.

"Yeah," he said. "I've still got plenty of money. Let's go."

"Thanks." She could manage without money, but she was

really getting to like restaurant food she didn't have to find in the trash.

Captain Nemo's had thick, white crockery coffee mugs, turquoise vinyl–covered benches in the booths, white Formica table tops patterned with small gold boomerangs, and wooden brain-teaser puzzles at every table. Matt smelled frying bacon and fresh coffee and a faint undertone of Lysol. Happiness flooded her.

When she had her hands around a steaming mug of coffee muted with lots of cream and sugar and she knew hot eggs, bacon, and toast were coming, she said, "So. These thoughts?"

Edmund drank water. He set the glass down and stared at Matt, then smiled. "All right," he said. "I'm jealous. I took you to see my best friend, and you were better friends with him than I was."

"Oh," said Matt. She sipped coffee and thought. She and Nathan had hooked up immediately; it had taken longer for Edmund to reconnect with his friend, and his connection was shakier than hers, despite shared history. "I can't help that."

"It's not your problem," Edmund said. "Yesterday it wouldn't have been my problem. I wouldn't have minded. I would have seen the whole thing in a different light, understood and appreciated it. Adolescence! I feel like I'm sitting on needles." The waitress set a big plate of hash browns in front of him and gave him a smile. Matt watched Edmund's return smile, automatic and beautiful. The waitress's eyes widened. Edmund's smile faded. He blinked. "Carol?"

"Huh?" she said in confusion, then glanced down at the nametag on her chest. It said CAROL.

"Carol Maddox?"

"Do I know you?" She glanced at her nametag again. No last name.

"Maybe not," Edmund said. "We went to high school together, though."

"Oh, honey, I think not, unless you're older than you look . . ." She stared at him a moment. "Edmund?"

"Am I so different?"

She bent her head to the side and studied him carefully. "Yes," she said slowly. "You look . . . you look like a kid priest. Way too young, way too serious, and not dumb enough."

He snapped his fingers and produced a red paper rose and a silly smile. Her eyes lit as he handed the rose to her. "Oh, yeah!" she said. "Now *that* I remember. Where you been?"

"Uh . . . seeing the world," said Edmund.

"I used to think about doing that," she said, "but I was too practical. Never could figure out how to make it work." She glanced at Matt for a moment, then blinked. "Order up. Sorry." She vanished kitchenwards, then returned a minute later with a plate full of breakfast for Matt.

"Thanks," Matt said, trying a smile of her own.

"I don't already know *you*, do I?" asked Carol.

"Nope. I'm Matt."

"Carol. Nice to meet you," Carol said, shaking hands. Someone called from the kitchen. She turned her head. "Gotta get back to work. Don't leave without saying good-bye, Edmund." She rushed off, tucking the paper rose's stem behind her nametag.

Matt bit perfect crisp bacon and sighed with happiness. "I love breakfast!"

Edmund smiled at her. "So anyway," he said.

"Yeah. Thanks for telling me the thoughts. I understand it's the boy thinking. It's okay."

Edmund shook his head, staring after Carol. "The boy has lots of ideas."

Matt salted and peppered her scrambled eggs. "She liked the rose."

"She always laughed at my magic tricks, but she never said yes when I asked her on a date."

"Try again now."

"But—" He frowned. "It's not important, and we have places to go."

"Ask her for a rain check," Matt said. "Let the boy find out that things have gotten better."

"I know that," Edmund said in a different voice. "Don't you think I'm poking around in here, checking stuff out?" He leaned closer to her across the table, and Matt leaned forward in response. "This guy is such a stiff! He backs away from tons of opportunities," he whispered.

"Maybe you can get him to change that," she whispered back.

"I dunno. What if he locks me up again?"

Matt frowned. "Do you really think he'd do that? He's a nice guy. I don't think he'd do that."

"Uh—" Edmund licked his lip, then reached for one of her pieces of bacon. "Can I have this?"

"Sure."

"Thanks." He lifted it toward his mouth, then froze. "Nope," said his older self. "I'm a vegetarian." Then, "But it smells so good." Then, "Forget it."

He didn't put it down, though. Matt sat back, ate eggs, and

watched him. He wasn't arguing with himself out loud anymore, but she could see the conflict in the way his face kept shifting.

"Everything eats everything else, so you might as well eat that," Matt said when she had finished the food on her plate and his hash browns were getting cold.

He took a bite. For a moment bliss transformed his face. Then it melted into horror. He sat still for a long time with his eyes closed.

Drew in a deep breath. Let it out.

Looked at her and took another bite of bacon.

"It tastes better when it's still warm," she said.

"It tastes good anyway," he replied. "You wouldn't mind if something ate you after you died, would you?"

"No, and neither would you. I know this is different. Its whole life was being raised to be eaten." She shrugged. "Spirit wasn't exactly providing me with food in recent years. I took what I could find, and I know what I like. Not usually things that went together, but hey. Didn't spend any time figuring out what *not* to eat."

"Mm," said Edmund. He finished the bacon and ate cold hash browns. "One way or another, everything turns into everything else," he murmured to himself.

"That's what I figure. That could turn into you or me or garbage, or maybe somebody else is casing the trash cans behind this place and it could turn into them. Or a cat or a dog or a rat. Or bacteria, whatever."

"It seemed important to me, in a spirit sense, not to eat things that used to think like animals."

"You ate that ham sandwich I gave you when I met you."

"Huh." He sat back for a moment, frowning. "Oh, yeah. I hadn't eaten in months. It tasted great."

"How can you not eat in months?"

"When you turn into something that doesn't eat . . ." He set his fork down on his empty plate. "Spirit provided."

Carol came back and put their check on the table. "Are you in town for a while?" she asked them.

"We're leaving right away, I'm afraid," Edmund said.

"Well . . . it was nice to see you. Nice to meet you," she added to Matt. "Come back soon."

"Thanks," said Edmund in the boy's voice, slightly surprised.

The car was where they had left it, a block past the bakery. Matt felt in her pocket for the sack of yesterday's doughnuts. Down to two. Matt glanced back over her shoulder at the bakery. Edmund looked too. "Something you want?" he asked.

"Food for the road?" She held up the bag and shook it so he could hear she still had some left.

"Sure," he said. "I don't think we're leaving the planet, though."

"Huh?"

"Food is everywhere." She wasn't sure if it was the boy or the elder Edmund talking, but she knew he was teasing.

"These are good," she said.

He stroked the top of the car—Matt heard its comforting, welcoming murmur—and turned to walk with her to the bakery.

As they crossed to the counter, Matt watched a woman behind it—the same woman as last night, Mrs. Danvers, a large comfortable-looking presence. She smiled cheerfully and served a ten-year-old boy who asked for a chocolate-frosted chocolate doughnut, wrote down instructions from a woman ordering a birthday cake, looked up as Edmund paused in front of the display case and studied choices.

Matt watched surprise inform her face. "Eddie?" said Mrs. Danvers.

Good, thought Matt as Edmund raised his gaze, startled again.

"Eddie! Where have you been?"

"Uh, hi, Mrs. Danvers," he said. He handed her a daisy, a real one, and asked for six mixed cake doughnuts, then explained to her that he had been traveling and that his sister lived in California and his parents lived in New Mexico now.

"You left town right in the middle of all that—" She shook her head. "Best let it rest, I suppose," she said.

"Wait. What do you know?" Edmund leaned forward.

Mrs. Danvers looked around at other people waiting for her attention. She put on a service person's smile and said, "Never mind. Glad to see you looking so well, Eddie. I did wonder how you were."

He stepped out of the way and went to the register to hand money to the second counter person, a young woman who looked tired already. Nobody he knew, Matt guessed.

Then he went to a low counter in front of the window where you could sit, eat pastry, drink coffee, and watch tourists walk by. He sat without any of the other verbs, and Matt sat next to him, waiting. Presently she felt like she really wanted to leave the bakery. She stood up. Edmund touched her arm, and she lost the impulse to leave but watched every other customer desert the place, some without having been helped. Even the girl behind the cash register vanished into the backroom.

Spooky. Matt had had no idea Edmund could do things like that.

They went to the counter again.

"My morning rush," Mrs. Danvers muttered. "What's happened to my morning rush?"

"Please," Edmund said to her.

She focused on him and blinked. "What is it?"

"Please tell me what happened when I left town. Mr. Backstrom—"

Her eyes widened. "That—that—"

"Did he die?"

"Would that he had, that disgrace to the human species," she said, then covered her mouth with her hand. She glanced everywhere around the store, then back at him. "What are you making me say, Eddie? A person can't say such things. At least . . . no, I suppose it's all right now. He's gone. Can't threaten anybody anymore, the bastard."

Matt felt unease stirring. She had met another witch before she met Edmund. What she had hated most about her first witch was the way the girl had forced Matt to say things when she wanted to keep silent.

Matt laid her hand on the counter. —Hello. Do you sense magic?— she asked it.

"He threatened *you*?" Edmund asked Mrs. Danvers.

—Magic?— asked the counter, confused. —Bakery magic. Boring powders turned exciting by fire and water and magic. Doughnuts!—

Mrs. Danvers said, "Didn't he threaten everyone, whether they got in his way or not? Every morning on his way to work, an old-fashioned doughnut, a cup of black coffee, a nasty remark, and an evil smile. Oh, what a creeping pestilence he was on this town. And what a trial to his poor wife. Oh, my tongue, my wicked tongue, saying things better left quiet."

—Do you sense talk magic?— Matt asked.

—No,— thought the counter. —Talk talk talk, but nobody's talking about these lovely fresh doughnuts. Get them now, when they're perfect. Wait too long and the magic leaves.—

Matt couldn't tell if the counter had any idea what she was asking it. She patted the counter and waited, trying to sense truthtell in the air, but that wasn't a sense she had.

"I'm sorry," Edmund said. "I really need to know. Is he dead? If he isn't, where is he?"

"What's it to you?" Mrs. Danvers asked, not as though she resented his question, more as though she were truly curious.

If she could resist a direct question and ask one of her own, Matt thought, Edmund wasn't using truthtell on her. Truthtell made you answer without letting you do anything else.

Edmund said, "Whatever happened to him, I . . . I think I was there. But I can't remember."

She studied him in silence for a long moment. "They said it was some sort of stroke."

"Stroke," he repeated, and stared down at his hands.

"You think you were there? Why wouldn't you know a thing like that? A stroke it was, or some sort of heart attack, or some other thing that made him different. He couldn't speak. God's mercy on us all, though I say it as shouldn't. I think he's in a nursing home in Salem if he's still alive," she said slowly. "Nobody at Blessed Heart would touch him. They'd all seen his wife's

X-rays and medical records enough times. Oh, I shouldn't be talking this way!"

Edmund touched her hand where it lay on the counter. "Don't worry. I won't tell," he whispered.

Her face relaxed.

"And Susan?" he asked.

"Susan," she said slowly. "The girl? They say she went south. The Bay Area—had relatives down there, on her mother's side of the family, thank the Lord. Haven't thought about her in years. Tragic life, that one."

The bell over the door rang as people flooded back into the store. "Thanks, Mrs. Danvers," Edmund said aloud, and she, back in service person mode, nodded, smiled, and looked at her next customer.

Still clutching the bag of doughnuts, Edmund led Matt out into the morning air, sea-scrubbed and sparkling.

"Hmm," she said when they were half a block from the bakery.

"I can't believe I did that," he said. He shuddered. "That's one of the things I threw away. I had just learned how to do things like that before . . . whatever it was. It was exciting, but it was creepy too. That's no way to treat other people. I never meant to reclaim that part of the craft. I feel like I'm moving away from spirit."

Matt walked a few steps without speaking, thinking about her own discomfort as she had watched him in the bakery. "Did you use truthtell on her?"

Edmund's eyebrows rose. "Truthtell? What do you know about truthtell? That I've never done. No. I used a thread of opening. She didn't want to say those things aloud."

"Opening?"

"A strong invitation to drop a mask for a moment."

"An invitation, but not a forcing?"

He glanced away from her and sighed. "An enticement."

Matt sucked on her lower lip and thought for a little while. "Are you going to use any of what she said to hurt her?"

"No."

She punched him lightly in the arm. "Quit torturing yourself, then."

"Hey!" He rubbed his arm and stared at her for a long moment, until she worried that she had crossed some line she hadn't known about and wrecked their whole relationship. "Quit that," he said after a moment in the boy's voice. He sounded shaken.

"Did I hurt you?" she asked.

"No. Of course not. I'm—" He shook his head, grabbed her hand. "Come on. Let's go to the beach."

"Huh?"

The car had rolled a window halfway down by the time they reached it, and Edmund tossed the bag of doughnuts inside, then crossed the highway and headed down to the sea, pulling Matt with him.

She ran, resistless, his grip firm on her left hand. Past the highway, buildings turned residential or hotel, and the black-green wind-warped shore pines grew everywhere, bent away from the sea. A faint smell of dead fish tainted the air. She and Edmund came to a beach access, sand-coated asphalt going down between the wings of cliffs, and Edmund pelted down that too.

At the bottom lay a broad beach stirred by tire tracks, with frozen waves of rocky reefs beyond it reaching out to meet the sea. Edmund dropped Matt's hand and went to a large driftwood log. He sat, unlaced his hiking boots and jerked them off, dropped balled-up socks in them, and then slipped out of his pea jacket. He left everything by the log. He rolled up his pants cuffs and raced to the rocks.

Matt sat on the log and touched Edmund's jacket. "What's the matter with him?" she asked, feeling desperate.

—Tattered inside,— the jacket answered. —Ripped, re-sewn, ripped.—

She stood. He had already climbed up on the weed-slicked rocks. He jumped from one to the next, heading out to the farthest point of land. She had a strange, sickening sense that maybe he was going to jump in, let the sea bash him against the rocks.

Was this her fault? Troubling the waters of his tranquillity. He had been perfectly happy before he met her.

She couldn't change anything that had happened. She thought of dead pieces of people that followed them around. She wasn't sorry she'd showed Edmund one of his. All she could do now was try to help him live with it.

—Wait,— the jacket said.

—Wait,— said something from inside it.

The portable devotions kit.

She laid her hand on the jacket. —It's okay for me to take it?— she asked.

—Please,— said the jacket and the kit together.

She reached into the right pocket and pulled out the Chinese silk, tucked it into one of her own pockets, and headed after Edmund.

She hadn't hiked around tide pools in a while, but once she had spent part of a summer in Southern California with a marine biologist who had tried to teach her about sea life. Matt didn't care about being able to tell one fish or seaweed from another, but she was good at keeping saltwater tanks running, and she had loved the lab equipment, especially the microscopes.

The rocks were slippery. Tide pools lay between and among them, and thin channels let the sea rush booming and splattering in here and there. The air tasted of ocean, slightly electric. Mussel colonies clung to the sides of rocks, and dark red-purple seaweed lay in iridescent ribbons and pods on top. In the pools, big aqua anemones bloomed. An occasional orange or purple sea star clung to the rocks along the tideline, and crabs scuttled with claws upraised. Keyhole barnacles made rough patches on the rocks, good grip for the soles of her combat boots, and less slippery than other places.

She didn't find the going easy and wondered how Edmund had done this so quickly and barefoot. She slipped and barked her hand against rough rock. In another place she slipped and went up to her knees in a tide pool, wetting her boots and jeans.

He stood out where waves crashed against the rock, facing out to sea, his head down. He looked thin and dark against the wide horizon, blue sky touching down on silver distance.

Matt grunted and kept working her way out. Sometimes she had to backtrack around places where water ran ice-blue and deep, and sometimes she had to jump and hope she wouldn't land on anything slippery.

She reached him just as he slid down to sit cross-legged. He turned and noticed her before she said anything. She sat too, almost touching knees with him. Her wet jeans clung to her calves, cold and salt-sticky and unpleasant. Her boots squished.

Edmund looked worried.

A wave crashed against the rocks, throwing spatters of spray over them.

"I didn't mean to . . ." he said.

"You're not going to jump in, are you?"

"What?" He glanced seaward, then looked at her with wide eyes. "Oh, no. No." He shook his head. "Nothing like that! I just needed to . . . touch base." He put his hands flat on the wet rock to either side of him. "I need to sit here for a while and reconnect, if I can. Slow down, find myself. If I can."

"Sure you can," she said. "Spirit's everywhere. You told me that."

He smiled.

She pulled his devotions kit out of her pocket. "This wanted to come to you," she said.

"Huh," he said, surprised.

"Is that okay?"

He took the kit and glanced at her. "What do you mean?"

"I took something out of your jacket without asking."

"It's fine." He reached across and touched her cheek. His fingertips felt cool on her skin. "So much stuff we haven't talked about yet. If something of mine asks you for a favor and you feel like doing it, that's okay with me."

"Good. I'm not talking to your stuff, mostly. I know talking to people's stuff is an invasion of privacy."

"I appreciate that."

"But I was worried."

"I understand."

She climbed to her feet. "Okay. I'll go wait on the beach."

"Matt."

"What?"

"Don't go yet."

She dropped down again. "You sure? Don't you need solitude to, you know, talk to spirit?"

"I don't know. Let's try it while you're here."

She settled and waited. Not much for her to connect with out here—rocks shaped by sea, scoured by sand; things lived on them, natural, nonhuman things; waves responding to wind and weather half a world away. All she could really connect with were her own clothes, and maybe Edmund's.

Well, there was Edmund. But he needed to connect to himself.

She waited. Wind blew. Waves came, crashed, went. Sun shone, sparkled off the blue water, warmed her against the wind. Gulls cried above. The air smelled damp and salty and clean. She felt everything inside slow down.

Presently she heard a strange sound, like a chord struck from a bodiless instrument. She turned and looked at Edmund. He sat with eyes closed, his hands flat on the rock, everything about him still except for his curls, which drifted in the wind's touch. His face held no expression, but she knew he was deeply happy.

A moment later, his eyes opened, unshadowed green, and he smiled at her.

"You're okay," she said.

"It says it won't leave me, no matter what I do," he murmured. "It says if I feel it going, that's because *I'm* turning away. It says I know the way back."

"Good."

He straightened, stretched, then picked up the kit in his lap. "So we need to figure out where to go."

"Nathan said Susan was in San Francisco. So did Mrs. Danvers."

"That was half a lifetime ago. She could be anywhere by now," Edmund said. He frowned down at his toes. "Salem's closer. We could go find out what happened to her father."

Matt frowned. She glanced at the kit in his lap, then up at his face. "Ask spirit where we go next," she said.

He studied her long enough to figure out that she was serious, then untied the red cord around the kit. Wind played with the tasseled cord ends. He hesitated, then opened a pocket and took out a pinch of something. "Spirit," he said. "Please help us. Give us a direction."

For a moment the wind stopped; the sea lay quiet between waves. Edmund placed something in his palm, held his hand up.

Gold sparkles blew up from his hand, hung in the air a moment. Matt leaned forward, eyes on them, feeling a strange painful intensity at letting glowing specks make a choice for her. She had handed that choice over, though, and it was more deliberate than a lot of her decisions had been.

The wind freshened. The sparks streamed south, over Matt's shoulder, and vanished as a wave crashed and sent up spray into their path. Matt turned to look behind her and saw the beach meandering off between sea and hotel fronts, vanishing into a sun-beaten haze.

"South," said Edmund. "Susan."

Chapter Five

· · · · ·

EDMUND stood and walked to the sea-edge of the rock, then knelt there and leaned down. The sea rose up with the next wave, and he thrust his hand into foaming water. "Greetings. Thanks," he said. The sea roared in retreat.

He came back and held his hand out to Matt. She gripped its cool wetness and pulled herself to her feet. "Ready?" he asked.

"Uh-huh."

"Thanks for staying with me."

"Sure."

He steadied her over the rocks on the way back to the beach. "Don't your feet hurt?" she asked as they crossed a width of sharp-topped keyhole barnacles.

"Huh?" He looked down. She looked down too. He gripped her shoulder for balance and lifted one foot so that they could both see his sole. It looked pink and clean and callused. "Nope," he said. He grinned. "I'm walking on sunshine."

She slugged his arm, and he laughed.

As they drove south away from town, she felt tugs on her heart. Nathan, and House—Home—moved farther and farther behind her. And those moments on the rocks, where she had not felt at home, but she had felt comfortable. She wanted to go to those places again. She could consider returning without flinching.

She touched her chest, wondering if she was all right.

She thought about some inland Oregon places she had been before, ones she hesitated to return to. The witch she had met before she met Edmund was a girl named Terry Dane who had used truthtell on Matt, put a tether spell on her, kept her trapped for a couple of months, and made her wary of witches. Matt had gotten loose and told Terry she'd consider her a friend, but she wasn't sure she wanted to see Terry again anytime soon.

The drive down the coast showed them sea and sky and land in ways Matt had never seen before. Sometimes Edmund stopped the car by the road just to stand and stare. On a headland they looked down at miles of beach stretching south, edged with the lace of foam, and the blue ocean reaching out forever below a forever blue sky.

Other times the road edged inland a little, away from the sea. Sometimes hunched dark trees hemmed the road, and sometimes tall ones that blocked the view. Sometimes dunes spread away from the road, and sometimes salt-scrubbed houses and stores staggered alongside. Matt had never spent any time on the Oregon coast except for the past couple of days. Some of the places they passed whispered to her to stop and see. She watched them dwindle and thought, *someday*.

At Reedsport they turned inland. "We'll make better time on I-5," Edmund said, and then, "There's a thing I never imagined myself saying. I love this coast, and I haven't seen it in ages, but—"

"Is something pushing you?"

He thought about it, then nodded. "It's not strong yet, but it's an undertone."

"Let's go." Matt studied the map and saw they would come out on I-5 far enough south that they'd miss Terry's town by more than a hundred miles.

Early in the afternoon, Edmund stopped at a rest stop and made a phone call.

Matt filled their water bottles at a drinking fountain and sat at a picnic table, watching kids playing with a dog on the grass.

Edmund hung up the phone and walked slowly back to the car.

Matt followed. "Something wrong?"

"I called my sister Abby and asked if we could stay at her place tonight. She lives on the way to the Bay Area."

"Yeah? What'd she say?"

"She says okay."

"She must of said something else." Otherwise why would he look so distracted?

"I've never brought anybody with me before. She was really surprised."

Matt thought about that for a moment, then put the water bottles in the cooler and said, "I'll be right back."

She went into the women's rest room and stared at her image

in the cloudy stainless steel mirror above the sink. What did he tell her about me? she wondered. Who does he introduce me as? Does his sister know I'm a girl? For a moment she wondered if Carol, the waitress at breakfast, had known one way or the other. The last haircut Matt had had, she had shaved her head. Spiky brown-blonde prickles were growing out again, a thistly fuzz that felt softer than it looked; not a boy's or a girl's haircut. Her face was not pretty, ugly, or handsome. It just looked like a face to her. She was thin and usually passed for a boy, though she hadn't felt guarded enough around Edmund to be careful of her projections.

Who does he think I am? she wondered. She had slept on him, beside him; he took her hand now and again, hugged her, and leaned on her shoulder, and she didn't shake him off.

To her, he was beautiful. She loved the way he smelled. She felt safe with him. She felt strange wanting more than conversation from someone else, but something in her wanted.

She shook the feather bouquet out of her sleeve and studied it a moment. Part of him knows I'm a girl. These to me, a rose to Carol, a daisy to Mrs. Danvers. He knows I'm a girl.

It hadn't made her feel twitchy, though, the way most male–female attention she had gotten since she woke up did. He wasn't like any man or woman she had ever known. She touched a flower to her lips, then hid the bouquet again.

She washed her hands and went out to the car.

"You okay?" he asked as she settled beside him.

"Uh huh. Who did you tell her I was?"

"My friend Matt."

"Huh," she said. That worked okay.

"She's really excited to meet you. I didn't ask you about this before I called her. Is it okay to stay with her?"

"Sure," said Matt.

"I think she thinks I don't have any friends," he said as he started the car.

"She knows you're a witch."

"Yeah. She figured it out before I did. She was great about it. Even though she was just a little kid, she let me talk to her about it, and that was a huge relief. I mean, I could talk to Julio about it, and sort of to Susan—not as easily to Deirdre, she was too logical. But Abby was the only one who just listened."

"She know what you've been doing with your life?"

"I've never been able to adequately describe my life to anybody but you," Edmund said.

Matt smiled. "Bet my sister thinks I don't have any friends, either."

"Do you have friends?"

"I make lots of friends. I just never see them again," Matt said.

"Same here."

They drove in silence for a couple minutes. "That sounds real depressing," said Matt, "when I think about it."

"But you never feel alone, do you?"

"Nope. Always something to talk to, and most of them are great." She touched the car's dashboard. She really liked Edmund's car. It was one of the nicest cars she'd ever talked to, and she liked most of the ones she'd met.

"Exactly," he said.

Edmund didn't talk to cars, though. "Spirit," Matt guessed.

"Right."

"Just makes us seem crazy," Matt said after a minute. Then she grinned. "Hey, you ever wonder if you *are* crazy?"

"No," said Edmund. He smiled at her.

"Huh. I have once in a while."

"Why?"

"Because, used to be other people always believed it. They'd see me and right away they assumed I was crazy, and I couldn't even figure out why for a while."

"You figured it out? What was it?"

"Nobody else hears the voices." She leaned back and sighed. "Doesn't that sound like what every nutcase says? Someone who walks around talking to things that aren't there, definition of a crazy person. Yo." She tapped her chest. "Everything talked to me. I answered back. Other people only heard my side of the conversation." A couple of times well-meaning people had hospitalized her. Once she had even stayed for a while before asking a friendly door to let her out. She liked the bed and regular food and showers, but she hadn't liked the way other people controlled her, made decisions for her; she especially hadn't liked the medication. What if it worked? What if it closed her dream-eyes and made her stop hearing things? She didn't want to go back to being deaf and blind.

"But that doesn't happen anymore." Edmund made his statement half a question.

"Naw. I know more now. I don't have to talk out loud to things that aren't talking out loud to me. We can have the whole conversation where other people can't hear it. It's so cool." She stroked the dashboard. "And some other times when people saw me talking to things, they could tell it was real. Or they sort of could, anyway. My sister didn't get it, but she got that I could do *something*. She wanted me to live with her and get a job fixing appliances after I repaired her dishwasher and her vacuum cleaner." Matt grinned. "I've done cars before, too. Maybe it's like you and that cemetery wall. Lots of stuff feels better when it's working right."

"So it's a job you might like?"

Matt watched trees go by outside, trying to figure this out. "If I had a regular job, that would mean I lived someplace."

Edmund let silence lie between them.

"I'm okay for a month, sometimes six weeks in one place," Matt said in a little while. "But I can't, I just can't stop moving." The very thought of it made her anxious and shuddery.

"Why not?"

"Could you stop?"

His eyes met hers, and she saw an echo of her unease there. "Not yet," he said. "I've stayed places when spirit led me to it. Half a year or longer, sometimes, depending on the task. It was okay; I knew I was going to leave afterward."

"Sometimes I think I'm leaving to find something better. But sometimes things are just fine, and I leave anyway. Can't stay nailed down. Makes me itchy."

"I wonder if you have a spell on you."

"What?" She gripped the sides of her seat, remembering Terry Dane's spells: cages Matt had chafed against. Misery. "Who'd do that? Why would anybody do that?" She had been wandering long before she ever met Terry, wandering before she could remember to pay attention to where her steps led her.

"I don't know," he said. "But I can at least find out if it's there."

They pulled into the Valley of the Rogue rest stop in southern Oregon. It was a park in a forest. Edmund grabbed his kit and led Matt to a place away from the rest room building where they could sit on the grass.

"Will it hurt?" Matt asked, half-joking, as Edmund untied the red cord.

"No. Of course not." He studied the white silk pockets. "Do you mind if we do this?"

"It's okay." She hunched her shoulders.

"Put your hands out, palms up, then."

She placed her hands palm up on her knees. He took something from his kit, placed it in the palm of his left hand, murmured some words Matt didn't catch, and rubbed his palms together. Dark dust sifted down over Matt's open hands. For a second small blue diamonds flared in the centers of her palms. She gasped, glanced up at Edmund.

"Huh," he said. "Spirit, we thank you, we bless you, release you." He slid his hands across each other a couple of times.

"What was that? Was it a spell?" Matt asked, holding her hands out to him. "Can you take it off?" She didn't know if she wanted it taken off. She liked the way she lived. What if this were connected to dream-eyes and thing-talking? No. She didn't want to lose those no matter what else happened.

"I don't know," Edmund said. "I've never seen anything like that before. It didn't look like a spell. Maybe I should have done the seek over your feet instead."

She stared at her salt-coated combat boots, then glanced at him again.

"But I think maybe it's better if I just leave it alone. Want some doughnuts?"

"Oh, yeah."

They ate in the car, driving south.

• • •

Day was sinking behind the Coast Range and night spreading up from behind the distant Sierra Nevadas when they pulled off Highway 505 and drove to the little town of Summers where Edmund's sister lived, thirty miles and a mountain range away from the east side of San Francisco Bay.

Matt's palms began to sweat.

Summers started with a couple gas stations and a little grocery store near the highway, then turned into a real town a little farther on, wide streets with head-in parking places, few buildings taller than two or three stories, a lot of architecture left over from the previous century, and an air of being friendly, warm, and small.

Edmund drove slowly, and Matt looked all around: two movie theaters in one block, with fancy marquees from the thirties, maybe; taverns and restaurants under the orange streetlights, a small hotel with a café in its ground floor, scattered chairs and tables on the sidewalk in front of it. People coated and scarved against the winter chill walked and talked.

Edmund took a smaller street to the right and drove past a park and some turn-of-the-century houses, then right out of town. A mile past dark empty fields and the occasional glint of barbed wire fence pacing the road, and then up a dirt driveway to a dark-shingled house with lots of little pieces sticking out here and there, fans of fancy woodwork under each crook of roof, and porches wrapping around the sides of the house Matt could see. Yellow light spilled across the porch from a fixture near the front door, and light shone through gauzy curtains in all the downstairs rooms.

Dogs barked and ran out to meet the car. Edmund pulled up

next to a white minivan and climbed out to be engulfed in dog embraces. "Hey, hey, hey," he said as the German shepherd licked his face. "Haven't you guys grown out of this yet?" The shorter dog, an odd-eyed Australian shepherd, sat back and woofed.

Matt had had good and bad experiences with dogs. For the most part, she didn't trust strange dogs, but ones that people introduced her to, she could deal with. She climbed slowly out of the car.

"Off," Edmund said to the German shepherd. It dropped to all fours. "Dogs, this is Matt."

Matt came around the car and held out a hand. The Australian shepherd approached first, smelled her hand top and bottom, then sat back and let its jaw drop, its tongue hanging out in what looked like a dog smile. "That's Heliotrope," Edmund said, "and this one is Pox." Matt let the German shepherd, Pox, smell her hand too.

The front door opened and people poured out of the house. "Hey!" cried a woman's voice, and, "Hey! Uncle Edmund! Hey!" cried children's voices.

"Hey," he said, catching a boy and a girl and lifting them. The third child, a girl, wrapped herself around his legs. "Didn't I just see you a couple months ago? How come you all got so much bigger?"

"Last summer," said the woman, hugging him kids and all. A stocky dark-haired man stood on the porch, watching and smiling.

The woman let go of Edmund and turned to Matt. "Hi," she said, holding out a hand. "I'm Abby." She was a little taller than

Matt and had soft brown shoulder-length curls, hazel eyes, and a wide smile. She did look older than Edmund.

"Matt. Short for Matilda," said Matt, taking her hand. It was something she almost never told people, but she didn't want to start her relationship with Edmund's sister with a deception.

"Ah," said Abby, and smiled. "I'm delighted to meet you. Up there is my husband, Tony."

Tony came down the porch stairs and ambled over. He was compact and short-haired and looked mid-thirtyish and kind. "Hi," he said, pumping Matt's hand. "Just thought I'd wait till things calmed down. Hey, Edmund."

"Hey, Tony." Edmund peeled children off of him and set them on their feet. "Matt, these are my nieces and nephew. Oldest is Keith, then Iris, then Sara."

"Hello," Matt said. She shook each small hand and exchanged solemn glances with them. All the children had light hair and large dark eyes. Matt hadn't spent much time with children and wasn't sure of their ages, but guessed about six and under. Iris had pigtails, and Sara had short, curly hair. They all wore overalls.

"You guys hungry? I have stew on the stove keeping warm, and we waited dessert until you got here," Abby said.

"I'm starving," said Edmund. "What kind of stew is it?"

"Beef," she said, and then, "Oh, no, I forgot! You don't eat meat. But I have lots of fresh bread, and some really good cheese."

"Sounds great," Edmund said. Abby gave him a sharp look: it was the boy who spoke.

Keith grabbed Edmund's hand. "Come on," he said, tugging. Edmund laughed and let himself be led into the house, Abby, Iris, and Sara following after.

"You have anything you want to bring in?" Tony asked Matt.

She glanced back at the rusting Volvo. "We can get it later."

"Come on in, then." Tony led Matt up three stairs, across the porch, and into a front hall floored with a series of mismatched doormats and crowded with pairs of many-sized shoes and boots against the wall, a coatrack bearing layers of many-sized coats, and a spiky, bare-branched tree-shaped metal sculpture with an array of things hanging from its branches that ranged from a black doctor's bag to a sparkling purple jump rope with glitter-tassel handles. There was something incredibly graceful about the way the tree's branches curved upward. At the same time, it gave the strange impression that it liked being an everything tree.

A low table nearby supported a Coca-Cola tray buried in opened envelopes that still contained mail and a silverware tray that held three sets of keys, an assortment of men's and women's watches, two pair of tortoise-shell-rimmed glasses, and a few rings and brooches.

A brick fireplace cut across the inside corner of the room. Arches flanking the fireplace led off in two different directions.

"Uh," said Tony as Matt glanced around. "It's kind of our air lock where we suit up before we go out to face the world."

She smiled. Edmund, Abby, and the kids had already vanished through one of the archways—Matt didn't know which.

"Want to hang up your coat?" Tony pointed to the tip of one of the metal tree's branches.

Matt took the feather bouquet out of her sleeve, put it in her deepest pocket, shrugged out of her olive-green army jacket and hung it on the tree. She touched a metal branch and said, —Hi. You like it here?—

—I was born here. I have purpose here. I will stay here all my life.— It sounded silky and certain of itself.

—Thanks for holding my coat.—

—I love holding things!—

—Cool,— Matt said. Destiny worked out for the tree.

"One of my wife's pieces," Tony said. For a minute Matt couldn't imagine what he meant, but she glanced at him, realized he was smiling at the metal tree, and finally put it together: Abby must have built this tree somehow.

Weird!

Tony led her through the archway under the staircase and from there into the kitchen, where a huge stove stood against the far wall, windows to the right showed night untroubled by civilized lights, cupboards stood or staggered along the walls, a bookshelf supported standing and leaning books, and a rectangular table with a pale lavender tablecloth took up the space in the middle of the room. Fresh-baked bread and simmering beef stew scented the air.

"Give us something sweet! Please, Mom, please!" Keith cried, dancing around his mother. Abby stood at the stove, stirring something in a pot. Edmund pulled yellow bowls and plates from a cupboard and set them on the table. Sara and Iris had already taken chairs.

"Matt, you want stew?" Abby asked, turning to look at Matt. Her eyebrows looked anxious.

"Sure," said Matt. "Smells great."

Edmund took two bowls to the stove. Abby glanced from the

bowls to his face, her eyebrows up. "What is it?" she asked. "What's going on?"

"I don't know," he said in the boy's voice.

She put down the ladle and reached up to feel his forehead with the back of her hand. "You sick?"

"Am I ever?" the boy asked, half sarcastic, half scared.

"Edmund!" She gripped his shoulder. "What is it?"

Sara, the littlest child, left her chair and ran over to wrap her arms around Edmund's left leg. He handed the bowls to Abby and leaned over to lift Sara into his arms. "I don't know," he repeated, then said, "Maybe I do. Kind of an identity crisis, I guess. That sure smells good, and part of me wants some a lot."

Sara buried her face in the crook where his neck met his shoulder. "Stars," she whispered into his chest.

Matt teetered halfway between the table and the stove, wondering if Edmund needed help, and if so, what kind. He sure looked tense, and he sounded confused.

She opened dream-eyes. The house glowed with a certain golden spirit that was not quite awake the way Nathan's house was, but not very deeply asleep. Some of the golden glow surrounded Abby's hands. A thin skin of it lay over parts of the people who lived here, and threads of it crept up Matt's legs. It left a cleared ring around Edmund.

In Abby's mental landscape, Matt saw a much younger Abby, an eleven-year-old girl, tugging at her big brother's arm and demanding answers. Dream Edmund looked just the same as present-day Edmund did to Matt. He was saying, "Help me! I don't know what's happening to me!"

Sara's dream showed her snuggled in Edmund's lap, and her Edmund opened a hand and tossed shining stars out. They flew around her room and settled on the ceiling and her stuffed animals and shone at her.

Keith was thinking about food: a vision of peach cobbler, it looked like, with vanilla ice cream melting on it.

Iris had a sleepy, stretchy image of a blue dog beside her, a stuffed animal, but it was alive. She yawned and laid her head on the table.

Tony's thoughtscape looked like a lie detector record or a seismograph or brainwaves, a long sheet of white paper, graphs of little wavering lines for what looked like miles, and then sudden seismic disruption, the pens scratching up and down over the page in wild disarray. He sighed.

Edmund had three images in his mental landscape. A venerable tree in full leaf reached branches down toward two men: young Edmund and tranquil Edmund, who stared at each other with tension between them. No sign of the red boy.

Matt couldn't see any answers. She stopped looking and went to the stove.

Abby dished up two bowls of beef stew, handed them to Matt. Matt carried the bowls to the table. She glanced briefly at the table with her other eyes to see where everyone usually sat, which was something the chairs knew and could image: Abby at the head, Tony at the foot, kids where they were already sitting. Yep, two extra chairs had been added. Matt set the bowls in front of the guest chairs and sat.

Edmund brought spoons, settled Sara in her own chair next to Tony, and dropped into the chair between Matt and Abby. Abby brought other food to the table: peach cobbler in a Pyrex pan, a carton of gourmet vanilla ice cream with a scoop stuck in it, a golden loaf of unsliced bread on a bread board, and a wedge of pale yellow cheese with the wax rind still on its outside edge. Tony brought dessert plates and silverware and a bread knife.

"Thanks for the food," Matt said, and ate a bite of stew. Herbs spread strange but pleasant flavors on her tongue. "Wow!" She ate another bite. Just as good.

Edmund held his hand above the stew for a moment, frowning down at it. Abby stared at him. Tony gently took the cobbler and the spoon to dish it with from her hands and started serving dessert to the kids.

After a minute, Edmund took his spoon and dipped it in the stew. Then he put the bite in his mouth and closed his eyes. Pain and then delight flickered across his face.

He opened his eyes and stared at Matt.

"It's really good," she said. "Isn't it? Delicious."

"Yeah," he said in a faint voice, and took another bite.

"What is going on here?" Abby cried.

"Leave him alone, honey," said Tony. "The man's diet is up to him. Keith, ice cream?"

"Yeah, lots, Dad."

Tony put a big scoop of ice cream on top of the cobbler and handed the plate to Keith. He dished more dessert for the girls.

"You had something to do with this?" Abby asked Matt suddenly.

"Uh-huh," Matt said.

"What? What's happening to my brother? Tell me or I'll kill you!"

"Stop it, Abby," said Edmund. This voice was tranquil but firm. "I'm changing a few things. Experimenting. That's all."

She touched his hand. "Are you okay? Are you really okay?" she asked.

"Yes," he said. "You're a great cook, you know that?"

"Yes, of course I know that." She watched him eat more stew. She looked at Matt again, her pupils wide.

Matt's stew began to taste like anger. She put down her spoon, sighed. "He's a grownup," she said. "Or maybe not all the way, but he can take care of himself."

"Right." Tony nodded. He shook Iris's shoulder gently. "Baby? You want this or do I give it to the dogs?"

"'M too tired, Daddy," Iris mumbled and lowered her head.

"This is none of your business, Tony," Abby said.

Tony straightened, stared at his wife. His genial face lost expression and color. After a moment, he bent and lifted sleeping Iris, then turned and left the room.

Keith sat with a spoon halfway to his mouth. He stared at his mother. Ice cream dripped off the spoon.

Sara left her half-eaten dessert and came around the table to crawl up into Edmund's lap.

"Fastest I've ever worn out a welcome," Matt said. She patted the table, then stood, pushing her chair back. "Guess I'll go sleep in the car."

Chapter Six

· · · · ·

EDMUND'S fingers closed around her wrist. "Wait, Matt. Please sit."

Matt took a breath, blew it out, and settled beside him again. She opened dream-eyes, checked the house's energy. If it was as mad at her as Abby was, she didn't want to spend the night in it.

The gold energy lay over everything, but it didn't seem to have an emotional charge to it. Threads of it had come farther up her pants, though it still avoided Edmund. She rubbed her thumb across her fingertips and reached out to dip her index finger in the nearest thread.

—Seess deess deess deess deess?— Its voice was light and friendly and curious, but she didn't understand what it said.

—Hello? You understand my language?— Matt thought.

—Strooss strooss strooss stroooss strooss.— The

golden thread thickened, spread, covered her hand like a weight-less, room-temperature skin. She felt it advance up her arm under her sleeve by the prickling of her hairs—up her arm, across her shoulder, to the back of her neck, and then the prickling spread across her scalp in a flash like fever. Her head burned for a moment so short she almost thought she imagined it. Then the light voice said, —Ahh? Yess? You?—

—Me? Who or what are you?— She wasn't sure she liked it touching her without asking, but it wasn't hurting her, and she could tell it wasn't mad at her. It didn't want her to leave.

—Op-por-tu-ni-ty,— it thought.

"Abby," Edmund said. He stroked Sara's hair. "Whatever happens in the house is Tony's business. Whatever happens between me and Matt, that's our business: we're working on it. It's not your place to defend me from my friend. Whatever happens to me . . ."

"You're my brother," Abby said.

"And, like Matt says, I'm old enough to take care of myself. I've been doing it for years. You helped me a lot when I really needed it. I love you. Whatever happens to me can affect you and our relationship. Still, it's my business. It's my place to take care of it. If you don't want Matt to visit, we'll leave now. What do you want?"

—Opportunity for what?— Matt asked.

—She calls and we come. We come. We come. She calls and we come and we wait and we wait. She calls. We come. She shapes us not.—

—Shapes you, huh. How does someone shape you?—

—Ask ask askaskask.—

"I want you to stay," Abby said. She sniffled and rubbed her eye. "I don't want you to change."

"Don't you?"

"What do you mean?"

"You've known me for years. Why beef stew, if you don't want me to change?" He took another bite and smiled at her. "You can make anything."

She looked away. Her gaze fixed on Keith, who sat completely still and stared at his mother while his ice cream melted.

"Hey," Abby whispered to her son.

"Stop making a mess," he said, his face clouding. "Don't be so mean to Dad." He jumped up and ran out of the kitchen.

—What shapes could you make?— Matt wondered.

—Op-por-tu-ni-ty,— the gold whispered. —Ask. Shape!—

Matt didn't know what to ask for. Before she could articulate a thought, a shape formed on the other side of the table, a golden man. Jubilant, the gold energy poured into the outline, packed itself densely and filled out details. Matt blinked into normal vision. She could still see the golden man. Color ran and flickered over the man's surfaces, finally set. No longer golden: it wore the same outfit Tony had, beige slacks, white shirt, suspenders, and its skin looked tan, with a golden undertone.

"Let's try this again," said the image of Tony that now stood beyond the table.

I asked for that *shape?* Matt thought. *Huh?* It really looked like Tony, including details she didn't remember noticing. It sounded like him, too.

Edmund and Abby stared at the image.

"Wha—?" Abby murmured. "How'd you—?"

"Let's try this again," Tony said. "Matt says Edmund is a grownup. I say right. Abby, what do you say?"

"Where did you come from?" She turned to Edmund. "What are you doing?"

He shook his head, his eyes wide.

"What do you say, Abby?" Tony asked.

"I say . . . I say, yeah, right. I'm *so sure* my idiot brother is a grownup." Abby spoke slowly. Sarcasm and confusion edged her words.

Tony smiled. "That's better. Much better than telling me it's none of my business."

"Daddy?" Sara said. "Not Daddy?" She climbed down from Edmund's lap and went around the table. She stared up at Tony. "Sort of Daddy?"

"What do you want me to be, princess?" He knelt and touched two fingers to her forehead.

"Hey," said Matt.

"No, I'm getting it," said Tony. "A bear? A really, really big bear?" His edges fuzzed, turned golden, spun out to reshape into something much bigger.

"Wait a second!" Matt cried. She looked around, saw that her hand was still coated with gold, felt it in the prickling at the back of her neck. "Stop it!" She made a fist with her golden hand and tugged. The spinning and shaping golden threads that had been building Sara's bear snapped back to wrap around Matt.

—Thank you for the language,— it said, and kissed her.

"Cut that out!" She smeared a hand across her mouth, brushing gold threads away.

"Matt, what are you doing?" asked Edmund. The boy's voice, and he was half laughing at her.

"This stuff was lying around," she said, trying to shrug it off. It clung. It laughed. "All over the house. I thought maybe it was like Nathan's house. House spirit."

"Yes?" Edmund said.

"But it's not. It's, I don't know what the hell it is, something Abby summoned, and it's all frustrated because she summons it but she never tells it what to do."

"I what? I—what?" Abby was on her feet now.

"It's all, it wants you to shape it," Matt said, shoving it away as it tried to kiss her again. "If you won't shape it, it wants anybody to shape it, and it's not patient. Stop it!"

"You shaped Tony?" Edmund asked.

"I don't know! It's on my neck, and it knows what I'm thinking before I do. Will you get it off me?"

"How?"

"You're the witch, you figure it out! It avoids you, but it hasn't told me why yet. Maybe if you just grab it . . ."

He rose and reached for the golden mass. It zipped away from him, reformed as soon as his hands passed. He couldn't close his fingers on it. "Slippery," he said.

"It's your stuff," Matt said to Abby. "*You* do something about it."

"How in the world is that my stuff?" Abby cried, her voice young and forlorn.

"You called it. Tell it to be something. Please."

Abby shook her head. Then she said, "Be an oriental carpet."

Gold wrapped Matt's head for a minute, blinding her. She felt as if she was suffocating, then realized that even though she knew it was all around her, she could breathe through it.

It pressed against her forehead with phantom fingers, riffled through her thoughts.

An instant later the gold left her and formed a carpet an inch thick, red, with squiggles of white and black and blue, on the kitchen floor, with Sara sitting on top of it. She laughed.

"What is that?" Abby asked.

"I don't know what an oriental carpet looks like," Matt said, "and it only asked me. Hey, you dumb stuff, why don't you ask Abby?"

An end of the carpet unraveled into golden threads, which spun toward Abby and twisted toward the back of her neck. She cried out and backed away from it, but it could move as swiftly as light. It splashed against the back of her neck, capped her skull, spread across her forehead, and clung while she made small, scared noises.

The carpet changed. It thinned and stretched until it covered the kitchen floor completely, easing under Matt's and Edmund's and Abby's feet. A picture wove itself against a background of dark red, a tree with wide branches, bright-colored birds on every twig, leaves forming a halo around the tree's edges. Intricacies multiplied, swirls of bark, feathers on birds, veins on leaves.

Finally the carpet stopped changing.

Sara crawled over it, touching bird after bird. "Wa," she said with each finger poke.

Matt felt strange as she stared at the carpet. Something wonderful, startling. Something she had watched make itself. How had Abby known? Was this idea just lying around in her head, waiting for its chance to come to life? Musta been, considering how the gold acted, huh? Amazing!

She glanced at Abby, who sniffed and brushed a tear off her cheek with the back of her hand. "What happened?" Abby asked, staring at the tree on the floor.

"It's great," Matt said. She dropped to her knees and looked closely at tree and birds. "Wow!"

"What happened? Tell me," Abby said. Her voice shook.

—Now we can talk to her,— the carpet whispered to Matt through her palms. —Thank you.—

—You're welcome, I guess. Hey. Don't hurt anybody, okay?— Matt didn't know what sort of bear Sara had been thinking about. Probably just a fairy-tale bear, but . . . what if it was a man-eating bear? Even fairy-tale animals ate people; what about the wolf in Little Red Riding Hood? This gold stuff could do anything.

—Shaper's choice,— the carpet thought.

—Abby shapes? Not the kids.—

—Shaper's choice.— The whisper faded.

Edmund touched her shoulder. "Matt."

She glanced up. Well, it wasn't her gold, or her family, but it was Edmund's. How could she help them deal with this stuff? She wasn't sure she knew enough.

Abby stared at her. "Please," she said. "Please tell me. Where did this come from? What is it? What just happened?"

"Umm . . . I can see stuff." Matt frowned and sat back on her heels. "Stuff other people don't notice, usually. And talk to things."

"You're a witch too?" Abby asked.

"No. I just talk to things." She bit her lower lip, glanced around, then met Abby's gaze again. "I came into this house and saw gold lying all over the place. Never saw stuff like this before, didn't know what it was. It's on the floor, it's over the furniture, it's a little bit over the people, but it doesn't touch Edmund at all. There's a lot of it around your hands, Abby. During dinner it came up my pants. So I touched it, and it, like—" She clapped a hand to the back of her neck. "—it jumped up to my neck and started messing around in my mind. Like, before that, it didn't know English, so it couldn't say what it wanted, or understand what other people wanted, or anything. And I guess regular people couldn't see it. But then it figured things out. Smart stuff."

She shook her head. "It said it was opportunity. It said you called it and it came, but you never told it what to do. You never shaped it. So I said, how do people shape you? It said all you do is ask it for something. Then it wanted me to shape it, but I didn't say anything. I didn't even have time. It just turned into Tony. I didn't tell it to do that. Honest."

"But it *was* Tony," Abby said. "It sounded like him. It acted like him."

Matt felt past the carpet to the house. —House? You awake?—

—Awake. Watching. Confused. Been nice and comfortable and sleepy for a long time, and this new color all over me made me sleepier, but now I'm awake. Scared. Don't want it to hurt me or my humans.—

—Bigness talks too?— said the carpet, surprised.

—Sure,— Matt thought.

—Bigness shapes?—

Matt felt the house's awareness startle. It hadn't done much thinking, only enjoyed its below-the-level-of-thought existence for a long time as people lived in it and cared for it. Some families it had liked better than others. The current family had only lived inside it for three years. It liked them, though it wasn't sure about this strange energy that accumulated with them.

That it could talk to the energy—or to anything at all—surprised it. That the energy offered to let the house use it . . .

The house woke even more.

Edmund touched her shoulder again. "Matt?"

"Just a sec."

"It wasn't Tony?" Abby asked.

Matt remembered what she had wanted when she began this conversation. —House, where is Tony?—

—Reading to the children in the kids' room.—

"Tony's upstairs reading to Keith and Iris," Matt said. "That was a fake Tony."

"It sounded just like him," Abby said again in a small voice. "I need to apologize." She gazed toward the door.

"This stuff can make a bear?" Edmund asked.

Abby blinked. "Oh, yeah," she said, and checked Sara, who was still creeping along the carpet tapping birds and uttering tiny "wa!"s.

"I bet it could," Matt said. "It's really smart. I mean, a thinking, talking man is a complicated thing to make, and it did that in a second. This is the most beautiful carpet I ever saw. And this stuff . . . I'm not sure it understands rules. I've been asking it."

Abby's eyes widened. She went to Sara. "Honey?"

"Look, Mommy." Sara patted one of the birds, and it opened its beak and sang.

"Beautiful," whispered Abby.

"Come out!" Sara said, stroking the bird's woven back. It

fluttered its wings and flew into three dimensions, a gold and red and black flash. Singing, it flew around the room, then dropped to Sara's shoulder. Sara laughed. She held up cupped hands and the bird dropped to nestle in them. Its bright eyes stared up at her face.

"Booja," she said. "That's her name, Mommy. Can I keep her?"

Abby's face lost color. She stared wide-eyed at Matt.

Matt felt frozen inside. Bears. Birds. What next? Something that bit? Something that killed? She should never have come into this house. She should never have touched the gold. But she hadn't known—how could she know what it was before she even met it? She held out her hand and said, "Booja, come here a sec."

The bird whistled and flew to her finger. —Do you ever stay in one shape?— Matt asked it.

—Don't know.— As a small piece of the gold, it didn't sound as ominous or overpowering as the main mass. Or as smart. —Everything's new. Can't tell.—

—Could you be this shape and just stay this shape? Act like this shape? For a long time?—

—Might. Say firing word.—

"Firing word?" Matt muttered.

—Firing word. Set word.— The bird sang a short trill. —Final word.—

—What is that word?— Matt asked, her mental voice a whisper, stalking something she didn't want to scare away.

—Seesstroosstraass,— the bird sang.

"Booja," Matt said, cupping her hands around the bird. "Seesstroosstraass."

Heat flared through the bird. It sang a liquid fire song. Then it pecked her hand until she opened it. "Ouch!" It flew back to Sara's shoulder and sang a very sad warble. Sara petted it.

"What happened?" Edmund asked Matt.

Matt licked her lip and looked at Abby. "It says there's a word that makes it stay in one shape. What I just said. At least, I think that's what it said. I think it's all right now. It should just be a bird. Or whatever it is."

Abby heaved a huge sigh. Her shoulders relaxed. "Oh, good. Will that work on the carpet too?"

The carpet rustled under them. Matt placed her palms on it.

—No,— said the carpet. —No. Don't say that to me. I have many more shapes to try.—

—Shapes that hurt people?—

—Shaper's choice,— said the carpet.

—And anybody can be the shaper?—

—Anyone who knows to ask.—

—How did Sara know to ask?—

—I touched her and knew her and felt her desire.—

Matt lifted her palms and sat back. Touched, knew, felt. What if it touched somebody dreaming? What if it touched somebody having a nightmare? What if it touched, knew, felt before the person could even form a wish, the way it had when it took her vague wish for Tony and made it solid? What if the person was making a really wrong wish? You didn't expect wishes to work, so you didn't worry much about what they were. What if it touched somebody who couldn't think through to consequences, like the kids?

Well, who could think through all the consequences, anyway?

Matt would try. That wasn't enough.

She gripped Edmund's jeans. "I need you," she said. If anybody could think his way past a world of consequences, Edmund probably could.

He dropped to sit next to her.

"I can't figure this out." He put his hand down, and the carpet made a hole in itself so that he touched the hardwood floor. "Why is it avoiding me?"

Abby picked up Sara. The bird stayed on the child's shoulder. "I'm taking her upstairs to her father," Abby said. "Don't do anything until I get back."

"Okay," said Matt.

Abby raced from the room.

—Give me some of yourself,— the house said to the carpet.

—Why?—

—I can use you. If something pokes a hole in my roof, or breaks a window, or eats my wood. You could be any of those things, couldn't you? You could plug a leak in a pipe. You could be a waterproof shingle, or a wood so strong no rat could gnaw through it. You could be skin and eyes, nerves and bones and organs to me. Couldn't you?—

—Yes,— said the carpet.

—Be part of me. Wherever I need you,— said the house.

—Yes,— said the carpet. Half of it melted away.

"Whoa!" Edmund cried. "What just happened?"

Matt smiled. "That part's good. The house is shaping it."

"The house?" Edmund stroked the floor with a fingertip.

"That part is really good. The house thinks it can use this stuff to repair itself. So it takes some for later. Or maybe now?" She cocked her head and looked around.

—A few things need doing right away. This family tries to keep up. Some problems it doesn't know about yet.—

"The house is awake." Edmund looked sideways at Matt.

"This stuff scared it and woke it up."

"This house always felt comfortable to me, but never particularly lively. I've never found a concentration of spirit here before," Edmund said. He reached toward the carpet and it moved away from him. "Spirit never told me about this stuff. I wonder how long it's been here?"

"Maybe spirit figured it wasn't your job to deal with it." Matt wondered if it was *her* job. Or was she just messing things up?

"This is something Abby made?"

"I don't think she made it, exactly. It says she called it."

"Ask it where it came from and how long it's been gathering."

—Where are you from? How long have you been here?—

—We follow her, the caller, since she—since she became a crafter, maker, mother. Since she called. Some comes. Some goes. Some dies. More comes. She called us and she shaped most of us not, until now. Thank you, talker. Thank you.— Still a carpet, some of it crept up her arm, hugged it.

Matt felt rooted and trapped. —Okay. You're welcome. Would you stop that, please?—

—But we— —It wove itself around her, not tightly, but like a tent. From inside she could see it was like stained glass: colored light came through the birds, the trees, the leaves to lie along her arms and legs in echoes of the carpet patterns. Beautiful. Spooky. She felt as if she was inside a very small cathedral.

"Okay. All right. Okay. All right. Stop it." She lifted her hands and pushed at it. It no longer felt like carpet. It was something smoother, almost liquid, infinitely strong, warm to the touch. It let her push it away; as soon as she stopped, it flowed back. She punched it and it closed around her fist. "Stop it!" she yelled, close to panic.

Edmund's hands came right through the carpet and pulled her up out of its embrace. He was standing. She clung to him, wrapped her arms and legs around him and pressed her face to his chest, letting none of herself touch the floor where the carpet was. "Oh, God. Thanks." Even as she held him tight, she felt something weaving around her left forearm. He felt it too. He looked back over his shoulder to where her arms gripped his back, but couldn't turn his head far enough to see what was happening.

—But we want to thank you,— the gold said to her through her arm. —You gave us life and power to do what we have longed to do for an age.—

"You don't thank people by hurting them and trapping them and doing things to them without asking," she said. She felt utterly tired. A long day's drive, an emotionally charged visit, not much food, and a series of difficult arguments with something whose nature she didn't even understand. Gradually she relaxed her hold on Edmund, let her feet touch the floor. Supporting her with hands on her shoulders, he helped her step away from him.

They both looked at her left arm. Like her right arm, it was encased shoulder to wrist in an olive-green waffle-weave sleeve, part of her shirt. It looked normal.

She shoved the sleeve up and gasped. From elbow to wrist, her arm was sheathed in fine, woven gold. "What are you for?" she said.

—Thanks,— it said. It spoke in the smaller voice of a piece cut off from the rest of the gold. —I'll be whatever you want. I'll be whatever you need. I won't hurt you.—

She touched it with her fingertips. It was slippery-smooth. She could barely feel it against her skin. She lowered her sleeve over it and stood for a moment, trying to decide if she could feel it or not. Pretty much not. She almost liked the idea of having some of this stuff. Like the house: home repairs. It might come in handy. Use it for a bandage? At least it could keep part of her arm warm. "Okay," she said gruffly. "But that's it! No more!" She stamped on the carpet. It laughed under her feet.

Abby came into the kitchen, followed by Tony. "Oh!" Abby cried. "Where did the rest of it go?"

"Wow," Tony said. "Beautiful!" He dropped to his knees and stared. The carpet had adjusted its pattern to a smaller size: birds and leaves were just as ornate and gorgeous; there were fewer of them. No sign of Matt's fight with the carpet remained. "I can tell it's your design, Abby. Gorgeous. But you're saying—there was more?"

"About half of it went off to let the house shape it," Edmund said.

"The house?" Tony asked.

"The house wants to be self-repairing," Edmund said.

"The house wants something," Tony said slowly. His brow furrowed. "How can a house want something?"

"The house," Abby whispered. She went to the wall and touched it. "The house! Oh. That's wonderful! The house should be safe, huh?"

"It's a really nice house," Matt said. "It cares about you. I think it'll be safe."

"The house," muttered Tony. He glanced at the ceiling. "The house cares about us? Better than being haunted, I guess."

"Much better," Abby said.

"This is a terrific carpet." Tony stood and dusted off his knees. "But I don't get the rest of it. The carpet was me? It's hard to picture. I must say, in however many years of visits we've had from you, Edmund, this is the weirdest one yet."

Edmund put his hand on top of Matt's head and smiled. Matt sighed.

"How do you get it to work?" Abby knelt and placed her palms flat on the carpet. "Just make a wish?"

"It says ask," Matt said. "I guess you don't have to ask out loud. It knew what Sara wanted, and she didn't say much of anything."

Abby grunted and lifted her hands. "You do it. Make it be Tony again, huh? So he can see. I'm not sure I could make as good a Tony as you did, Matt."

"You've known me for years, Abby," Tony said.

"That's the problem. I know you so well I don't see you the way you are anymore. You're all the yous I've ever known you as, and I think that would be confusing and messy."

"I don't know if making it be Tony again is a good idea," Matt said.

"What's wrong with it?"

"I'm not sure." She slipped out from under Edmund's hand and paced around. "It says it'll do whatever you want, but then it does other stuff." She scratched her left forearm. She couldn't feel her fingernails through the golden sheath. "It makes a really great carpet. We could ask it to stay like that."

"But that wasn't a real choice," Abby said. "It was a spur-of-the-moment thing."

"The Tony thing was even shorter notice," said Matt.

"Matt, did it ever answer my questions?" Edmund asked.

"Huh? Oh, about where it came from and how long it's been here? It said . . . something complicated. About following Abby around since she called, or became a mother, or something. It never said where it came from."

"I'd like to be able to talk to it," Edmund said slowly.

Matt sighed. She dropped down onto the carpet. —I have a shape request for you,— she thought.

—I can hear you from anywhere,— it said.

—I know.—

—But I like to listen to you here.— A corner of it unraveled and reached up in a snaky golden twist to grip the back of her neck.

Fury flooded her. She could feel heat in her face. —All right. You won't be nice. I'll shape you. I'll shape you. Take any shape, so long as it doesn't hurt anybody!— "Seesstroosstraass," she yelled.

The carpet whimpered. The gold of its arm lost some luster and sagged, but it didn't let go of Matt's neck.

"So this *isn't* a rule?" she asked, frustrated. "About firing words? Does that just work on birds?"

—It's a rule,— the gold whispered, its joy dampened.

"You fired it, Matt?" Abby asked, her voice sad.

"I don't know!" Matt said, and thought, —Let go of me!—

—I'm not hurting you.—

Matt growled and pulled it off her neck. It wound around her hand instead. But it was right. It wasn't hurting her. Not physically. "God, you're slippery!" She wondered if she should order it not to annoy people, but that seemed too restrictive. On the other hand, her last direction was too loose. What if it tied people up for hours? That might not hurt them directly, but they could still starve to death. —Please take some kind of shape that talks,— Matt thought.

—Delighted,— the carpet said, and turned back into Tony's image, holding her hand. He smiled.

"*That's* what I look like?" said the other Tony. "Jesus. What a dork!"

Tony's image straightened, let go of Matt's hand. It looked down at itself, held its arms out, flexed its biceps, and smiled.

"God," said Tony. "I hope I never do that. This is way too weird." He sat down on a chair at the table, shaking his head.

"You fired it, but it changed?" Abby said. She no longer sounded forlorn.

"I don't know what it did," said Matt. "I told it it could be any shape so long as it doesn't hurt anybody. But I don't know if that'll work."

"It's a great thought," Tony said.

"Do you have a name?" Edmund asked the image.

"No," it said. "Call me Gold, maybe."

"Where did you come from, Gold?"

"I don't know."

"How long have you been here?"

It walked to Abby and lifted both her hands. Matt opened dream-eyes and saw that more threads of gold streamed from Abby's hands even now, flowing from her to spread across the floor. Gold Tony stroked fingers through its stream but didn't absorb it. It pooled around him, though, and crept up his legs the same way Gold had crept up Matt's legs. "Not long here. But near the caller." He rubbed his thumbs across Abby's palms. "Since a long time," he said. He glanced toward Edmund. "Since you left, maybe. Some of me, anyway."

"Since I left?" Edmund asked. He tapped his chest, his eyebrows up.

"Or later. She called me because you were gone."

Abby stiffened. Her eyes went wide.

And Gold changed. Not all at once, but not slowly. He grew taller; his hair grew curly and thicker, and his form slimmed. His clothes shifted from Tony's white shirt and slacks to Edmund's dark green shirt and black jeans. His face shed age and emerged young and perfect, smiling faintly, Edmund's most enigmatic smile. All the while his thumbs stroked Abby's palms. "Mm. Finally. This feels right," he said, and his voice had changed too.

Matt recognized it.

Young Edmund.

Abby snatched her hands away from him. "This is sick," she said, backing away. Her hands crept to her cheeks.

Tony stared at Gold's new shape, his brows lowered in concentration.

Gold shook his head, then rolled it; raised each shoulder in turn, bending his head toward them as he lifted them; shook his arms, shivered his legs. "No. This is what you want. Since a long time." He strode over to stand in front of Edmund. "Eh?" He held out a hand, palm up.

Edmund held out the opposite hand, and their heads bent, comparing. "So she remembers this," said Gold, tapping the base of Edmund's thumb, "but not that." He stroked the curve of Edmund's heart line. "This," Gold touched a tiny scar beside

Edmund's left eye, "but not that." He tapped a thin white slice on Edmund's upper lip.

"Got that one later, after I left," Edmund said. "So now you can touch me. Can I touch you?" He lifted an index finger toward Gold's lips.

Gold wavered, flickered out of range without taking a step.

"Why not?" Edmund asked.

"I don't know," Gold answered in Edmund's voice. "You terrify me."

Edmund's eyes narrowed. His hand shot out and closed around Gold's. Gold screamed and tried to jerk away. He struggled, but he was caught. Matt understood Edmund had done something extra to touch him this time.

It took Gold a jerking, shimmering, shrieking couple of minutes to give up on getting away. He didn't change, though. Finally he stood still except for his trembling and stared at Edmund. Sweat gleamed on his forehead.

"What are you scared of?" Edmund murmured.

Gold closed his eyes and turned away.

Edmund laid a hand on top of his head. "Oh," he said in a surprised tone after a little while. "That? I don't think so. Don't worry." He let Gold go.

Gold wiped sweat off his forehead with his sleeve, then ventured a faint smile.

"What *is* he scared of?" Tony asked. "We might need to know."

"It's private," Edmund said. "Sorry. I think Matt's instruction to it not to hurt anybody should work."

"Hope so." Tony drummed fingers on the tabletop. "The

upshot of this is that this guy showed up because of Abby? And she wants him to be another Edmund? Have I got that right?"

"I don't," Abby said. "It's not specifically Edmund I wanted."

"What *did* you want?" Tony asked.

Abby hugged herself and stared at the floor. Finally she glanced up and said, "Magic."

"Oh," Tony said slowly. "Ah. I see." He looked at Gold for a long moment. Gold smiled. "Edmund's shape means magic to you . . . but this being, this Gold, can be any shape? And other people can want him to be other things?"

"Until you say the final word," said Matt. "The firing word, like clay. Then he's stuck."

"Hey, buddy," Tony said. "You know how to be a rototiller?"

Gold shook his head and smiled.

"How about if I take you to look at one? Would that work?"

"I could touch it?"

"Yeah."

"Yes. I could do that."

"But would you?"

"It's something you want? It wouldn't last forever?"

Tony nodded. "Just need one for a little while in the spring. Usually have to rent it."

"I could do that," said Gold.

"Hot dog!" Tony said. "Let's nobody say that firing word, okay? I have a lot more ideas." He muttered, "Flying carpet? Witch's broom? Window-washing scaffolding? Pony?"

"But, Tony—" Abby said.

"He can't hurt us, he can do farm equipment, he makes a nice rug. I say we keep him," Tony said. In a lower voice he continued, "Let's talk about the rest of this upstairs." Then, to everyone, "I think the kids have the right idea. Let's go to sleep, huh?"

Matt looked at the food still sitting on the table and sighed. Gold walked over, picked up her stew bowl and spoon, and brought them to her.

"Thanks," she murmured.

"Sorry," said Tony. "Forgot about dinner. Shoot. Ice cream's totally melted, too. Eat whatever you want. Edmund, you know where the guest room is. See you all in the morning." He gripped Abby's arm and led her away.

Matt's bowl of stew was steaming. How had Gold done that? He had set it on her left forearm, and it stuck there without burning her. She walked back to the table and sat down. A jiggle, and the bowl came loose. She set it on the table.

Edmund joined her, sliced bread and cheese, and ate. "This is definitely the strangest homecoming yet."

Gold sat down across from them and picked up a slice of cheese. "Food," he said. "Food?"

"Taste it," Edmund said.

Gold took a tiny bite of cheese. He rolled it around in his mouth a moment. He frowned.

"Well, I like it," said Edmund. "Do we have different senses of taste?"

"How much are you like Edmund?" Matt asked between bites of stew. "Is it just the way you look, or inside too?"

"I don't know," Gold said. He took a bigger bite of cheese. "I don't know how to like this. I never ate anything before. Is this what it's supposed to taste like?"

"You made the stew hot," Matt said. She glanced at Edmund's bowl, and saw that a skin had formed on the stew in it. "Are you a witch?"

Gold bit a piece of bread, then choked, coughing crumbs. "Yaiii! Why eat this? Dust!"

"He's not a spirit seeker, but he's a witch," Edmund said. "In a couple of ways. He's Abby's idea of my witch self, and he's his own kind of shape-shifter. Abby never knew just what I was doing, so it's kind of mixed up in there. He can probably do things I can't."

"That's very weird." The stew still tasted wonderful. Matt finished it and ate some cheese. It was some flavor she hadn't tasted before, not cheddar, American, Swiss, or jack: pale yellow, smooth and buttery, with little bubbles all through it. She wasn't sure she liked it.

Gold dipped a finger in melted vanilla ice cream and tasted. "Mm!" He buried his face in it, lapping and sucking.

Matt had seen many more disgusting things, but it had been a while. She glanced at Edmund just to make sure he wasn't the one up to his eyebrows in ice cream.

He hunched his shoulders. "Disconcerting," he said.

Gold finished licking the ice-cream container. "That was a good taste. Is there more like that?" Vanilla streaked his nose, cheeks, and chin.

"Try the cobbler," said Edmund.

"Don't eat like that when Abby's around," Matt said. "She won't like it."

Gold frowned at her, thought for a moment, then lifted a napkin and wiped his face with it. "I forgot to be human. But my mouth is big, and a spoon is too small." He held a hand above the peach cobbler. His hand melted into shimmering gold and flowed down over half the dessert. His eyes closed. He groaned with delight. "This is a good taste too."

Matt rose and collected dishes and flatware. She and Edmund cleaned up the kitchen while Gold finished off the cobbler.

"Now I feel strange," Gold said presently. He put a hand on his stomach. His other hand looked normal again. "I don't want any more tastes."

"You're full. You'll get over it," Matt told him.

"Huh!" He stood up, slightly wobbly. "All this time I've watched people and food and behavior, and I never understood it. My head feels weak!"

"You need sleep," said Edmund. He took Gold's arm over his shoulders and slid an arm around Gold's waist, then helped him stagger across the hall and into the living room, where he laid Gold on a large couch. "Lie here for now. We'll see you tomorrow."

"Sleep?" Gold muttered drowsily. "I don't want to sleep. Sleep is stupid."

"Human bodies do it," Edmund said.

"I don't like it," Gold said. His breathing slowed and he drifted off.

Edmund opened a cupboard and pulled out a quilt, tossed it over Gold. He studied Gold's sleeping face for a minute. Then he glanced at Matt.

"No," she whispered. "He doesn't look exactly like you. Especially not now. You don't sleep like that."

He smiled at her and brushed past on his way to the front door, taking her hand. She let him lead her outside. The dogs lay on the porch and greeted them with sleepy tail thumps. The night felt frosty; thousands of stars glittered in the ink-blue sky. The air smelled of rank weeds. In the distance, coyotes yipped to each other. Edmund dropped to sit on the steps, and Matt sat beside him.

"This is not," Edmund said after a few moments, his breath visible, "exactly what I expected from this visit."

"I didn't mean to mess around with that gold stuff. I'm sorry."

"It's not your fault. How can you help talking to things? It's one of your best qualities. And tonight has been very interesting. I love my sister. I love my nieces and nephew. I like Tony. I stop by and see them once or twice a year, and we're all pleasant together—I think of their house as a place to rest and recover from things. I've learned more in the past three hours about all of us than I figured out in the past fifteen years."

"Will they be okay?" Matt asked.

"I'm sure they will. Might have to make some adjustments. Tony surprised me tonight. He's always been suspicious of my craft, kept his distance, didn't believe. I never tried to convince him, or anything; he put up with me for Abby's sake, and I did my best to be a good and undemanding guest. Tonight, all these strange things happened right in front of him and he didn't get thrown off balance. I underestimated him . . . I can't believe I've been coming here for years and never noticed that gold stuff before."

"It avoids you," Matt said. "She's making more of it, too. It comes off her hands all the time. How come it avoids you?"

"It thought if I knew about it, I'd destroy it."

"Why would it think that? It must of seen you before. You don't destroy things, do you?"

He stared into the night. "If I thought it was dangerous and couldn't be controlled, I would do something about it. Not just because I'm afraid for the family. Gold is my responsibility. That's what he didn't want me to know. I don't remember doing this, but it makes sense: I put some kind of spell on Abby when I left. I wanted her to be safe and happy no matter what happened. Wanted her to have whatever she wanted. And what she wanted—I never knew this—what she wanted was her own magic."

Matt sat and thought about this. Edmund left Abby a wish. Abby wished for magic. Magic came, but it didn't know how to talk to her or do what she wanted. How sad was that?

Matt watched her breath rise in the chilly night air and wondered why she wasn't cold. She had left her jacket hanging on the metal tree in the hall. She felt a strange rustle over her skin, and lifted her shirt to peek at her stomach.

Gold. Her small piece of gold. Now that she was conscious of it, she felt it all over her except on her hands and head. Sneaky, but effective. She lifted her sleeve and stroked the gold down over the back of her hand. It swathed her palm and fingers and closed over her other hand without prompting, then moved up her neck, stopping just below her chin. Creepy. But so nice and warm.

"You tamed the first gold," Edmund said. "But you say there's more wild gold?"

She opened dream-eyes and looked at the house behind her. "It's thin, but it's everywhere." She squinted at the window of a room on the ground floor she hadn't been in yet. It glowed. Matt pointed. "Most of it's in there."

"Her studio. Ah," said Edmund. "So she did figure out how to use it. Does the new stuff know how to talk?"

What if it didn't? Matt looked at the thin layer of gold lying on the porch. What if she started the cycle all over again? Taught this new gold to talk, had it attack her with friendliness? Had it erupt, had to tame it before it did anything rash . . . She was too tired to deal with it tonight.

Still, she dipped her fingers into it before she remembered her fingers were covered with gold. She could feel gold talking to gold, but she couldn't hear what it said. The gold lying over everything glowed bright as sunlight for a second, then faded to its former barely-there sheen.

"I don't know what that was," Matt said to Edmund.

"What what was?"

Matt blinked. "I forgot you couldn't see it. It just did something, but I'm too tired to figure out what." She felt gold rustling against her skin again, changing, but still warm. Maybe a little thicker.

"Let's get some sleep. You must be freezing. I'll get the stuff." Edmund rose and went to the back of the car, which opened for him. He took out his duffle and Matt's black plastic garbage sack. "Thanks, car," he murmured. The door shut softly.

"I'm not cold," Matt said, climbing to her feet as Edmund returned. She yawned and covered her mouth with a gold hand.

"Wah!" Edmund said. "What's it doing?"

"Keeping me warm." Matt grabbed her sack from him and followed him inside and up the stairs. At the top, a small hall held an array of closed doors. Edmund turned to the one on the left, and it eased open. "Whoa," he muttered. "Oh yeah. The house woke up, huh? I wonder if that's going to be trouble for them?"

"How could that be bad? It's a really nice house." Matt went through the door and found herself in a pleasant bedroom with twin beds, ruffled curtains, and a few pieces of battered wood furniture. Large watercolor paintings on the walls stopped Matt in her tracks.

A wild, beautiful seascape with gulls above, sun struggling through gray and orange clouds, green-gray waves below, and a glint and hint of something strange in the water—all caught in a moment that leaned toward movement.

On the other wall, an evening forest, some of the trees older than time. They reminded Matt strangely of things she had seen in Edmund's mental landscape. She stepped closer and recognized that they reminded her of the tree on the magic carpet in the kitchen, too. Again, though she couldn't see any overt animals, she got the sense that the forest was full of mysterious creatures.

"Abby did those," Edmund murmured. "She's really good."

"I'll say."

Edmund put down his duffle. "Bathroom's over there," he whispered, pointing to a door across the hall from the guest room. "You want first shower?"

"Maybe I better, before I fall asleep," she said. "Need to use the head first?"

"Yeah. I'll only be a minute." He vanished through the bathroom door.

Matt took her sack to one of the beds and rummaged around until she found the smaller plastic sack she kept her toothbrush, toothpaste, and deodorant in. She grabbed an oversized T-shirt to sleep in and stashed her luggage on the floor at the end of the bed. Sitting on the bed, she took off her boots. She shucked out of thick white socks, then sat, staring stupidly at golden feet.

She checked her hands. Flesh-colored again. She checked her stomach. Still gold. "Not so much coverage, okay?" she said. "I mean, thanks for keeping me warm. That was great. I'm okay now." She patted her stomach. How was she going to get clean if this stuff didn't uncover her?

She was still trying to work it out with a fuzzy brain when the gold zipped up her like a windowshade. She tingled all over. The only places that didn't feel fizzy were her forearms, which she checked. Instead of one gold sheath, she had one on each forearm now, which somehow seemed more workable. "Are you wash and wear? Guess I'll find out."

Edmund came back. He handed her a towel and washcloth. "You okay?"

Matt yawned.

"Golden arms?" he asked. She still had her sleeves pushed up.

"It's better than it was," she said, "all over gold. If I'm not back in half an hour, would you check on me? I might fall asleep in the shower."

"I'll check," he said.

She stumbled across the hall.

Stripped for the shower, she took a look at herself in the mirror. Yes. The gold was only on her lower arms now. Good. She had been wondering about going to the bathroom, too. Not a problem at the moment.

When she stepped under the pounding water, gold shrank to inch-wide wristbands, but it didn't let her take them off.

She managed to shower and brush her teeth and make it back to the bedroom before collapsing into sleep.

She woke up in bed with someone. She wasn't expecting it, and she didn't like it. For half a second she thought it was Edmund, then recognized Gold. He was awake. He lay facing her with his arms around her. "What are you doing?" she growled, pushing at his chest.

Chapter Seven

. . . . .

"NOT hurting you," he murmured, glancing over her shoulder toward the other bed. She looked too. Gold let her turn over. Edmund still slept in the other bed, and the quality of light against the thin gingham curtains at the window made her think it was either early morning or a dark day. Matt rolled back to face Gold. His arms weren't human—no bones she could feel, and too much stretch to them. Still, they held her tight enough that she couldn't get away from him without a fight, and she was pretty sure he could outfight her.

"What do you want?" she whispered.

"Little sister needs to learn," Gold murmured. His hand gripped the back of her neck. She felt a layering of touch there, his and something else, something warmer and less solid. She opened dream-eyes, realized that she and Gold lay under a quilt of wild gold, thick, glowing, fuzzy, enveloping.

"Why does she have to learn from me? You can talk just fine now. Why don't you teach her? Why can't Abby do it? Or even Edmund? Aren't you guys all part of each other anyway?"

"I don't know why," he murmured. The fingers of his free hand trailed down her cheek, stroked her chin, rested on her collarbone. He pressed his lips to her forehead. "You're the only one who can do it."

"That sucks," she said. She lay still while he stroked her face, fuming inside. She felt the new gold nudging gently at her thoughts, felt it touch until the touch connected. A strange sensation, like a piñata full of light breaking open; different from the flash of fever when the first Gold had read her thoughts.

Matt sighed, relaxed, let go of her anger. She was going to teach, whether she wanted to or not. Might as well do a good job. She gave the wild gold language instead of having it pulled out of her unasked, and something new happened. It felt more mutual, as though she were receiving something too, mostly images of light she had no words for, bright split-second-long bouquets.

Another language. Her gift was speech. She drank the light, and it tasted strange and wonderful.

She lay tangled in this strange exchange for an age, for an instant, a breath's length, a life's. Then the flow slowed and stopped. Matt felt peculiar, hollow and light inside.

Wild gold grew delirious with delight. Only moderately solid, it embraced her, embraced Gold, rolled around under the covers in a snaky, half tangible form, grew eight arms to hug her, shifted into cloud-light blanket, then a dog, then a woman.

—Hey,— Matt thought at it.

—Hey!— it answered.

—I shape you.—

—Shape me!— It sounded silly with joy.

—I shape you into something that can teach any other gold what you just learned from me.— "Seesstroosstraass!"

It kissed her, and its kiss was warm and sweet and gentle. For the first time in a long time Matt thought about wanting something like this, a closeness beyond thought. Before her mind flipped over into resentment, the kiss ended. Wild gold leaned its forehead against hers. Matt felt it nudging at her mind again, frantic but gentle. It made Matt feel drowsy, and its touch went on and on, shuffling and sorting through her mind in a tingling but soothing way. There was something strangely pleasant about it. Matt sank toward sleep.

Alarm jerked her awake just as wild gold broke contact.

What had it done to her? What if it had hurt her? Wait a second. She had forgotten that part.

Matt thought, —I shape you to take any shape so long as you don't hurt people!— "Seesstroosstraass!"

It laughed. Its voice was low and warm and familiar.

"Matt?" Edmund asked in a sleepy voice. "You all right? What are you doing?"

Matt groaned and sat up. Gold sat up, and Gold Two did too, her arm draped around Matt's shoulders. Matt saw Gold Two's profile from the corner of her eye and turned to look into a face that mirrored her own. Short spiky brown-blonde hair. Narrow, genderless face with sharp cheekbones and a well-defined jaw. Deep-set hazel eyes under thin but definite dark brows.

"Stop it," Matt said.

Gold Two smiled wide, showing strong white teeth. For a strange whirly second Matt thought, *But she's pretty. She looks great.* She blinked that thought away.

"Who is she?" Edmund asked, awake and sitting up, covers pooled around his waist.

"I guess she's whatever gold Abby made since Gold," Matt said in a monotone. "It's not safe for me to sleep in this house."

Gold Two stroked a hand across Matt's bristly head, then jumped to her feet on the bed. She even wore a giant T-shirt identical to Matt's sleepshirt. "It's okay," she said in Matt's voice. "I can teach talking next time. We'll stop bothering you now."

"Would you please stop being me?" Matt asked.

"Sure," said Gold Two. She leapt from the bed, and by the time her feet touched the floor, she was someone else.

In a way.

She looked twelve, or maybe a scrawny fourteen. She had long wavy brown hair that tumbled to her waist, and the T-shirt draped over a ballerina's muscular, sexless body. She still had Matt's face, edges softened by childhood. She posed on tiptoes, arms outstretched, and said, "Okay?"

"How did you—"

She tapped her temple with an index finger. "I snooped. I had to, so I could know how to do what you do. Okay?"

"All right," Matt said after a moment, breath tight in her chest. She used to look like that a long time ago, before her life collapsed.

Gold Two danced to her and touched her face with long slender hands. "It's not okay. It hurts you. I'll change."

"Don't," Matt choked.

"I mustn't hurt you," said Gold Two.

"I don't think . . . it's a bad kind of hurt."

"Doesn't matter." Gold Two spun on her toes and shrank again. When she stopped, she had short red hair, ginger freckles, and brown eyes, and she looked about eight years old. She resembled one of Matt's childhood friends, Ginny. "How about this?"

Matt sniffled and knuckled her eyes. "Cute," she said.

Ginny dimpled. Matt remembered that, vaguely. The details were sharper in front of her than they were in her memory. "How much do you know?" she asked.

Ginny looked away. "I needed to know a lot to take that teacher shape you gave me." She crumpled the T-shirt, now miles too big, between her fingers. "I don't really *know it* know it yet, but I understand about not hurting people."

Matt opened her arms a little way. Ginny ran to her and hugged her tight. "People suck," Ginny muttered against Matt's chest.

Laughter startled out of Matt. "Some of them."

Ginny sighed and let go of her. "Oh. Yeah. Maybe most don't." She turned a couple of cartwheels. "Well, I'm out of here for now," she said, and vanished.

"How did she—what did she—" Gold looked around the room, frowning. He climbed out of Matt's bed and stared at the floor. "What did she do?"

Matt opened dream-eyes and looked at the floor too. No layer of gold lay there now.

"That's not fair. She came second, and she's a better human than I am. Then she disappears!" Gold stomped out of the room, slamming the door behind him.

"I dunno," Matt said. "Maybe he's turning into a better human. He got mad pretty good."

"Are you okay?" Edmund asked.

Matt let herself fall flat on her back. She stared up at the ceiling. "I woke up and he's in bed with me. He's such a brat. He really irritates me!"

"You could shape him into something less irritating," Edmund said.

"Huh. Guess I probably could."

"I'd like to myself. I don't like it that he looks like me. I'm trying to be calm about it, but these thoughts . . ."

"The boy," Matt said.

"He's not even a *good* me," said the boy.

"He doesn't know how to be like you. He only knows how to look like you. Guess Abby's memories weren't specific enough."

"That girl looked a lot like you," the boy said.

"She *is* a lot like me. She's got a bunch of my memories. She's much more me from the inside."

"Is that okay?"

"Yeah. I really like her."

"That's cool," said the boy. After a moment, he continued, "Wish I could like Gold. I almost could last night. Hey, if you could turn Gold into anything you want—and you probably can—what would you choose?"

Matt rubbed her hand across her face and wondered if she'd gotten enough sleep. It didn't feel like it. "I would have to think about it for a while."

Edmund rolled over onto his back and lay staring at the ceiling too. "Maybe a life-size concrete dinosaur," said the boy. "With a staircase inside, and a little room up in the head where the kids could hide out."

Matt giggled, surprising herself.

"Or a vacuum cleaner. He could suck up dust."

"Rude," Matt said.

"How much worse is that than rototilling?"

"I think a rototiller is a big machine. Guys like big machines. A vacuum cleaner is too small to be impressive."

"You think Gold'd like being a big machine?"

"Yeah. Don't you?"

The boy laughed. "Guess he might. He could be a Humvee. Or a Jeep."

"You'd want him to test-drive himself before you got in."

"Gawd. What a concept." They were both laughing when a knock sounded on the door.

"Come in?" Edmund said, sitting up. Then he glanced at Matt. She nodded.

Tony slipped inside. He wore a red terrycloth robe and a worried expression. "I've been lying awake all night thinking about it. Can it really turn into anything?" he asked.

"We don't know," Edmund said.

"I'm sorry I started this," Matt said. "I'm really sorry, Tony."

"*You* started this?"

"Uh-huh."

"I got the impression last night that Abby was behind this."

"She made it come, but it was asleep until I talked to it," said Matt. "It didn't know how to, uh, activate itself."

"But it was always here." Tony shook his shoulders. "I felt it. It was in the other house too, huh? Our San Francisco house? Used to get the willies in midwinter there. This sense that something was always waiting around the corner, and I couldn't figure out what it was waiting for. Creeped me out. I was worried about the kids, too. What if it was an angry ghost? What if it scared them to death? Thought about asking Edmund to do an exorcism or something."

"Why didn't you?" Edmund asked.

Tony smiled and shrugged. "I kind of figured you were, you know, off your rocker."

"Thought so," said Edmund.

"Abby talked a good game for you, but I never saw you *do* anything."

"I didn't want to disturb you."

"What? You were pussyfooting around so you wouldn't bother me? Jesus! I kept hoping I'd catch you doing something impossible. I mean, I love Abby. I hated to think she was so wrong about you."

Edmund slapped his forehead with the heel of his hand.

"Could you do something now?" Tony said. "All you did last night was talk. I'm still not sure."

"This is a frivolous use of power. But then, I'm not in spirit seek mode," Edmund said. He drifted up into the air and sat there a moment cross-legged, naked except for dark blue boxers. "Yeah, lighten up, bozo," the boy said to himself. Edmund shot up and bumped his head on the ceiling. "Ouch! Not that light!"

"What's with all these voices? Are you actually having an identity crisis, like you said last night?" Tony asked.

"Uh-huh." Edmund rubbed the top of his head and drifted low enough so that he wasn't nudging the ceiling.

"But you can still float."

"Uh-huh."

Tony clapped his hands together. "This is so much better!" He did a little dance. "I'm not crazy because I think we're being haunted, and Abby's not crazy because she thinks you're a witch. I'm so relieved! Now if we can just be sure that that Gold character isn't up to too much mischief . . ."

"He's hard to control, and he has a creepy side," Matt said.

"You told him he couldn't hurt people."

"He kind of thinks of that like, it's got to be physical hurting. He won't hit anybody or cut them or anything. He's harder to pin down about the mental stuff."

"In a way, he's just a baby," Edmund said. He floated down to rest on the bed again. "He's excited about being able to do anything besides lie around waiting for Abby to figure out what to do with him. It's been a long, boring existence for him up until now, always looking, never being able to touch."

"Huh," said Matt. "Guess he is like a baby. A really smart, superpowerful baby."

"Can you teach me that freeze word?" Tony asked Matt. "Just in case he has the mother of all tantrums or something?"

"I hate to think about that. Even though Gold is creepy, it would be creepier to trap him. I hate traps. I guess you need it, though." She pronounced the firing word, and Tony mimicked her. Three tries, and she was satisfied he knew it.

"We should tell Tony about the other one," Edmund said to Matt.

Tony straightened, eyebrows up.

"Abby's still leaking that gold stuff," Matt said. "A bunch of it turned into another person this morning. That's how I woke up. Gold was sucking my brain."

"Yowch," said Tony. "Did it hurt?"

"No, actually. And I like the second one a lot better."

"She modeled herself on Matt instead of on Abby's idea of me," Edmund said. "Much more complete and caring."

"Could I meet her?" Tony asked. "Is she going to live here? How many of them are there going to be? I mean, I'm a doctor, but in a town this small, that doesn't mean big enough bucks to feed an army. Are we going to get a new one every day?"

"I don't know where she went," Matt said.

"You're right. Maybe I could stop that leak," Edmund said at the same time, "but Abby uses some of that stuff in her work."

"Oh, jeeze," Tony said. "Of course. I always thought her pictures looked kind of haunted. Jesus."

The air near Matt's bed shimmered. Ginny popped into view, her hands clasped behind her back. She no longer wore a big T-shirt; now she had on a dress, soft knit cloth in spring green. "Hello," she said.

Tony blinked. "Hi."

"I don't really have to eat," she said.

"It's all right. I could feed you." He came and knelt in front of her so that their eyes were level. He held out a hand. "I'm Tony."

She giggled. "I know. I'm Ginny." She shook hands with him.

"Ginny?" he said.

"Well, for now."

"You're a shifter too?"

"Uh-huh."

"I could ask you to be something and you'd be it?"

"Maybe."

"You have limits?"

"I'm a teacher," she said. "That's my main shape already. Matt fired me into it. And the 'don't harm people' one. And somewhere in the middle of that, I get to choose my shapes, and choose shapes not to be. If it's something that doesn't teach . . ." She raised her eyebrows.

Tony sat back on his heels. "How do you feel about 'baby-sitter'?"

Ginny smiled. "My favorite!"

"What would that look like?"

"What's wrong with this?" She held out her hands, looked down at herself, then gazed at him again.

"You look like you're about eight years old."

"Yes."

"The kids wouldn't take you seriously."

"They'd learn," she said. "But I can be bigger."

Ginny closed her eyes, shimmered a moment, and grew two and a half feet taller, her dress keeping pace. Her hair lengthened. Her face and body matured, though the freckles stayed. She looked like a sixteen-year-old version of Ginny, someone Matt had never seen; they had moved away from each other when they were ten.

Teenage Ginny brushed long, crackling auburn hair behind her shoulders and looked down at herself. Not as muscular as the Matilda ballerina she had been earlier, not as compact; a gawky, long-limbed adolescent with freckled arms, and bumpy, beautiful, awkward knees and elbows, hands and feet. She smiled. Her eyes glowed soft amber.

Tony rose to his feet. Ginny was almost as tall as he was now, and taller than Matt. "That's great," he said.

"Thank you," she said.

"Will you come meet my wife? The kids?"

"Sure." She followed him out of the room.

"Is your head okay?" Matt asked Edmund.

He gave the top of his head a final pat. "It was worth it. Wow. Spirit, where were you when I needed to know about Tony?"

"There's an easy answer to that," Matt said.

"Oh yeah?"

"You didn't need to know until now."

"What a gyp!" said the boy. "Tony and I coulda been good friends a long time ago."

"Maybe not," said Matt. "You weren't too playful until recently."

"Oh, yeah. I forgot." He stretched. "Ready to get up?"

Matt pulled the covers up over her head and wondered if she could get back to sleep. After a little testing she decided she couldn't. As she lowered the covers, she saw Edmund slip a dark red sweater on over his head. She got out of bed and dressed under her T-shirt, even though he wasn't looking at her. She straightened the covers on her bed. Would they spend another night here? Just in case the answer was no, she repacked her bag.

"Before all that gold stuff happened, I planned to do a search for Susan," Edmund said as they pulled on their shoes. "Thought we'd find some quiet space in the house and do some casting. I have a map of the Bay Area."

"I wonder if there's quiet space in this house anymore," Matt said.

"I used to think the whole place was quiet. What does the house say?"

—House?— Matt thought.

—You could use the basement,— the house responded.

Matt told Edmund.

"Oh, good. Thanks, House," he said.

Matt looked around. For half a second she expected the house to answer aloud, the way Nathan's house had.

—Tell him he is welcome,— the house said, so Matt did.

"But first, let's get some breakfast," Edmund said. They went down to the kitchen.

Iris, Sara, and Keith were at the table. Sara and Keith were eating bright cereal; Iris had pancakes with syrup.

"Want something fried?" Tony asked from the stove. He wore dark slacks, a white shirt, and a dark-blue tie. He flipped pancakes with a spatula.

"Those pancakes smell good," Matt said.

"Pancakes I can do. Also eggs and sausage. You'll have to speak fast, though. In about twenty minutes, I gotta take Keith and Iris to school and then go to work."

"Pancakes, please," Matt said.

"For me too. Did you guys meet Ginny?" Edmund asked.

The children looked up, smiling and nodding.

"She talked to Booja," Sara said. The bird sat on her shoulder, nibbling Froot Loops that Sara held up to it.

Keith frowned. "Hey!" he said. "How come Sara got a pet and I didn't?"

"I want a pet too," Iris said. "It's not fair."

Maybe Gold could give them each a pet, Matt thought, but would he? Maybe Ginny would do it. Maybe Matt shouldn't say anything about it. She glanced at Tony.

"We will discuss this after school," Tony said in a firm voice. "This is the third time I've told you that. I mean it."

Iris huffed and finished her pancakes. Keith frowned. He looked like a kid who could hold a grudge.

Abby, pale and tired, entered the kitchen. Her smile was brief and unconvincing. She took her seat at the table and Tony plopped a plate of pancakes down in front of her without asking. He served Edmund and Matt, then went to the counter and made school lunches for two. Matt liked watching him buzz around the kitchen. He seemed to be having a good time, and he did everything with practiced efficiency. Presently he packed the lunches in two small, brightly colored backpacks, filled a thermos with coffee for himself, kissed Abby, and led the two older kids out of the kitchen. "Bye, guys. See you tonight. If you need me for anything, give me a call."

In the silence he left behind, Edmund and Matt watched Abby eat. Sara stroked Booja with her index finger.

"Didn't sleep very well," Abby said eventually. She set her fork on her syrupy plate with a click. "Was that stuff really my fault?"

"Mine," Edmund said. "That's what it told me. When I left, I gave you a wish, and your wish was to have magic in your life. This gold is the magic that came. Until Matt taught it, though, it couldn't understand you. You had magic. Just no way to use it. Or, well, it came out in your art, but—"

"My magic. You gave me magic and didn't tell me?" Red stained Abby's cheeks.

"I didn't know that was what I did. I couldn't even tell it was here. It kept slithering away from me. Every time I came here, it stayed away just so I wouldn't find out about it."

Abby bit her lip. Her eyes shimmered. "I wish I'd known."

"You know now," said Matt.

Abby studied Matt for a long moment. "Yes. Where is he, anyway, my dream man?"

"Gold?" Edmund called softly. "Where are you?"

Gold stepped out of the kitchen wall. He glided to the table and sat down in Tony's chair. He looked calm, almost as tranquil as the Edmund Matt had first met. Worried, Matt opened dream-eyes and looked at him. Nothing but a sea of quiet gold.

"Have you chosen?" he asked Abby.

"Chosen?"

"Did you choose a shape for me today?"

"What's wrong with the shape you already have?" Abby asked.

"It upsets people." He looked down. Sara stood beside him, her hands on his knee, and stared up into his face. "What is it, princess?"

"Here's Booja," she said. She held her hand up to her shoulder and the bird stepped onto it. She set the bird on Gold's lap.

"I see," said Gold. He lifted the bird in both hands and stared into its eyes.

"She's the neatest thing I ever had. I love her. I love how she talks to me."

"Good," Gold said.

"Would you make boojas for my brother and my sister?"

He stroked a finger across the bird's head and down its back. It chirped and settled.

"I can do that, if it's all right with your parents." Gold looked at Abby.

"Puh-leeze," Abby said. "They've been going on and on about how unfair it is that Sara got a pet and they didn't."

"Uh . . . Tony said he'd discuss it with the kids after school," said Matt.

"Oh, yeah," Abby said. "Maybe we better wait. Thanks for being willing, Gold."

"I'm here for you," he murmured. He held up his hand with the bird perched on top. The bird flicked its wings, sang a little pure-noted warble, and fluttered back to Sara's shoulder.

"What do you mean?" asked Abby.

Gold frowned at Matt. Matt felt a sinking in her stomach and thought, okay, he can walk through walls. He can *be* a wall. Even after he slams out of a door. What had she and Edmund said about him after he had left the room?

She had called him a brat, and creepy. Edmund had called him a baby. And those silly plans for what to turn him into. Did he know enough to be hurt or offended by that?

She licked her upper lip and set her hand on the table next to Gold. He hesitated, then put his hand on top of hers. —What happened to you?— she asked. —Are you okay?—

—I'm— — And then a whirl of pictures, information that wasn't language, some of it in the same language she had learned that morning from Ginny.

Matt gasped. When the flood ended, she sat back and tried to sort through it.

He'd been doing a lot of thinking, some of it in nonhuman ways; but then, he wasn't human.

Yes. He had heard them talking about him. Yes. It had hurt. How could it hurt? How did he know enough to have it hurt, to have feelings at all? Mysterious. (Tight-strung gold cloth with small red spatters appearing on it.)

Sleep? (A colored wind blowing.) Tastes? (A forest of splinters.) Desires? (A gold tsunami that swept everything away.)

He had talked to Ginny, blended with her and tried to understand what she knew and how it was different from what he knew. (Heat rose from a lighted crack in dark Earth, and as he leaned over it, it blew his hair upward.)

He understood a lot. Absorbed lots of information. (A hidden stream flowing from an unknown place into the bottom of a lake of warm something-that-wasn't-water.)

He knew what he was here for. Playing at being human, at

having human desires and flaws, those weren't his purpose, though his immense delight at his liberation from pointlessness had tripped him over into them. He was here to do impossible things. He was here to be shaped, to grant wishes, to use his power as someone else directed it. Finally that was possible.

All he needed was direction.

His eyes looked peaceful.

—I'm sorry,— Matt thought.

—*You're* sorry?— He smiled. —Hey. I was a brat.— He edged his hand up her wrist and touched the gold wristband there with his first two fingers. —Do you want me to take this off of you? I didn't understand before how thanks could hurt.—

—Naw. I like them.—

—Them?— His eyebrows rose. She placed her other hand in front of him and he peeked under her sleeve. "Huh?" He touched the second wristband with his other hand. She felt it talking to him. Felt him talking back.

"They can go invisible," he said out loud.

Abby came over and plopped down in the seat across from Matt. "What were you guys talking about? When are you going to answer my question? What *are* those?"

Gold lifted his hands, and Matt pushed her sleeves up to show Abby the wristbands. "They're sort of a present, but he gave it to me without asking. But they're actually pretty neat." She stroked one wristband with a finger and it responded, spreading to glove her hand in gold.

"Pretty," Abby said, touching Matt's gold hand.

"I went outside last night and it made me a whole suit thing. It was really warm." Matt stroked it again and the glove turned back into a wristband.

"Can I have some of those?" Abby asked.

"Of course." Gold gripped her wrists for three seconds. When he took his hands away, she had wristbands like Matt's.

She looked at them and they changed: Greek key patterns stitched around them. "Oh!" Abby said. She rubbed one and it grew up over her forearm. She stirred it with her finger and strange abstract images chased across it, streaming, intertwining lines that reminded Matt somehow of wind. Abby pulled at the lower edge of the band and it stretched across the back of her hand to her fingers. She touched it to her middle finger. It made a ring, connected to the wristband by a gold chain. "Wonderful," she murmured. With shining eyes she looked at Gold. "Thank you!"

"My pleasure."

She played with the gold on her arms some more, making spiky science-fiction jewelry and smoothing it out, pressing thumb-print whorls on the surface of the metal, then rubbing them away. "Does it hurt you to give up pieces of yourself like this?" Abby asked Gold after a moment.

"No," he said. "That's what I'm for."

"That can't be right. Edmund—"

Edmund touched Matt's hand. She met his gaze. No way she could think all the stuff to him that Gold had just told her.

"Tell us," Edmund said to Matt.

"It's okay," Matt said. "He gets it. He's your magic, Abby. He wants to do what you want."

"He's mine?" She gripped Gold's hands. "You're mine? But anybody can shape you?"

"If you want them not to, change me that way."

"What does that mean?"

"Not what I said?" Gold asked. "I mean what I said." He looked frustrated.

Abby looked at Matt.

"He can do physical shapes," Matt said after a moment's thought, "and then other stuff inside. I shaped him, but you can't see that part. I told him he couldn't hurt people, no matter what outside shape he takes. I bet you could tell him to take any shape so long as you're the one who's telling him, and then nobody else could change him around."

"Or you could tell him that," said Abby.

"But I won't. He's *your* magic. Only thing is, you shape him, that doesn't automatically shape the other pieces, I don't think."

"Other pieces?"

"The house has a big piece—" Even as she spoke, she heard the house telling its scattered pieces of gold that only the house could shape them, seesstroosstraass. "It just shaped its gold to work only for it. And then there's Ginny, kind of another wild card. And . . ." She blinked dream-eyes and looked at Abby's hands. A trickle of wild gold still came from her. "You're still calling more of it."

"Ginny's gold?" Abby let go of Gold's hands and rubbed her eyes. "Tony brought her in this morning and introduced us before I was awake. I thought he said she's the new babysitter. Figured she was some neighbor kid."

"Nope," said Matt. "More of your magic. I did shape her some, though."

"What did you do to her?"

Matt took a gulp of orange juice. She was doing too much talking. She'd much rather listen. She sighed. "See, Gold thinks I'm the only one who can teach them to talk," she said. "So he brought the new gold to me this morning and made it figure out how to talk by, you know, grabbing the back of my neck and flipping through my brain. Gold figured out how you think about oriental carpets yesterday, so I don't get why it has to be me, but he says it does. Anyway, I was pissed. I told the new gold to take a shape that could teach all the other gold how to talk. So she's gold, she wants to take whatever shape I give her, but the only way she could turn into something that teaches other gold how to talk was to read a bunch of my mind. Much more of it than Gold did. I didn't know she'd do that before I shaped her. Anyway, I gave her the don't-hurt shape too, and that's all I did."

"Is she here in the house too?" Abby asked. "Where is she?"

Matt glanced around with dream-eyes open. Ginny sat at the table two chairs down from Abby, sleeping Sara cradled on her lap. Matt blinked into regular sight and Ginny was still there, long-limbed and coltish, a perfect imitation teenager. "Here," Ginny said.

Abby turned, startled, and almost fell off her chair. "Whoa! When did you get here?"

"While you were distracted with jewelry," Ginny said. She smiled.

"Who do you look like? It's so definite."

"A friend of Matt's from when she was a little girl."

"Tony—Tony introduced us. I wonder if he's all right. Does he know you're gold?"

"Yes."

"That's beyond odd. He's so calm about all this stuff! Calmer than I am. I—" Abby glanced at Gold. "I had this wish in my heart for so long. I never told anyone. It comes true, and I—" She lifted one of Gold's hands and stared at it. "I'm a little . . . staggered."

Gold gently turned her hand over, held his hand above it for a second. Clinks sounded. "Go ahead," he said, lifting his hand.

Abby stared. Six large gold disks lay in her hand. Coins, thought Matt, magic coins she could use to buy anything she liked. She placed them gently on the table and covered her face with her hands. A moment later she was crying, quietly but with shoulders jerking.

Edmund rose and went around the table to her, pulled up a chair and sat with his arms around her. She leaned into his chest and cried.

Matt went to the counter and talked to the coffee machine. Tony had made a pot of coffee earlier, but he had used most of it to fill his thermos. With help from the coffee machine and the ingredients, she figured out how to start another one. After that she cleared the table and worked on dishes. She loaded the last juice glass into the dishwasher just as Abby stopped crying. Matt took her a glass of water.

"I'm sorry," Abby said.

"For what?" asked Edmund.

"Falling apart. Thanks." She accepted the water from Matt and sipped it.

"It's a good thing to do," Edmund said.

"Oh yeah?" She sat back and glared at him. "You never do it, do you?"

"Me?" He tapped his chest with his palm. "You'd be surprised."

"I'd be flat-on-my-back astounded if you did any such thing."

"I fell apart years ago. Maybe not in a good way. Matt's putting me back together."

"What?" Her gaze sharpened. "Are you serious?" She glanced at Matt, then touched Edmund's face. "I *thought* there was something different."

"Mm." He smiled at her.

"You look older and younger at the same time. Or maybe just different."

"It's a long story. What are these things?" He touched one of the disks.

Abby swallowed and picked up the top disk. "This is an idea I had." She looked at Gold, still sitting at the end of the table. He nodded. "The way this stuff responds to my thoughts—" She looked at her wristbands, which were now heavy domed bangles, "—I thought I could design jewelry. God. It's so simple without having to weld and mold and melt and smelt and etch and all those things. Just—" She pinched a piece off the disk and dropped it on the back of her hand. It flowed around her middle finger in a wide gold band. She stared at it a moment, and lines flowed across it, stretching it broad in some places and thinning it in others. She pulled up a thin piece, curled it over, rolled a ball on the end, pressed it back. "Seesstroosstraass," she murmured.

Then she slid the ring off her finger. It rang as she dropped it on the table. Solid. Set. Fired. Strange and beautiful.

"I've already got gallery connections," Abby said, breaking a short silence. "I've been selling paintings and sculptures for some time now."

Matt lifted the ring, glanced at Abby to see if it was okay. Abby nodded. The ring reminded Matt of the ocean, though she couldn't figure out why. She slid it onto her index finger. It gleamed against her tanned skin. "It's really great." She took it off.

Abby said, "I could make a lot of pieces, send them out and sell them. If it's all right with Gold."

"I am yours."

"Don't talk like that," Abby cried.

"Why not?"

"I'm not—not a slave owner."

"I am not a person," said Gold.

"I don't believe that."

"I am material for you to shape."

"How can that be? We're talking to each other right now!"

"I can stop talking, if you prefer." He climbed up onto the table, curled up, and turned into stacks and stacks of gold disks.

"Stop it!" Abby cried. "Come back! Stop that right now!"

The disks melted into each other and turned back into a human. He sat up. He looked less like Edmund this time: his curly hair was golden, and his eyes amber-brown. His face looked more perfect and generic. "I want to do your bidding," he said.

"My bidding is keep acting like a person for now! Okay?"

"Okay." He picked up two of the disks and tossed them into the air, caught them. "Look. There's plenty of this. You keep calling more. Ginny teaches it how to know what you want. You could do this." He set a disk in her hand.

She licked her lip and pulled at the disk. It stretched, opened in the center. She smoothed it into a band, pinched peaks into it, rubbed it, stroked it, set it on her head. A crown, a small, tasteful one, suitable for everyday wear. She took it off and studied it. "What if . . ." She tapped it in three places, and rainbow-casting jewels appeared. "Oh!"

She stared at it, then looked up at Matt and Edmund. "Is this crazy? It's so easy. Art's supposed to be hard."

"You already did all the prep work," Edmund said. "You've been studying for years. You've developed your style. This is just a more flexible medium."

She turned the crown over, stroked its inside, then pressed with her little finger. A small square design appeared. She held it up and stared at it. "It's my chop," she whispered.

She stood up and set the crown on Gold's head, then stepped back to study the effect. Three more touches, and small silver bumps appeared. She lifted the crown off Gold's head and held it in her hands. "Seesstroosstraass."

"Beautiful," said Matt.

"It is. It's so great. Put it on." She tossed the crown, and Matt caught it.

Putting on a crown struck Matt as one of the weirdest things anyone had asked her to do in a long time. She lifted it and set it on her head, though. Featherlight, like her wristlets. She couldn't tell she was wearing it after a minute. "Don't I look stupid?"

Abby grabbed another gold disk and stretched it, stroked it, silvered it. A moment later she held up a mirror.

Matt stared at her image. She didn't look stupid. She looked like a prince. It made her whole face look regal and distant.

"Suits you," Abby said.

"I don't think so." Matt took off the crown. "'S cool, though."

"Here's a big question. If I take it to a jeweler, what does he find out? What kind of metal is it? Are these jewels real or cubic zirconia? Does this last, or does it turn to leaves after someone buys it?"

"Whatever you believed when you made it, just before you fired it," Gold said.

"So we're sitting in a house with piles of treasure?" Abby stroked the impromptu mirror, winding gold ivy leaves around its silver reflecting surface.

"Nice, huh?" Edmund picked up the crown and tried it on. It fit. "This still adjusts."

"Oh! I wanted it to. I want these pieces to fit whoever tries them on. Then if they really like them, they can wear them right away. But—"

Edmund took off the crown. "Might be a problem in the real world. People might notice they change."

"Just call them magic jewelry," Matt suggested. "Say it's your secret technique."

"I don't know if that'll work."

"But you *are* leaving some of the magic in. I wonder if that could cause trouble later on," Edmund said.

"I have more work to do. Lots to plan, lots to think about. But this is so exciting!" She jumped up and hugged Edmund. "I know I'm years late saying this, but thank you. Thank you. Thank you!" Then she hugged Gold. "Thank you, too!"

"You're welcome."

"Mommy?" Sara rubbed her eyes and sat up in Ginny's lap.

"A crown for the princess!" Abby grabbed a pinch of gold and shaped a simple circlet, then placed it on Sara's head. "Ta-da!"

"Mommy, can I have a glass of milk?"

"That's a tricky one." Abby picked up a whole disk and turned it into a cup, then stirred its interior. White frothy liquid appeared. "Wow," she said. She held it out to Sara.

"Wait," said Edmund. "You didn't fire it. You don't know what it might do inside her."

Abby jerked the cup back, her face alarmed.

"I'll get you some milk, gingersnap," Ginny said, carrying Sara to the kitchen counter and setting her there while Ginny looked through the fridge.

"Magic is great. You have to be careful with it," said Edmund.

"Uh." Abby stared at the cup in her hand. "I don't even know what this is." She closed both her hands around the cup and smashed it back into a disk. "I'm—I think I better sit down."

"Want some coffee?" Matt asked.

"Oh, yeah. That'd be good." Abby sounded dazed. She slumped in her chair.

Matt poured fresh coffee into a mug. Ginny added milk to it without asking, then dropped in two spoons of sugar before pouring a cup of milk for Sara.

"That's how she takes it?" Matt muttered.

"Mm-hmm," said Ginny. She stirred the coffee with her index finger.

"Ouch," said Matt.

Ginny smiled and sucked on her finger. "Doesn't hurt."

Matt took the coffee to the table and handed it to Abby.

"Oh, yeah," Abby said, and drank half of it. "I'm punch-drunk. I'm slaphappy. When am I going to wake up?"

"Do you want to?" Edmund asked her.

"Uh . . ." Abby scanned the kitchen. Her gaze halted at Ginny, who held a cup of milk up to Sara's mouth at the counter, and Gold, who still sat beside her at the kitchen table. "No. I really don't."

Edmund cupped her cheek in his hand. She smiled at him, her eyes misty. "Tell me if you change your mind," he murmured.

"I won't change my mind. I might have more questions, though."

"Let me know." He rose. "Matt and I are going down to the basement for a while. We need to do some dowsing."

"The basement? Oh, okay. See you later, I guess." Abby finished her coffee and picked up another gold disk.

Matt followed Edmund through a door and down some stairs into darkness that smelled of fabric softener, damp, and dirt. He flipped a light switch at the bottom. Space opened up around them, dimming with distance. Ahead, a washer and dryer stood, with a clothesline stretched above them. A basket of folded laundry sat on the dryer. To the left the bulk of the basement spread out, interrupted here and there by pillars, and cluttered in the distance by a big furnace with heat conduits radiating from it. Jam-packed storage shelves stood in crooked rows, and there was a canning bay with jars of preserves. The floor was rough cement; the ceiling was missing, revealing pipes, wiring, beams, cobwebs, and the underside of the floor above.

—Here,— the house said. Light brightened back by the furnace.

Edmund walked there without waiting for Matt to interpret. He pulled some things from his pocket and sat on the floor. Matt dropped to sit across from him.

"I had a dream last night," he said in a quiet voice.

"What was it?" She guessed it wasn't a fun one like the others.

"I put my hands into fire. They turned black."

"Yuck," Matt said. "Did it hurt?"

He hunched his shoulders. "It hurt terribly, and then I liked it, even though it hurt."

"Creepy," she said.

"It was scary."

"Not all of your dreams come true, do they?"

"The others haven't. Yet."

Matt reached across and took his hands in hers, turned them palm up and looked at them. His hands were beautiful, long-fingered and strong. She opened dream-eyes. Edmund's hands stayed the same. "They look okay," she said.

He turned them over and gripped her hands, and she gripped back, staring into his eyes. *Whatever's in the fire*, she thought, *we can survive it.*

They sat for a long time just looking at each other. Then Edmund sighed and released her hands. "Guess we better get this done," he said.

"All right."

He opened a California map, flipped it over to show an enlargement of the San Francisco–Monterey area, and folded away all the other enlargements. He flattened the map on the floor. Then he sat quiet, breathing slowly. Matt sat still too, wondering if he actually needed her here, and if so, what she was supposed to do. She guessed he would have briefed her if there was anything she needed to know. She slowed her breathing, closed her eyes, and tried to relax.

Things Gold had told her glinted through her mind: A fish leapt above a lake, and never came down. It had jumped into a lake of something else above. Dazzling energy traveled along a wire, came to the end of the wire, flashed out into nothingness and died. Image of a hand from the inside: sparrow bones, webs of nerves and blood vessels, muscles, and under the center of the palm a pooling place that called: come, be here, next you'll be used, shaped, cast out into the world. Blue diamonds on her palms. What? Why?

Edmund stirred, the slide of jean fabric against cement. Matt opened her eyes. Slowly he picked up something, held it between index finger and thumb. Fishline swung from his fingers. A battered lead fishing weight hung at the bottom. Edmund held the line above the map and murmured something low and musical. The sinker swung in a circle above the map. Matt watched it, lulled by its neat, slow rhythm.

Presently it stopped, pulling the fishline at a slight angle. Edmund leaned closer and studied the map. "Palo Alto or Mountain View," he murmured.

The sinker circled slowly again in the opposite direction, finally came to the bottom of its arc and stilled.

"Thank you, spirit," Edmund said. He coiled the fishline, folded the map, and sat back.

"That's dowsing?" asked Matt.

"Not technically, but sort of. I asked where Susan was. I need a better map of Palo Alto and Mountain View for the next part. We can pick one up when we get there."

Susan, Matt thought. Will she have answers? Will she remember something so awful that Edmund can't look at it? Will this help or hurt? "Are we going today?"

"I feel—" He glanced around, listened. "Oh! We should go soon. Something's happening."

She smiled. "A lot's happening here, too."

"I think Abby has a handle on it now."

"I'll say. What about Tony, though? The kids?"

He relaxed, put his palms flat on the floor, and closed his eyes.

Matt relaxed too, and waited. She thought about Gold. Even though he had told her in various ways that he wasn't a person, she found it hard to understand. Everything seemed like a person. Lots of the things she talked to had little freedom of movement and no say in what use they were put to, but that didn't mean they had no personality.

He was a person, she decided. He just accepted that somebody else got to tell him what to do.

Well, he seemed to accept it. Before that, he had done a lot of things on his own, like grab her neck and get in bed with her. Maybe because he didn't understand no. Or at least he didn't understand no the way Matt had meant it. Before he understood himself, he had had a lot more freedom.

Matt remembered that she hadn't heard Abby shape Gold so that nobody else could shape him. Better remind her to do that. Maybe.

Why did Matt think kids couldn't handle magic? Had she watched too many Disney movies? So far Sara had done all right. Though Matt had interrupted the bear.

What about Ginny? Definitely a person; but then, Matt had shaped and fired her into a person without even trying. Tony thought she'd make a good babysitter, but how could you trust your children with someone you knew so little about? Just because Ginny had read Matt's mind, that didn't make her trustworthy. Or did it? A person made of magic. They didn't know enough about what that meant.

Well, it was like every choice you made. You never knew enough, but you had to choose anyway.

Edmund sucked in breath and opened his eyes.

Or maybe spirit would always tell you the right decision to make. But Matt didn't believe that.

Edmund said, "Whatever's happening with Susan, we have until tonight to catch up to her. That's as much as spirit tells me. You want to stay here and see if the kids and Tony are all right when they come home? Cutting it kind of close. We've got about a three-hour drive to even get to Susan's neighborhood, and then I'll need to do some more seek spells to find her."

"What do you want to do?" Matt asked.

He put the coiled fishline and sinker on his palm, pushed it so it turned in a circle. "There are other options. Other ways to travel, faster ones, but they make me really tired, and I've never used them with another person, so I'm not sure how that would work. There's all that magic upstairs: if Abby let us, we could take some and use it to streamline the car, make it invisible to radar, whatever we need. Or we could split up. If you have concerns, you could stay here and I could go on."

"No. I came on this trip to be with you."

He smiled at her. "Thank you. Thank you again. Okay. To answer your question: what I'd like to do is pack our stuff and hit the road, even though we're leaving a lot of things up in the air here. I'll talk to Abby about developing a way to keep in touch with me in case she needs magic advice." He grinned at that. "So strange. My little sister and all that magic."

"I want to talk to Ginny," said Matt. "Then I'll be ready to go."

"Okay. Good." He grabbed the map and got to his feet, took

her hand and pulled her up. She dusted off her jeans and followed him upstairs.

Nobody was in the kitchen when they got there. Matt heard a murmur of voices coming from the curtained doorway to the living room: Ginny and Sara. —Where's Abby? Where's Gold?— Matt asked the house.

—In her studio,— the house answered. Matt relayed this to Edmund.

"Come with me," he said. She nodded, and he led her out of the kitchen to a door under the stairway, where he knocked.

"Come in," Abby called.

Smells of oil paints and pungent turpentine, the dusty scent of tempera, the fresh cedar of pencil shavings greeted them. Matt stepped past Edmund into the room and stopped. Finished and blank canvases stacked against the wall, right-side up, upside-down, and sideways, all the images drawing her gaze; watercolor pages tacked to the walls above them, each painting another demand, another delight, a different collection of image and color; a table with mat cutting and paper cutting equipment on it; several easels; a sectioned shelf unit with paint stuff shoved into its cubicles and stacks of paper on its longer shelves; another table with a water jar and brushes, and lots of other things Matt didn't know how to name. In one corner near the windows, a huge old overstuffed armchair covered with a paint-spattered sheet.

Abby stood by one of the easels, a brush in her right hand and a palette in her left. On the palette was only one color: gold.

"Look," she said in a low voice. She dipped her brush into the gold, then brushed paint onto paper. Colors bloomed in the wake of her brush stroke. She painted a sunlit tree: dark green in shadowed parts, with scraps of blue sky or dark branch showing through, and lighter green ranging up through gold all the way to white on all the surfaces light struck. "I just have to think it and it comes," she whispered. "And—" She touched an already painted part, and it changed, lightened. Turned suddenly violet. She tapped the brush over the tree. Violet flowers appeared wherever she touched.

"They say you can do this with computers," she said, "but this is beyond anything I—" She swayed.

Edmund leapt forward and caught her.

"I'm so tired," she said, leaning heavily against him.

"I forgot to tell you." He lifted her and carried her to the big chair, eased her into it, knelt before her, holding her hand.

"What? What did you forget?"

"Magic makes some things easier, but it makes demands, too. You use it, it uses you. It takes a while to build up to using it full-time the way you have been today. I forgot. I'm sorry. It's been a long time since I used a lot of it."

"I'm so sleepy," she said. "That's why I'm so sleepy? The art comes better than ever. But I—"

"Better if you ration it. Do some every day and stop. You'll be able to do more with practice, but you can't spend a whole day doing it. It'll steal your muscle tone, leach the calcium from your bones, deaden your nerves if you're not careful."

"What if I made myself a magic tonic? One that makes me strong enough to handle this?"

He stood. "It will want something back," he said.

Matt hugged herself and wondered. Was she paying some kind of price for dream-eyes and thought-talk? Sure didn't feel like it. She'd watched Edmund doing his own kinds of craft. She had never seen him exhausted the way Abby was. Then again, he never did such splashy things, either. Spirit might be a different kind of master from magic.

"It will want something back?" Abby asked in a sleepy voice. "Like what?"

"I don't know. Maybe your creativity. Something about you that's your own kind of magic. Abby, will you be careful?"

"I'm so sleepy. I— Will you make sure Sara's okay?"

"Yes. After that, Matt and I have to leave, Abby."

"You're leaving? You can't. I need you. I don't understand this yet." Her voice got slower and slower.

He kissed her cheek. "You'll work it out."

"No," she moaned. "Don't go."

"I have to. I'll work something out with Gold so you can call me, though, okay?"

"Oh . . . kay . . ."

Edmund knelt and slipped Abby's shoes off, straightened her arms so the sleeves didn't bind them, tipped her head so she wouldn't get a kink in her neck from sleeping upright.

"How can we leave if she's asleep?" Matt asked. "There's a little kid here."

"Maybe we can't." Edmund sighed. "I have to talk to Gold."

Gold whipped from the wall, fluttering watercolors as he passed through them. He went to Abby and knelt beside her chair, his face anxious. He had shifted form again: his skin's flesh tones were overlaid with golden tan; his hair had straightened and lengthened and was now a golden mane; and his body looked whippet thin, whippet strong. He no longer looked like Edmund.

"Working with me hurts her?" he asked, after staring at

Abby's sleeping face. "No one told me. We could have slowed down."

"I'm sorry," Edmund said. "I'm really sorry, Gold. I forgot."

"I'll have to watch her now." Gold brushed a strand of hair off Abby's forehead.

"Is that a problem?"

"Telling her she has to stop, when what she's doing feels so good?" He sank to his knees, laid his cheek against the chair arm. He laced his fingers through Abby's. She never stirred. "I've been waiting forever for this. I never want to stop."

"It's not a permanent stop. It's a stop and a start and a stop," Edmund said. "And a start. If you wear her out, she won't be able to work with you at all."

Gold closed his eyes and sighed.

"She tell you she's the only one who can work with you yet?" Matt asked.

"No."

"I think it better get done." Matt looked at Edmund. After a moment, he nodded.

"What you do to me won't affect the wild gold," Gold said, glancing up at her.

"I know. That means if Abby doesn't agree with it, she has some other stuff she can let the rest of them use. Is it okay if I give you this one last shape?"

His lips thinned and he looked away. "Help me, Matt," he said after a moment. He sat up, releasing Abby's hand.

"How?"

"Tell me I have to help her go slow, too."

Matt sat on the floor and thought for a while, then held out her hands to Gold. He took them. "Take any shape you like, so long as you and Abby choose it," she said. "Take any shape she chooses, any use she uses, until she starts getting tired. Then stop, and you'll feel good. Stop working with her until she's back to full strength. Unless she really, really needs you because it's an emergency." She glanced at Edmund, then at Gold. Was that all right?

After a moment, they both nodded.

"Seesstroosstraass," Matt said.

Gold shivered, gripped her hands, then let her go. "Thanks," he said.

"So there's an out for him," Edmund said.

"Mm?"

"If Abby chooses something and Gold doesn't, he doesn't have to do it. Unless the second part contradicts that part."

"I tried to get that to work," Matt said. "Did I screw up? You were supposed to tell me how to fix it before I said the firing word."

He shook his head. "I don't know."

"It's better than it was," Gold said.

"Gold? If Abby has problems working with you, if there's something Matt or I can do to help, we need to set it up so that she can get in touch with us."

"Yes?"

"We won't be reachable by phone, and—" Edmund broke off, looking at Gold's uncomprehending face. "Can you give me a way that you can call me?"

Gold's gaze moved from Edmund to Matt. Matt tried to figure out how to explain this to Gold. (Dazzling energy traveled along a wire, came to the end of the wire, flashed out into nothingness and died.) Then she said, "Well, he can't, actually.

We're not Abby. We can't shape him anymore. Maybe we should get a cell phone?"

"Maybe Ginny—"

"Yeah." Ginny would understand, at least, and she wasn't bound to Abby. Matt wondered if she should be. "Or, you know, we could just call from Palo Alto or Mountain Home or wherever when we get there and find out if everything's okay."

"Hmm," Edmund said. "Gold, will you make sure Abby is okay?"

"Yes," said Gold. He curled up on the floor beside Abby's chair and closed his eyes.

Edmund led Matt out of the studio.

In the kitchen, they could hear Ginny and Sara, still talking. Edmund paused and said, "You have a good feeling about Gold now?"

Matt nodded.

"You think Abby's really safe with him?"

"I'm not a hundred percent sure. How can anybody ever be that sure? I think he likes her and doesn't want to hurt her."

"Okay." He headed for the curtained doorway, and Matt followed him.

They passed through a pantry with well-stocked shelves and on into the living room, a comfortably disarrayed room with a fireplace in one corner, a TV in another, a piano in a third, and an un-matching collection of couches sprawling everywhere, with an occasional comfortable-looking chair tossed in and little tables here and there. Sara and Ginny sat on the floor in front of a coffee table. They were building something with wooden blocks and Legos.

"I don't know if it'll stay," Ginny said.

"Put stickum on it." Sara placed a big orange wooden block on top of a slender tower of Legos.

"Do you think that's fair?" asked Ginny.

"Uh-huh. Go on." Sara held the block in place. Ginny flicked her fingers at its underside. Gold flashed. Sara crowed with laughter and let go, and the block stayed balanced on the tower. "That's their place where the bird people have a home," Sara said. She lifted Booja from her shoulder and set the bird on top of the orange block. The bird sang and walked from one end of the block to the other.

"Hey," Ginny said to Matt.

"Hey."

"We're making a city," said Ginny.

"Booja-rooja," Sara said. "That's its name."

"It's nice." Edmund dropped onto a nearby couch.

"Give me a star, Uncle Edmund. I'll put it right here." Sara tapped the side of a blue block.

Edmund closed his hand for a moment, then opened it. A star all light sat on his palm. "Yaaay!" Sara said, and took it. It shone pink through her fingers, darker through the shadows of bones. She pressed it against the block. Glowing, it stuck. "This is the best city!"

"It just might be," said Edmund.

"Ginny, can I talk to you?" Matt asked.

"Sure."

"Edmund and I have to leave. We left Abby asleep in her studio. Do you actually know anything about babysitting?"

"How many times did we do it?" Ginny tilted her head back and stared at the ceiling. "Almost every weekend all through eighth grade for the Gundersons, and their kids were much worse than S-a-r-a. Ninth and tenth and eleventh grade we had gigs almost every Friday and Saturday all over town, huh? Made it hard to date. But we did save up enough money to buy a used car. That's a lot of babysitting, Matt."

"I forgot." Matt's hands gripped each other. "I don't remember that."

"It's in there."

A moment later, memories tumbled into her conscious awareness. The Gundersons had had four kids, all of them brats of different calibers. First few times were terrifying, but then they worked out a system of compromises, and it was smooth. The Gundersons said they never found another sitter as good as Mattie. She remembered running into Ingrid, the oldest kid, at a supermarket a year or two after she had stopped babysitting them. Ingrid said they missed her.

But she'd rather babysit smaller, wealthier families. Less hassle, more money. She'd had an appointment book and everything. Pam kept griping, said Matt should get her own phone line. Too many calls, and none of them for Pam.

Her car. An ancient forest-green Volkswagen Rabbit. She sure loved it. Why had she left it behind when she ran away? She would have had a place to stay if she had taken it. Oh. Yeah. It had been in the shop that weekend, for a repair she couldn't afford. She wondered what had ever happened to the car.

And what, exactly, did these memories have to do with Ginny being able to teach wild gold to talk? She'd probably never know.

"Tony left his work number by the phone," Ginny said. "If anything comes up, I'll call him."

"Is there any way you can call us? We don't have a phone," Edmund said.

"Call you?" Ginny looked puzzled.

"Just in case something goes wrong and you need us to come back."

Ginny thought for a while. Sara built another spire of red and white Legos. "Matt, you still have those wristbands?"

"Sure."

"May I touch them?"

"Sure." Matt plopped down beside Ginny and held out her wrists.

"Look. If I put a strip of me in them, I can talk to you even if you're far away. Is that okay?"

"That'd be great."

"Okay." Ginny stroked her thumbs across Matt's wristbands. A streak of darker gold flowed around them, circled Matt's wrists.

—Can you hear me now?—

—Yes. Can you hear me?—

"Oh, yeah," Ginny said.

"So you can take care of Sara all right, huh?" Matt asked.

"Sure. She's a total Bink." They grinned at each other. Bink had been the easiest-going kid Matt had ever babysat. Interested in everything, but never whiny. She had really liked his parents, too.

"I shaped Gold so only Abby can shape him now—I think. That seemed safest. Also we found out that if she uses him too much all at once, she gets sick, or at least exhausted."

"Oh, man!" Ginny glanced at Sara. "She's not actually using me, though. We're just playing."

"She shaping you?" Matt asked in a whisper.

"Not at all."

"Can you not let her?"

Ginny hesitated, frowning. "I don't know."

"How about this? Kids can only shape you if you think it's okay and won't hurt them. If the parents say the kids can't shape you, you stop letting the kids shape you. For however long the parents say."

"I think the first part is all I need. If the parents don't want the kids to shape me, I won't think it's okay. And I'm already shaped not to hurt them."

"Oh, yeah." Matt smiled. She glanced at Edmund.

"Sounds great," he said.

"Okay," said Matt. "The kids can only shape you if you think it's okay. Seesstraasstrooss."

Ginny shivered once, then smiled. "Good."

"So Abby's asleep in her studio. She worked too hard and wore herself out. Gold's watching out for her. You know how I feel about that."

"No. I know how you felt this morning. I don't know how you've felt since breakfast, though. Seemed like you changed your mind about him."

"Oh, yeah. I did. Kinda."

"Ah," said Ginny. "I talked to him. I think he's all right."

"Oh, yeah," Matt said, remembering. The conversation with all the pictures in it: Gold had told her about blending with Ginny and learning more.

"So we just have to pack, and then I guess we're ready to hit the road," Matt said.

Ginny straightened, then leaned forward to hug Matt. "I—I don't want you to go. I'll miss you."

Matt felt a stifled something in her chest. She hugged this friend who never was. Where was the real Ginny now? She'd never know. This one was a good friend, too.

Feeling throat-tight and hot-eyed, Matt leaned away from Ginny and said, "We have to go find Edmund's friend, and we have to go soon or something else will happen. But I—" She lifted her arms to show the wristbands.

Ginny smiled. "Oh, yeah!"

Sara went to stand in front of Edmund. "You're leaving? Not fair."

"We'll be back," he said.

Sara frowned. "Takes you a long time." She stomped out of the room.

"Guess I better follow her," Ginny said. She kissed Matt's cheek and jumped up. She paused beside Edmund on the couch. "Bye, buddy. Thanks for being such a good guy." She ruffled his hair in passing and dashed after Sara.

It only took them a few minutes to pack, and they didn't run into any of the house's inhabitants before they slipped outside. Matt patted the door sill and thanked the house for everything.

—No, I thank you,— said the house. A brass knocker formed in the middle of the front door. A man's grinning face looked at Matt. She gasped.

Edmund studied it for a moment, then tapped the knocking ring held in the man's mouth. "Wow. Next thing you know, gold fixtures everywhere!"

The knocker's mouth opened and the ring dropped to the porch. "No gold. Not yet. Maybe later."

Matt retrieved the ring and held it up to the knocker.

"Thanks," it said, and opened its mouth wide. She eased the ring into it.

The dogs were nowhere in sight. Matt wondered if the active gold in the house had frightened them away.

Edmund stowed their things in the back of the car. "Let's go."

"This exit," Matt said three hours later, watching the lead sinker that dangled from the rearview mirror. It was definitely pulling to the right.

Edmund pulled off Highway 101 onto the University Avenue exit, drove past a liquor store and some tired-looking bars and barred storefronts. The sinker pulled them farther and farther away from the highway, indicating right and left turns. They wound past nicer and more expensive-looking residences, past venerable trees, one in the middle of the road.

It was almost one in the afternoon, and there was a lot of traffic in downtown Palo Alto. People in BMWs and Mercedes took a second look at Edmund's rusty Volvo.

The sinker finally shivered in place. Edmund pulled into the nearest parking lot. He took the sinker off the rearview mirror, and he and Matt climbed out of the car.

Susan was somewhere nearby.

Chapter Eight

· · · · ·

SOMEWHERE in the back of the restaurant, someone dropped something—a tray of glasses, Suki thought. The crash, smash, and tinkle of stray pieces cut through her daily haze, made her lift her head out of the menu. Across the table, her co-worker from Hot-Now Industries, Lyle, tried to catch her eye. He had porcupine brown-blonde hair, kind gray eyes behind his glasses, and a shy but friendly smile. With the ease of long practice, Suki avoided meeting his gaze and looked back at her menu, taking the crashing sounds inside her to replay later.

"Have you decided?" the pretty dark-haired waitress asked, pen poised above her order pad.

"Caesar salad." Suki folded the menu and handed it to the waitress.

"You always order the same thing," said Lyle. "Aren't you ever tempted to try something new?"

She met his gaze at last, putting ice into her eyes.

Usually Lyle responded to her social cues without much trouble, though initially he hadn't known her code. Today was different.

"You could go crazy. Try something spicy. Try something with actual protein in it."

Suki looked at the waitress. "He'll have the French dip and coffee with cream," she said.

The waitress glanced at Lyle, who shrugged and nodded. After grabbing Lyle's menu and making notes on her pad, the waitress rushed off.

"So okay, I guess I'm predictable too," Lyle said.

"Hey. Last week you had a garden burger with red onions. The Tuesday before that you had halibut."

"You noticed!"

"That's my job." Suki drank ice water. Well, okay. It wasn't exactly her job to observe everything and remember it, but her ability to do that made her much better at her job, which involved developing and memorizing promotional material about HotNow products and giving demonstrations and sales pitches for them at trade shows around the world. She had a sharp eye for her audience and could read people better than most of her coworkers.

Lyle was great at developing ad concepts, but terrible speaking in front of people. He said, "Maybe one of these times I'll find something I like better than French dip and switch. Why don't you ever try anything else?"

"Everything tastes the same to me." She almost never admitted this, but she had known Lyle for eight months, and she knew he didn't gossip. Maybe he would quit bugging her about food choices now.

"God, it's a waste to send you to the trade show in Paris."

"So true. Wish you could go instead."

Lyle frowned. "You mean you didn't even petition for this trip?"

"Nope. It's just a big irritation as far as I'm concerned. I hate packing. I hate long plane rides. I hate international customs. I hate direct current. I hate my passport picture."

"I lobbied for that trip! I gave Deedee a case of Twinkies. And I happen to know that Oliver went further than that. You didn't try one single bribe?"

"I never even applied. It dropped into my lap."

"I hate you," Lyle said. The waitress brought him a mug of coffee, and he poured two containers of cream into it.

"Take my place," said Suki. "I'll stay here and work on the Spodewar project and you go make the presentation at the trade show and eat a lot of good French food. No one will know."

"The company will know when they don't get any orders following the presentation. And besides, they check your picture ID when you get on planes these days."

"Let's switch driver's licenses. You get a blonde wig, and . . ."

They got out their licenses and traded them, studying pictures of each other. Suki seriously wondered if they could get away with switching places. She and Lyle were about the same height, both slender, though Lyle was built differently—the right padding could change that; both blonde, though Suki's hair was much paler, thicker, untangled, and several inches longer—a wig could change that. Lyle's eyes were gray; Suki's clear blue. Their faces looked very different, but how closely did airport personnel study IDs? As long as Lyle never needed to use his driver's license and his passport at the same time . . .

No. It was a ridiculous idea.

"This is your real name?" Lyle asked. "Susan Ellison Back-strom? How'd you get 'Suki' from that?"

Suki one-shoulder shrugged. "Nickname." Because she always observed and always recorded, she memorized Lyle's birthday: next month he would be twenty-four. So young. The men she got along well with were always boys. She felt comfortable with boys. They didn't scare her, and she didn't have to consider them her equals.

"I wish I had the guts to switch places with you, but this would never work. You're the ultimate presenter. You polish up real nice, you never get rattled, and you know how to use your voice to get people to do what you want. I'm okay behind the scenes, but I freeze in front of people. Besides, you're gorgeous, and I'm boring." Lyle handed Suki her license.

Suki put her license away, but continued to study Lyle's. If she could switch places with anyone . . . melt out of her own life and start living someone else's . . . Inside her something that had been awakened by the sound of breaking glass stirred and looked around. It almost got out of bed and went for a walk. Instead it sighed and turned over, switched off the light.

"Susan?"

She had seen them approaching, thought they were headed toward the back of the restaurant: a tall, smooth-faced boy, a shorter girl, both dressed casually and not entirely cleanly, one or two steps above street people. Catalogued, filed, dismissed. None of her business.

So why did this boy know her name?

Why did his voice sound—

Slowly she raised her gaze, starting at his dusty-kneed black jeans, traveling up over his soft red sweater, stalling as she noticed his chin, then his mouth. She couldn't look into his eyes. Her gaze skipped away.

"'Scuse me." The waitress bumped past the boy, laid loaded plates in front of Lyle and Suki.

The hairs on the back of Suki's neck prickled. A chill swept up her arms. The sleeping thing inside her woke, jumped up, looked everywhere for threat.

"Susan." His voice was gentle, warm, familiar. Terrifying.

He snapped his fingers. A larkspur spire of midnight blue flowers appeared out of nowhere. That hand, with its long, clever fingers, laid the flowers beside her silverware.

She lifted her hand away from her knife. She covered her mouth, pressed the scream back inside.

"Hey, buddy. What's your point?" Lyle asked, anger and upset naked in his voice. He stood up. "Get out of here, why don't you? You can see she doesn't want to see you."

"Susan," he said a third time. She heard the woodwinds in his voice, the warmth and welcome.

No. She couldn't go back there. It had taken her almost a year to claw her way out of that abyss, to build a wall over it brick by brick, to plaster this working surface over that wall, brilliant, smooth, and shallow, with no doors back to where she had come from. She'd been living almost comfortably in just this thin skin of surface all the years since. She didn't want to break through the wall to face all she'd left behind. She would rather die.

"Excuse me," she said, sliding her chair back, moving away from him without ever looking at him. "I think I'm going to be sick."

She ran.

• • •

Lyle knocked on the open door of her office. "They boxed your salad for you," he said, setting a white Styrofoam carton on a pile of papers on her desk.

"Oh. Thanks." Suki stared at the carton. She had clicked over into work-self, eliminating lunch-self and panic-self. It was an effort to dredge up the one who remembered what had happened less than an hour ago. "Sorry I left so suddenly." She pulled her purse from under her desk and fished out her wallet to repay him.

"What was the deal? I talked to them after you left, and they seemed nice. Not like the guys who hit on you here."

Suki smiled faintly as she handed Lyle twelve dollars. She had decided he was the least of all evils here about six months earlier. She did lunch with him every day, and he did his youthful best to send every other guy who seemed interested in her away. Suki never did anything with Lyle but lunch and the occasional after-overtime cappuccino (they couldn't afford to hurt their heads with beer, not when they'd have to get up early the next morning and be super-sharp at work). Lyle didn't push for more. Well, not often, anyway.

"Who was that guy?" Lyle asked, stuffing money in his pocket.

"What guy?" asked work-self, already submerging in the problems she had been dealing with before Lyle showed up.

"The guy who called you Susan."

Her gaze went to her monitor. "No one."

"Oh. Duh. Okay. Duh. Well, he said he didn't mean to scare you and he's sorry, and he'll try to catch up with you later."

Later she would be on a plane to Paris. For the first time she was glad she was going on this trip.

They were waiting on her aunt Caroline's porch when she went over after work to pick up a couple of outfits for the trip.

She stored most of her clothes in the closet of her old room at her aunt's house. Her aunt had invited her to stay on after Suki graduated from Stanford, but Suki had wanted to be alone by then, wanted to get away from all the things about her aunt she thought of as "sticky": the hugs when Suki got home from school, the concern in the questions about how Suki might be feeling, the endless invitations to talk about it, whatever "it" might be. The occasional awkwardness when Aunt Caroline offered to talk to Suki about Suki's mother, Aunt Caroline's sister. Aunt Caroline kept trying to connect to places Suki no longer had.

Suki found an apartment just far enough across town that she didn't have to deal with most of that. Her life had been smoother ever since. But Aunt Caroline's house still had much bigger closets. She didn't mind storing things for Suki.

Things like people Suki didn't want to encounter. She was already on the porch when she noticed them, though. Which shook her: Suki noticed everything. How had she gotten this close to them without seeing them?

She wouldn't look at the boy's face. The girl stood up. "Miss? Ma'am? Ms. Backstrom?"

"What do you want?" Suki said in a low, grating voice, keeping her eyes averted.

"Just to talk to you."

"Forget it."

"Just to ask if you're all right."

"Of course. Go away."

"Nathan wonders how you are."

A knife twisted in Suki's gut. She stared the girl full in the face. An unknown face, a stranger, how dare she say something like that? How dare she even say Nathan's name? Startling rage flamed through Suki. "Don't you dare try to manipulate me," she said.

"Manipulate you?" the girl said in a surprised voice, and then, "Huh! Guess I was trying to. Weird. Not my usual thing. What's the best way to get through to you?"

Her own laughter startled Suki, banished the rage. "Who are you?"

"Matt Black. You don't know me. I'm a friend of Edmund's."

His name. Now that she had heard it out loud, she had to remember it. She looked past Matt and for the first time met Edmund's eyes.

She didn't know what she had expected, but the look on his face wasn't it. She remembered how he had been, magnificent and huge in anger (don't think about that!) or before that, kind, sometimes silly, sometimes taking himself too seriously, but he could be kidded out of that, usually by Julio—Suki hadn't known how to kid people when she was a kid. A tall, gentle, helpful boy who seemed to accept her surface and like her just because Julio told him to. One of her four friends.

What looked back at her now was serenity with questions in it. No demands, just questions.

Still, an alert went through her. His presence threatened her wall.

"What do you want?" she asked Matt in a neutral voice.

Matt glanced at Edmund. He smiled at Matt, and his smile

surprised Suki too: tender, calm, sweet, with a swift undercurrent. So Matt was Edmund's friend? Huh.

Matt breathed deep and turned back to Suki. "What happened right before you left Guthrie? He doesn't remember, and—"

Suki walked past Matt then, into her aunt's house, and locked the door behind her. No way was she thinking about that particular piece of past.

"Hello?" she called, but she could sense the house's emptiness. Aunt Caroline wasn't even home. All the curtains were closed against the evening sky. A light was on in the kitchen, shining out a doorway at the end of the hall. Suki took two steps into the dark foyer.

The door opened behind her, even though she had thrown the deadbolt.

"I know it was something really awful," Matt said softly. "Sorry to be bringing it up, but—"

"How did you get in here?" Suki turned, wondering whether Matt was a ghost. Had she slipped through the door? But no. She closed it without a click behind her, leaving Edmund outside.

Matt's voice continued, low-key and neutral in the half darkness. "He kinda collapsed inside. Until we find out what happened, part of him stays dead, and that's not good."

"What are you talking about?" Suki wouldn't let herself remember, but she did know that if not for Edmund she would have, well, maybe died. Something terrible would have happened. Something terrible *had* happened, but not to her. No, she wouldn't think about it.

"After what happened, he changed into somebody else, same way you did. Cut himself off from the past and started over."

"Edmund? Why would he—?" Suki wouldn't let herself remember.

But she remembered.

Withering. Almost everything in her father's path withered sooner or later. Some things took longer to die.

That night . . .

And then, finally, escaping the house and her father, something she'd dreamed of all her life.

After she had spent some time falling apart at her aunt and uncle's house, unable to tell them why or to talk about any of the things that had happened, she woke up one day and realized she needed a plan. She needed to recreate herself. This time, she wanted to never feel so terrible again, either so terribly depressed or so terribly overjoyed.

Most of all she wanted not to be a person who needed someone horrible in her life to respond to because she didn't know any other way to live. She had felt that draw as she walked past certain people at her new school: had felt an attraction to those with submerged violence, confident that she would know how to be near them, seduced by the idea of feeling normal again. She fought away from it, but it was difficult.

So she built a mental model of who she wanted to be, and went to work becoming her.

Some of the things she had learned from living in her father's house, she kept: she knew how to maintain a perfect appearance, how to be quiet and pleasant, how not to be noticed for being odd or wrong. She knew how to listen around corners, not only to what a house could tell her about what was going on in it, but to what people said when they didn't know she was near enough to hear. She knew how to check the trash for vital information on things that could affect her that she wasn't supposed to know about. She knew how to keep her feelings invisible.

She had learned a range of household tasks from the housekeeper and from her mother. Her aunt appreciated the fact that Suki could and would do laundry, iron, wash dishes, change beds, cook meals, remove stains from all kinds of things, and pull weeds without complaint. She had supermarket coupon savvy and knew when to buy a brand name and when a generic thing would do just as well. She threw things out; she didn't collect anything; she never asked for anything to move or change. She was the perfect guest or servant: considerate and quiet and helpful, with no irritating habits.

The perfect guest or servant, though her aunt and uncle had wanted her to be family.

"He's been wandering around ever since," Matt continued as though there had been no pause in the conversation. "Which is not a bad way to live, except when something you can't see is chasing you and you can't get away."

"Chasing you." Suki wasn't following this very well. She didn't want to think about Edmund: he was part of everything she had left behind the wall. She frowned. What was this girl doing here? She should call the police or something, get them to take Matt away, or maybe just tell her to get out. Suki said, "As long as you're here, you might as well have something to drink, huh? Come on in the kitchen. I'm sure my aunt will have a pitcher of something in the fridge; she always does."

"What about Edmund?"

"I don't want to deal with him."

"'Kay. I'll be right there. You go on ahead." Matt slipped out the front door.

I do not want to be having this conversation, Suki thought. *I have things to pack, a plane to catch. A past to ignore.* She turned the deadbolt, but without hope; noticed the chain, and put it on. Then she went to the kitchen and got out two glasses and a pitcher of iced tea.

Matt was back in two minutes. Suki heard the deadbolt turn and the chain unhook, sensed the quiet footsteps; sensed also that Edmund still sat in the chair on the front porch. She hadn't used her house sense like this for a long time. She hadn't needed to. It made her feel strange.

"Are you a burglar?" Suki asked as Matt took a chair across the kitchen table from her.

"No. Not usually."

"You're really good with locks."

"Thanks." Matt smiled.

"Makes a person wonder."

"It's a survival thing. Same as your listening."

"My what?"

"How you listen to the house. I listen like that, only harder."

Suki poured tea and sat down across from Matt. "How can you listen and make locks unlock?" This was a much safer topic.

"It's more like talking listening. Like, I ask the house, hey, okay for me to come in? And the house says, you gonna hurt anything inside me? And I say no, and the house says, okay, come on in, and the door opens. You know?"

"I don't know," said Suki. "I really don't."

"I had this dream," Matt said. She sipped iced tea. "When I spent the night in the haunted house. I forgot it until I saw you today. It was a dream about you. The house really liked you. You would lean on the wall and think of what you wanted, and the house would do it. Open doors, shut them; lock them, sometimes with people on the other side. Pop the secret panel. Bring the furniture." She smiled. "That's the best house."

Suki sat back, blindsided. She had forgotten all of that, buried it deep, even though it was something she had really loved. Matt was talking about little lost Susan, pathetic little Susan, whose only place of power had been the haunted house, whose closest relationship had been with a dead boy. Little Susan was someone Suki would never go back to being. Much safer to collect many places of power, and not have close relationships at all.

"So when I met Edmund he was living half a life," Matt said. "And I think he was pretty happy, too, even though he was a shadow of his old self. I kind of messed him up."

"On purpose?" Suki asked. These lightning topic shifts confused her, but she decided to play along.

"I don't know. I really try not to mess people up. But ever since I met Edmund . . . Man. We were just visiting his sister, and I messed around in her life, too."

"Oh? How is Abby, anyway?"

"She's a really great artist. She has three kids and a nice husband. And a lot of magic loose in the house."

"Is that part of the mess you made?"

"Naw, it was in the house already. I just taught it to talk to her."

"That's a mess?"

Matt sat back and looked at the ceiling. "At first I thought it was a big mistake, but I think it's going to be okay now. I'm not sure about Edmund." Her gaze drifted down to Suki's face again.

"What's wrong with Edmund?"

"He was like you. A living shell. Kind of killed a couple of his old selves, same way you did. I woke one up and talked him into taking it back, and now he's all mixed up inside."

"What makes you think you know anything about me?" Suki asked in a neutral voice.

Matt drank iced tea and set the empty glass on the table. "I been looking at you. I'm sorry, but I did it. Edmund's worried about you, and I wasn't sure there was any other way to find out how you are."

"Looking at me?"

"At some of the pictures you have."

"Pictures?" Suki looked at the table between them, empty except for the pitcher, the two glasses, and their elbows. "What pictures?"

"Like the jigsaw girl."

Suki felt that she had fallen into something over her head. She felt stupid just repeating what Matt said and hoping for an explanation, so this time she remained silent.

"Like, there's this big horrible thing with your father." Matt stretched out her arms as far as she could, then dropped her hands to the table. "Then afterward the Alice you, you know, the blue dress, the headband, the long straight hair, she falls apart into jigsaw puzzle pieces, and then there's your ghost looking at the pieces and only picking up some of them to stick back together. And carving new ones to fit. Throwing the rest away. Except they don't go away. They lie around in the bottom of you and they keep sending you messages. You just pretend the messages come from somewhere else, or the messages aren't even there, but you're listening even when you think you aren't."

Suki blinked twice. She checked her watch. "Well, this has been fascinating, but I have a plane to catch."

"So people live in all these different ways, sometimes with the pieces in place and sometimes all torn apart, and it's not really my business to know which way is the best," Matt said, and frowned. "But sometimes I think about it anyway. Especially about people I care about. Then I want them to feel better, and I mess with them. I think it ends up helping. I hope it does."

"Does this have anything to do with me?" Suki asked.

Matt nodded. "Edmund loves you, and I love him. Nathan loves you, and I love him too."

Suki felt flickers of alien rage inside. Who was this stranger to take away her boys? Her boys. Oh my. How strange. More than Edmund and Nathan, Julio had been her boy, before she had even met the others. The first time she had seen Julio was when they were both about four: a little dark boy in the kitchen with Juanita, the housekeeper, and he hid under the table with Susan and they ate raisins while his mother made gingerbread cookies.

Pictures from the past spun, recrystallized in a new pattern. Had she really been special to them? To Julio and Nathan, definitely. They had done everything they could to protect her. Deirdre, the tomboy, had been a buddy to the boys, but Susan had been the princess.

Her father had owned Susan's shell self, every part of her that he could see. And Susan, she had had her deep self and her boys and her first and only girlfriend. None of whom could protect her against the whirlwind force that was her father.

Not true. Edmund had done that.

"Julio," Suki said slowly. Her first, best, and for a long time, her only friend. Where was he now? She hadn't heard from him in more than ten years. When she came to California, she had let everything else go, but for a while, she and Julio had exchanged letters. At least, he wrote her letters, and she sent back one-sentence postcards. When had that stopped? Probably she had dropped it as she let the past fall further and further behind her.

She wondered what had become of Deirdre, who had also had a hard time making friends, especially with girls. Deirdre was too strong and too rude to get along well with people who kept quiet about anything. Little Susan had admired that, even though she couldn't understand it.

What had become of them?

Edmund was on the porch. She could ask him. And chance toppling everything she had built.

Suki didn't need or want boys anymore, except Lyle, and she only wanted Lyle to keep the other boys away with the least effort. She didn't need or want other people to protect her. She could take care of herself. She had been training at a karate dojo ever since she moved in with her aunt and uncle. She trusted her hands and feet, arms and legs, to protect her from physical attacks, or at least to let attackers know they had been in a fight. She was not going to be like her mother, beaten many times and never fighting back.

Martial arts training didn't protect against Matt. It was just talking that this girl was doing. Talking. The most disabling art on Earth.

Walk away, Suki thought. She checked her watch and got to her feet. "I've got to go," she said. "Tell the boys you saw me and I'm fine."

"Naw. I try not to lie." Matt got up too and took her glass to the sink. "Thanks for letting me in, though."

"Letting you in?" Suki laughed, thinking of deadbolts turning, chains unchaining without any help from her.

"I'm not talking about the house."

"What are you, anyway? I thought maybe you were a ghost. But you're more like a leprechaun or something, aren't you?"

"A leprechaun? Like the Lucky Charms guy? I don't think so." Matt looked down at herself, checked her waffle-weave shirt, which was indeed green. "I don't think there's a word for what I am. Human, maybe."

Suki put the pitcher of iced tea back in the refrigerator. "Is that right?" she asked.

"Sure. Hey, you want a ride to the airport?"

The sheer effrontery of this made Suki turn around and stare at Matt in surprise. Matt smiled. "I could tell Edmund not to talk to you. He would just drive, if you wanted him to."

Suki considered what this said about Matt's relationship to Edmund. Matt seemed pretty sure she could get Edmund to do what she wanted. Suki had never had that kind of confidence, though people often would do what she asked. "What do you think any of this is going to do for anyone?" she asked.

"I don't know. We could really use your help, but only if you're ready to give it. And even if you're not, I just—I hate to lose you."

"Why is that? What does this have to do with you?"

"I told you already. People I love care about you."

"Well, they can stop worrying. There's not a mark on me." Suki posed, holding out her arms as though to display herself as merchandise.

Matt stared at her for so long Suki's eyebrow got tired of being raised. "Spit it out, Elf," Suki said.

"But there's marks all over you," Matt said in a low voice. "Your mom's death pushes down your shoulders, and there's bruises, all the ones she got that you felt like belonged to you. There's a big red scar over your heart, and slashes over your stomach. And kind of a halo thing squishing your head."

A chill iced through Suki. None of this stuff should be anywhere near her surface, and what was Matt doing with the information, anyhow?

"I'm going to get some clothes," Suki said. "Be gone by the time I come back downstairs, okay?"

Matt shook her head.

"I mean it. Get out of here."

Matt bit her lip and shook her head again.

"No means no."

Matt looked away. "I'm sorry," she whispered.

Suki's fury collapsed, but not her determination. "Suit yourself," she said, and went upstairs to her old bedroom.

In the closet she looked through a lot of formal clothes she had for fancier presentations, pulled out a couple of sleek evening gowns and some elegant-by-trade-show-standards daywear. She zipped them into her garment bag, making sure nothing would wrinkle.

She checked her watch. Three and a half hours before her flight. It would take her forty-five minutes to stop by her house, pick up her suitcase and laptop, and get to the airport. On international flights she was supposed to be in the terminal two hours in advance. This first leg of the flight would only take her across the country, though. Still, she had a little time.

She sat on the bed and opened her house sense.

Edmund still sat on the porch, but she could only tell that by the tiniest flicker of consciousness: he wasn't really present, somehow; maybe his shell was here and his real self elsewhere, though Suki couldn't work out how that could be.

Matt was in the kitchen doing something quiet and not invasive. The house made no protesting sounds.

Why had Suki let Matt inside? Talked to her at all? What was going on here? Why did she want to say yes to a ride to the airport with these two, even though she couldn't imagine anything good would come from it?

She pressed her hand over her heart and wondered about a scar there. She couldn't feel anything physical. She touched her stomach. Every once in a great while, her stomach hurt. Nothing else ever did. Suki didn't get sick and didn't get hurt. Occasionally, she cut herself by mistake, but the blood was always a surprise; she never felt the wound.

Maybe Matt was some kind of psychic. Maybe she was just a lunatic, and flat out wrong about everything. Maybe Edmund had primed Matt, told her things about Suki that Suki never wanted another human being to know. She felt a rush of bitterness. People never knew when to stop talking, and she couldn't make them stop no matter how hard she wished. She couldn't bury her past as long as other people who knew about it wanted to discuss it.

Matt said Edmund needed her help. That was strange. After that night, Suki had figured he'd never need anybody's help.

She didn't want to go back to that night. Couldn't even think about it without feeling bricks tottering inside. How much would it hurt her to help him? She touched her chest again, searching for scar tissue.

Still tuned to the house, Suki felt/heard the garage door open, a car come in and turn off, the kitchen door being unlocked and opened. "Susan?" called her aunt. "I saw your car. What are you— Who are *you*?"

Susan, thought Suki. Even though her aunt had given her her new name when Suki first moved to Palo Alto, Caroline still called her Susan most of the time. Suki was a good name: not connected to the past at all.

"My name's Matt Black. I'm visiting Susan. Sorry to intrude, ma'am." The conversation drifted up the stairs.

"Susan's friends are welcome here, she should know that. I'm Caroline Frost, Susan's aunt."

"Nice to meet you," Matt said. Suki suspected a handshake.

Now Matt would talk. Suki was sure of it, based on her experience. But no, a blank space went by.

"Where is Susan, anyway?" asked Caroline. "She's here, isn't she?"

"She went upstairs to get some stuff," said Matt. "She's leaving for Paris tonight."

Did I ever tell her where I was going? Suki wondered. *No, I did not. Who's she been talking to? How does she know this stuff?*

I know magic works. Magic saved my life. Even though Matt says she's not a leprechaun, she's some kind of something that knows way too much. I should get as far from her as I can.

Paris should do it.

"Susan?" Caroline called up the stairwell.

Suki sighed, picked up her garment bag, and went downstairs. Caroline met her at the bottom of the stairs; Matt was still in the kitchen. "I called before I came," Suki said, "but you weren't home. I left a message."

"It's all right," said her aunt. "How long are you going to be gone this time?"

"About a week. It depends on if I line up extra presentations and interviews. Thanks again for letting me keep stuff here."

"You're entirely welcome." In a lower voice, she said, "Who's this boy you've brought? Are you sure he's safe to have in the house?"

"Boy? What boy?" asked Suki, bewildered. Did Caroline know about Edmund on the front porch? But he was nearly invisible, in more than one sense, and Caroline had come in through the garage door.

Caroline jerked her head toward the kitchen.

"That's not a boy, Aunt Caro. It's just Matt. There's no way to keep her out, but I'm sure she'll leave with me."

Caroline blinked.

"Hey, Matt," Suki called. "Time to hit the road."

Matt came out of the kitchen carrying Suki's purse. "You forgot this."

"Damn! Thanks. Couldn't even get on the plane without my passport and my tickets. Let alone go to Paris without a wallet." Suki kissed her aunt's cheek. "Bye, Aunt Caro. See you later."

Caroline hugged her and let go, and Suki hurried from the house with Matt behind her.

On the front porch, Suki said, "If I get a ride with you, do you promise to go just where I tell you?"

Matt locked gazes with Edmund. After a moment he shook his shoulders, woke out of his dream state, and sat up straight. "I told her we'd take her to the airport," Matt said to Edmund.

"And that you wouldn't talk to her unless she said it was okay. Is that all right?"

Edmund nodded. He went down the front steps ahead of them and opened the passenger door of the rusty brown station wagon, held it for Suki.

A backdoor popped open before Matt even got within touching distance of the car. "Take your bag?" Matt asked. Suki handed it to her and slid into the front seat, which was covered with something synthetic, tiger-striped, and soft. Automatic car doors. What next? Suki glanced behind her and realized the car had no backseat, just a padded cargo area, with odds and ends of cargo along the left side. Matt laid the garment bag down carefully so that it stretched flat. Can't complain about the service, Suki thought. She studied the dashboard. All kinds of things lay on it, rocks, dried leaves, feathers, a snakeskin, seed pods of various sorts, even a couple of plastic dinosaurs and a small tangle of tinsel.

Edmund climbed behind the wheel and looked at her. She looked back. Same serious green eyes, absurdly handsome face—was that his real face, or had it changed after he got his powers? Suki couldn't remember—slightly shaggy, curly hair. A different smile, sort of a blessings-on-all-things smile that tempted Suki to punch him. She stared at his face for a while, thinking all sorts of things about it, then glanced at her watch. "Hey! We have to go. Don't you know how to start this bucket of bolts?"

The car started, though Edmund didn't move.

"You don't have to insult her," Matt muttered from the back.

"Sorry," said Suki. She laid her hand palm down on the glove compartment. Something more than engine noise thrummed against her skin. "Sorry! I didn't know you were listening."

Edmund touched her arm. His touch crackled through her like lightning. She jerked away, staring at him, but he looked just as surprised as she felt. "What! What was that?"

Matt leaned forward. "We don't know our way around your town. You have to tell us where to go, and he won't ask, 'cause I told him not to talk to you."

"This is so incredibly juvenile! Go to the corner and take a left." Suki tugged at a recalcitrant seatbelt, got it to buckle over her waist. No shoulder strap. "Okay, left on University. I have to stop by my apartment and pick up a couple things before we go to the airport. Edmund?"

He glanced at her, smiled. Not quite a blessings-on-all-things smile. Something less global, more personal, and a little sad.

"I don't know . . . I can't remember. Did I ever thank you?"

He looked confused.

"This is stupid. Okay, you can talk. I'm just kind of scared of your voice, okay?"

"I've been working on it," he said, and sounded like a normal person, almost like his old, pre-witch self.

"Oh! But in the restaurant—" Her old name, three times, so beautifully said and seductive it had almost persuaded her to fall into her old self.

"Couldn't help it. I was excited to see you."

She put her hand to her cheek. They hadn't seen each other in a long time, they used to be really good friends, he had saved her life—if not literally, he had rescued her from an intolerable situation, stopped her from killing herself, something that had been on her mind more and more toward the end of that part of her existence—and the first thing she said to him was she was going to be sick.

Remorse crashed down on her. The old horrible sense of never being able to do the right thing, to do enough, to be the right person washed through her.

God, she thought she had stopped doing that.

Matt smacked her lightly on top of her head. "Cut it out. He doesn't mean it like that."

"What?" Suki's voice came out in a wail. She looked back at Matt.

"He's just explaining. He's not blaming. Lemme—oh, man!" Strange shimmering gold lace spun from Matt's hand and draped over Suki's head. She could see through it. A couple of seconds later it glowed brighter and brighter, pinpricks of colored light sparkling all over it. Then it snapped away.

Suki's sense of total failure vanished with it. "Turn left here," she said, her voice solid, normal, calm. She turned to look at Matt. "What the hell was that?"

"I dunno." Matt shoved her sleeve partway up and looked at a gold-sheathed wrist. Tiny lights flickered across the golden surface, cityscapes seen from a mile up. After ten seconds the lights winked out, leaving the band dull gold behind them. "It ate it."

"Are you okay, Susan?" Edmund asked.

"Let me see," Suki said. "Thing one. My name is Suki now, okay? Thing two, yeah, I feel just fine. Thing three. Matt, what the hell is that? What did it do to me?"

"Suki?" repeated Edmund.

"That's right."

Matt stroked her fingers over the wrist band. "This is a piece of Abby's magic," she said. "It gave it to me."

"What?" Subject, verb, object, prepositional phrase, yes, but sense? No.

"Abby's magic gave a piece of itself to me. I don't know how it works yet. It just—it—it ate your mood."

Suki thought about that for a while. She felt fine. She probed the sore spot: Edmund had been happy to see her, and she had rebuffed him. Okay, that had happened, she was over it now. "Oh. Uh. Okay. We just passed my apartment building."

The car slowed and made a U-turn. Suki pointed out her building, an old art deco apartment house built in the late thirties and rigorously maintained ever since. It was full of spacious apartments with high ceilings and yuppies who never spent time at home. The car pulled into the driveway. Suki directed Edmund to her assigned parking spot. Her car was in front of Aunt Caroline's house, which should be okay while Suki was gone, and would cost a lot less than airport parking.

"I just have to run in for a minute." Suki climbed out of the car.

Matt rolled down the rear window. "Can I come? I gotta use the bathroom."

Suki stared at Matt's guileless eyes. Much as Suki wanted a couple minutes to herself to think about things, she couldn't say no. "Come on," she said gruffly. "But don't look at my things, okay?"

"All right."

Suki peeked through the passenger-side window at Edmund. "Do you want to come too?" she asked in an exasperated voice.

"No." He gave her a narrow grin. "I'll pee out here."

Sure! Have one of the neighbors arrest him for indecent exposure, and then there she'd be, nobody to drive her to the airport, unless Matt could drive, or unless Suki could drive Edmund's lively car. "God. Come on!" Why should she care if they saw how she lived? The apartment was clean, she knew that much. It was always clean: she cleaned whenever anything old tried to surface, which happened more often than she wanted to remember. Anyway, she had done an extra cleaning last night because she always did before she traveled; she hated coming back to left-behind dirt. "There's goddamn rest rooms at the goddamn airport."

"We're not actually stopping there," Edmund said, climbing out of the car, "unless you want us to wait with you, which didn't seem likely a couple minutes ago."

"You going to lock the car? My garment bag is in there." Along with other potentially intriguing things, an overstuffed duffel bag, a full plastic garbage bag that didn't smell bad, a cooler, blankets, pillows, and some sacks of groceries.

Edmund said, "No one will trouble it."

"You've never been here before. How can you know that?"

Matt touched her arm. "Don't worry about it, Suki."

The car made popping noises. Suki noticed that all the lock buttons had dropped.

"Oh. I forgot. Auto-car." She led them to the front of the building and unlocked the foyer door, wishing she hadn't made an inadvertent pun. She hated puns. At least neither of them had laughed.

They rode the old-fashioned elevator in silence. Suki was still thinking about the golden veil eating her bad mood. If she had that kind of technology, what would she do with it? She didn't feel bad very often these days. She took lots of precautions to keep her life streamlined: she never did anything after work with anyone but Lyle, who understood that nothing extra was going to happen, even if he didn't like it; if a book she was reading got too emotionally wrenching, she skimmed or stopped; she avoided newscasts or TV movies of the week; she never established relationships with people or exchanged greetings any deeper than wishing they'd have a good day/evening/weekend; and she always picked projects that challenged the intellect instead of the heart. With a few specialty replies for particularly sticky situations, she coasted through just about everything without effort or trouble.

Suppose she had a golden veil. She might try a few new things. The veil would act as insurance against suffering from them. She would get to vary her routine. Which, now that she thought about it, was pretty boring, if safe.

Her fingers tangled with Matt's just as the elevator door opened on her floor. "What?" said Suki, looking down in surprise.

"Hey!" Matt cried. Gold flowed over her fingers and enveloped Suki's hand. "Stop it! What are you doing?" Gold split down the center. Some swooped up Matt's hand to disappear into her sleeve, and some flowed up to form a ring around Suki's wrist. She lifted her hand and stared at the gold band. It looked like a flat, featureless bracelet.

"I'm sorry, I'm sorry," Matt said, "I don't know why it did that. It's not supposed to do stuff unless I tell it to, but . . . I'll try to get it off if you want."

Suki held her hand above her head. Come down, mood-eating veil, she thought, but nothing happened. Well, of course, she thought, I don't have much of a mood at the moment. "I wanted it," she told Matt.

"What?" Matt's hazel eyes were wide.

"It ate my bad mood. I wanted something that does that. It was a very neat thing." She laughed her best chilling, supervillain laugh. "With this bracelet, I can rule the world!"

"Someone else wants the elevator," Edmund said softly. He was holding the door open.

"Oh, of course they do," said Suki, stepping out, Matt right behind her. "Guess one mood-eating veil can't control everything." She led the way down the hall to her apartment, unlocked the door, and ushered them in. "The bathroom is through that door." She pointed to the right.

"Thanks," said Matt, running.

Suki stood in her living room and looked at Edmund. He studied her white couch with its white pillows, the white rug, the glass-topped coffee table on steel legs, and the three upholstered white sit-stools. The walls were cool, pale green.

He turned to her, his eyebrows up.

"It's very soothing to come home to," she said.

He nodded.

"Nothing sticks to it. It doesn't make any pictures."

"Mm."

"I'm comfortable here," she said, and wondered why she was saying anything at all. She surely sounded defensive.

"Good," he said.

She took a few steps forward and collapsed onto the couch. Despair swamped her. This was how she lived. She came home to nothing. She went to work and avoided connecting to anything. She called herself happy.

Her new bracelet moved against her wrist.

Defeated, she lifted her hand over her head. The dull gold

veil descended. Lights glimmered and brightened all over it. Then foof! It turned back into a bracelet, and she felt just fine.

"Wha—" Edmund edged forward, pulled a stool up to sit facing her, almost knocking knees. "What?"

"Yesss," said Suki, wrapping her hand around the bracelet. It was warm, almost hot, and it was a little bigger than it had been. She peeked at it and saw little lights twinkling at her for a moment before they vanished. "I love you!" She kissed the bracelet. A strange pressure kissed her back. She jerked her wrist away from her mouth and saw an outline of her lips against the gold. A moment later, that too faded. She wondered if she should fear the bracelet.

"It's just what I wanted," she said. Her voice shook a little, though she felt fine. She glanced up into Edmund's eyes, saw his intense concentration. "Edmund . . ." She opened her arms and leaned forward to hug him. He hugged her back.

Her uncle Henry had died a year ago. She couldn't remember hugging anybody besides Henry and Aunt Caroline in years. This felt different, but not scary. Edmund smelled like sage and campfire smoke and human. His embrace was firm but not tight, and he radiated comforting warmth. She knew, somehow absolutely, that he wouldn't hurt her. She pressed her ear to his chest and listened to his heart.

After a little while she murmured, "Sorry I've been so snotty since you showed up."

"It's all right," he murmured.

"I guess I'm still scared of a lot of things."

"Life wasn't safe for you."

"But it has been. It has been ever since you—since I came down here. Why can't I just get over it?"

"It doesn't seem to work that way."

"I just want it to be over. It *is* over. I'm someone else now. It still keeps hurting me somehow."

He didn't say anything. She wondered if it was hopeless. She felt the bracelet moving on her wrist, and thought, —Stop it. Not now.— Whatever she was feeling, she didn't want it to go away yet, even though she didn't know what it was. The bracelet froze into immobility.

Running. Running away, with something she couldn't see chasing her. Jigsaw puzzle pieces lying at the bottom of a well. If she stopped running and took another look at them, would anything change? Would it just hurt worse?

At last she sighed and let go of Edmund, and he released her too. They leaned back and studied each other's faces. "Matt said you ran away," Suki said after a minute. "And you've been running ever since. Or something like that."

He frowned and said, "I've been wandering and listening for work to do—helping people and things. It didn't feel like running away, more like drifting. I liked it. But now, I—" He looked away. Then he smiled. "I met Matt, and my life changed. I think she's right. I'm running from that night. I can't even remember it. Until I get it back . . ."

"You want me to help you with that?" Suki asked. She needed more plaster on her inner wall. More plaster and more bricks. "I can't. I can't do that."

"You don't have to," he said.

Matt came back and sat on the rug near them. "It's like a big burned place inside him," she said. "Hard for him to look at."

Suki hugged her stomach. The stabbing pains, gone for years, came back, and she groaned. Her mind slipped sideways.

She checked her watch. "My trip!" she said. She ran into her room, changed quickly into her traveling clothes—comfortable black slacks and a loose pink blouse, a lightweight gray blazer that made her look businesslike, flat black shoes and regular socks—and grabbed her suitcase and her laptop. "We have to go!"

"One minute," said Edmund. He disappeared into the bathroom.

"You can't look at it either?" Matt asked.

Suki paced back and forth on her white rug. "It hurts, Matt. It makes me sick."

"Okay." Matt sighed. "Okay. Let it go. We'll find another way. Didn't mean to hurt you." She stood up. She smiled and dropped the subject. "Let me help you with your stuff." She reached for Suki's suitcase. Suki thought about handing her the laptop, but it was delicate. Then again, the suitcase was heavy, and Matt was shorter than Suki. Suki shrugged and handed it over.

"When that thing happened with the gold," Matt said, hanging onto the suitcase, "that was because you wanted it to?"

"I really did," Suki said. "I kind of stole it from you, though, huh?"

"That's okay. I got more. Only, how could it know what you wanted? I guess it just could. Do you understand what it is?"

"A mood-eating veil."

"No. It's magic."

"Of course it's magic. How else would it work?"

"I don't mean—I mean, like a stick of butter is butter? This is a stick of magic. I don't know how it works yet or what it can do, but it can do lots of stuff." Matt bit her bottom lip and pressed her gold-plated wrist against the handle of the suitcase, then released it. The suitcase floated in the air, a small dot of gold gleam on its handle. "Using it too much makes you tired, though."

"Wow," Suki breathed. A troop of ideas for livening up presentations marched through her mind. If she could make things float, that ought to keep prospective clients awake.

"The other thing I don't know is if it runs out. Maybe you use it up, and then it's gone."

Edmund rejoined them. He studied the floating suitcase.

"So I did take something away from you," said Suki.

"Yeah, but look." Matt shoved both her sleeves up to reveal gold that covered her forearms halfway to the elbows. In the center of each band ran a darker band of gold. "Shoot. They're bigger than they were. Thicker. Shoot. How'd that— Well, anyway, Suki, I got plenty."

"Thanks, then, Matt. This thing is—I've only used it twice, but I can tell already it's a huge help." Suki wondered if it would work on her stomach pains. Too late, though; they had vanished when she stopped thinking about the past.

"Good." Matt headed for the front door and the suitcase followed her. Suki and Edmund trailed after. In the hallway outside, an older woman and a small white dog came out of another door. The woman wore a turquoise running suit. The dog, a poodle, wore only a plain leather collar. A slim chain connected the woman to the dog.

Matt grabbed the suitcase's handle just in time. "There's another thing," she said as Suki relocked her door with the three of them outside. "Be careful where and when you use magic, or people will think you're crazy."

"Wouldn't Mrs. Tompkins think *she* was crazy if she saw a suitcase floating, rather than thinking I was crazy?"

"You can't count on things like that. People's brains do flips to stop them from having to change what they think. Maybe she sees the suitcase in the air and her eyes slide past it and she never thinks about it again. Or she thinks we're doing a practical joke or something. People think you can do anything for a practical joke, no matter how impossible it looks. Or maybe she just thinks *I* think I've got a floating suitcase, and I'm crazy." They headed down the hall.

Mrs. Tompkins held the elevator door for them. Her poodle lunged on its leash, jumped up against Edmund's legs as soon as they were all in the elevator.

He knelt to pat the dog. It licked his face. "Oh my," said Mrs. Tompkins. "Fu almost never likes strangers. Suki, dear, who are your friends?"

"This is Edmund and Matt. Edmund and Matt, Mrs. Tompkins. Mrs. Tompkins, if you saw a suitcase floating through the air, what would you think?" Suki asked.

"Special effects? I've stumbled onto some sort of movie set? *Candid Camera?* Why, dear? What should I think?"

"Magic," said Suki in a dark voice.

"Oh. Oh, very well. That's what I'd think, then." Mrs. Tompkins smiled. "Are you a witch, my dear?" she asked Edmund.

He smiled up at her. Fu, panting gently and still leaning his forepaws against Edmund's arm, looked back over his shoulder at his mistress.

"My familiar is never this friendly with true outsiders, you see, and the elevator reeks of magic," said Mrs. Tompkins.

Edmund rose, lifting Fu on his left arm, and held out his

right hand. Mrs. Tompkins shook it and grinned. "I hope this means good things for Suki," she said. "Her life is far too quiet."

"I'm on my way to Paris," said Suki. "How quiet is that?"

"Are your friends going with you?" Mrs. Tompkins asked.

"No. It's a business trip."

"Then it's too quiet," said Mrs. Tompkins. "You need to stay with these people for a while, Suki. Check your horoscope if you don't believe me." The elevator door opened on the ground floor, and Mrs. Tompkins retrieved Fu from Edmund and disappeared.

"I've known that woman a year," Suki said, "and I never suspected anything about her."

"That's the other thing," said Matt. "People will surprise you." She left the elevator.

"Could you tell she was a witch?" Suki asked, following.

"If I was looking, probably I could. I wasn't looking, though, since you asked me not to look at your things."

"Huh." Suki worked this out. "Are you always looking? I guess not."

"Right," said Matt. "I call it dream-eyes, and I can open or shut them. Used to have 'em open all the time. Now I feel safer, and don't use 'em so much."

"Dream-eyes," muttered Suki. Edmund moved ahead and held the outside door for them, and they trooped through the cool night air to the car, which lifted its rear door as they approached. "The jigsaw girl." Suki slid her laptop into the car. "How did you get Paris, though? How could you see that?"

"Paris?" Matt put the suitcase in the car. She frowned. "Paris? Oh, your tickets told me."

Suki remembered leaving Matt in the kitchen with her

purse, Matt emerging with it. "You went through my purse?" Rage shot through her. One more invasion.

"No. I didn't go through your purse. The tickets talked."

"What?"

Edmund closed the car's backdoor and herded the women toward the front. Matt and Suki climbed in, Suki taking the front seat again.

"Well, 'cause they're excited. Paris. Paris. They just squeaked it."

"Listening," Suki said, remembering that Matt had talked about that early on too, how she could walk into locked houses because she listened. "Spooky," she muttered.

Silence answered her from the back of the car. Suki glanced behind her and saw Matt lying across the car on the padding, staring up at the car's roof, feet propped above the window.

Edmund backed out of the parking space and into the street. Suki directed him to the freeway and told him to head north. She leaned back against the tiger-striped seat cover, stroking her magic bracelet without thinking about it much. The metal heated under her fingertips.

What must it be like to be Matt? Suki spent a lot of energy insulating herself from stimuli she was afraid might upset her. Matt was looking at lots more things and hearing lots more conversations than most people did. What filters did she use? How did she sort all that information? Why didn't it drive her mad? Did it come at her whether she wanted it or not? No, she said she could close the special eyes. The eyes of intention? Could she see a person plan an evil act before it happened? Could she stop it?

What if she couldn't?

How did she decide when and how to use information she had? How much of it could she ignore or forget?

The tires sang on the road. They traveled from the illumination of one streetlight to the next, with an endless string of them shining on the freeway ahead, and city-lighted buildings and billboards charting the night landscape to the sides. It was late enough that traffic had thinned to bearable. *I live here*, Suki thought. *What's beautiful about it, what's irritating about it, what's ugly about it, it's all my home.*

My home. She thought of her apartment. She had never brought in a houseplant or put up a picture. There were home decor magazines on the white wicker laundry hamper near the toilet, with her name and post office box number on their subscription labels. After she looked at them she threw them away. As roots went, that wasn't much.

Her room at Aunt Caroline's had more personality, but most of it was applied personality: a poster of wild mustangs running across a plain, one of a pair of pink ballerina slippers, a small, fat ceramic baby robin: all things Aunt Caroline and Uncle Henry had put in the room before Suki got there in an attempt to make her feel welcome. They hadn't known each other very well; Suki's father hadn't ever taken the family traveling, and Caro and Henry had only come north once, when Suki was about ten. Suki had had glass horses on a shelf in her room, a collection of her mother's dolls that she never played with, and a porcelain statue of a ballerina. The horses and the ballerina were birthday presents from her father. They really had nothing to do with Suki.

She had grown used to the mustangs and the ballet slippers on her wall at Aunt Caroline's house. She even grew to like the horses. But they too had had nothing to do with her. Yet she had never cared enough to take down those posters or pick others she liked better. It was just one of a multitude of things she had considered outside her power. "I wonder what I'd put on a wall," Suki said out loud. Even in her room at Nathan's house, she hadn't decorated.

Or had she? She remembered walking through the downstairs of the haunted house, calling furniture from the past. She could have picked some pieces and banished others, but she had loved all the things that used to be there. Soft velvet chairs that had hugged her; cluttered tables with tiny treasures on them, and the old painting of Nathan's mother above the fireplace, looking so pretty and young.

"There are wonderful museums in Paris," Edmund said, as though he could follow her thoughts. "They probably have reproductions of artwork you could buy if you saw something you liked."

"Have you been there?"

"No, but I lived in a library for a while and looked at picture books all night."

To the right of the freeway, airport hotels showed. Then the airfield: giant airplanes lit from below by their landing and ground lights lumbered along runways, temporarily earthbound dinosaurs. Beyond lay the night-gray waters of San Francisco Bay.

"What were you doing in a library?"

"Solving some problems."

"What?" she asked, laughing a little.

"Like I said before, that's what I've been doing since I left Guthrie. Blowing around from here to there, waiting for things to summon me to do work. It's satisfying to help things fix themselves. An antidote to destruction."

Suki studied Edmund's profile. He looked young and strong and good-hearted. It sounded like a satisfactory life. "What kind of problems?" she asked.

"Mostly structural. Tired shelves, weary floors, spine-broken books, on-its-last-legs plumbing."

"You're a carpenter?"

"Not exactly." He smiled at her. "I fixed it witch ways. Find weakened things that want to be strong again. Summon and apply strengthening energy. It doesn't work quickly, but I didn't have anyplace else I wanted to be. And at night, when everyone was gone, the library showed me all its best things. It took me around the world."

She cocked her head. "You ever fly on a broom?"

That made him grin. "Not yet."

"Why not?"

"Had plenty of other things to do." He pulled off the freeway at the airport exit.

Suki checked her watch. Still two hours before her ten P.M. flight. Should be okay.

"Which lane?" Edmund muttered. There were six or eight.

"Get over to the right, and just keep in the departure lanes," Suki said. "The international terminal is the one in the middle." She felt a queer pressure in her chest. She had been talking with Edmund the way she hadn't spoken to anyone else in years, not just about lane changes, but about vital things and silly things. He was someone she didn't have to hide from, because he knew most of the worst things about her. Stranger still, she knew deep secrets about him. Then there was the somewhat forced intimacy she had with Matt, who could see through her and answer the unspoken. Even though she resented that, she craved it too:

someone who needed no explanations, who spoke to her reluctant heart. And in fifteen minutes, or ten if they were lucky, she'd be saying good-bye to both of them and flying off to a city full of strangers, where she would put on a false face, speak a foreign language, and counsel people to buy things she didn't care about.

"A broom," she muttered. She stroked her bracelet. She looked down at it and wondered. If she touched it to a broom, would a piece of it jump off and make the broom float the way her suitcase had? Could she ride a broom?

A tiny tendril of gold unfurled from the bracelet and lifted toward her. Its tip swayed back and forth. Terrified and exhilarated, Suki stroked it with her finger, and it curled around the tip. A stick of magic. It wanted to do whatever she asked. Maybe a nice upright vacuum cleaner would be easier to sit on. Or a carpet. How would you steer?

The car pulled over to the curb in front of the international terminal. Black men in airline uniforms stood by podiums in front of the terminal, waiting to check luggage. "United?" asked Edmund.

Suki blinked. She smoothed the tendril down into the main mass of her bracelet and looked blindly at the glass-fronted building. "Huh? Oh, yeah." She sat unmoving in her seat as her eyes unfocused and everything blurred.

She'd been coasting for so long. This trip was supposed to be just another coast, waxed surfaces sliding past polished surfaces, sleep on the plane or hide behind a fat thriller, hope no one in a nearby seat wanted to talk, change planes in New York, fly until Orly. Blur of events, blur of work, blur of surface smiles, slide on past, never engaging, come home again to more slipping and sliding. Bonus if sales of units spiked. Salt the money away, because the future had to be full of rain.

"Suki?" Edmund touched her cheek, his fingertip skating on a tear Suki couldn't remember crying.

She looked away, out the window.

An airport policeman was striding toward them. You couldn't sit at the curb for long without getting a warning, she remembered. When Aunt Caroline had dropped her off a while back and couldn't get herself to say good-bye, they had gotten into trouble for it.

"Let's get out of here," she said in a low voice.

"You sure?"

She waited a long moment, long enough for the policeman to come up and tap on the window. Was she sure? They could come around the departure ring road again and she'd only be a little late. She lowered her window.

"You gonna unload passengers and luggage or not? You can't park here," said the policeman. "If you stay here any longer we're gonna take you into custody and impound your car."

"We were just leaving," Suki said. She looked at Edmund.

He checked traffic. He pulled away from the curb.

"Where are we going?" he asked as they headed away from the airport.

"I don't care," Suki said, and then, "North."

Chapter Nine

· · · · ·

SUKI was coming with them. Matt felt her shoulders relax. She lay crossways behind the front seats, her knees bent, the toes of her boots against one back door and her head against the other, and felt tension drain from her. She wasn't sure what kind of help Suki would be, but she was miles better than no help at all.

But that reminded her. Matt pushed her sleeves up her arms and looked at her wristbands, which were stretching into forearm bands, even though she had given some of her gold to Suki. —Why are you growing?—

—You're feeding me.—

Feeding it. Huh. What did it eat? Suki's moods, that was one thing Matt knew about, but what else? Something she'd miss? How big would it get? Had she shaped this so it wouldn't hurt anybody? No. Out of the confusing rush of memories from the time she had spent at Abby and Tony's house, Matt remembered: Gold had given her the first wristband before she had told Gold not to hurt anybody. Part of the wristbands came from Ginny, though, and she had been shaped to do no harm . . .

—Are you shaped not to hurt anybody?— she asked her wristbands.

—We are shaped to follow your wishes.—

Matt's wishes. Huh. —How come you do what Suki wants?—

—You didn't tell me not to.—

Huh. Another puzzle. Should she shape her gold so it only listened to her? But Suki seemed so happy with it. Maybe what Suki needed most was some magic right now.

Matt's stomach growled. She sat up and rummaged through a grocery bag. "Want some Fritos?" she asked.

Suki looked back, wide-eyed. She nodded.

"Edmund?"

"Toss me a bagel."

Matt found a poppy-seed bagel and flipped it forward. It slowed as it approached him and dropped into his hand. "Thanks," he said. Matt grabbed the bag of Fritos and a couple of bottles of water out of the cooler and edged forward again. She opened the Fritos and set the bag on top of the emergency brake next to Suki, handed her a water bottle.

"Thanks," Suki said. She stuffed a handful of Fritos into her mouth, chewed, swallowed. "I forgot how long it's been since lunch. Which, come to think of it, I never did eat. Oh man. I left it sitting on my desk. If nobody cleans up in my office, it'll be an ugly thing to come back to."

"Are you going back?" Matt asked.

"What?" Suki blinked at her.

"Blowing off this Paris trip could be a problem if you want to keep your job. I'm just guessing. I never had real jobs besides high school babysitting—just some dishwashing gigs mostly, or whatever people asked me to do for food. But—"

"You're right," Suki said slowly. "I don't know. I feel so strange. I guess I just threw away everything."

"It's not too late," Edmund said. "Maybe too late for that particular flight to Paris, but it's not too late to turn around and get your job back."

Suki sat silent for a while. "I think . . . I think I'm not going back. Not exactly, anyway. If I go back to Palo Alto, I'll have to start over. I'm coming with you because things have to change now."

Nobody said anything for a while.

Suki broke the silence presently. "I better call them, tell them I'm not going to make the Paris trade show, that they have to reassign my projects."

"We'll stop somewhere soon," Edmund said. "You can phone then."

"Probably nobody's in the office now. Well, maybe a few diehards. I could leave a message. Or I could wait until tomorrow and actually talk to my boss. He's not going to like this. I guess I'd rather talk to a machine. I'll call Lyle too. That should do it."

Matt ate some Fritos. She uncapped her water bottle and handed it forward to Edmund, who took a drink and handed it back. "Where we going, anyway? Back to Abby's?" said Matt.

"Do you think that's a good idea?" Edmund asked. "We'd probably get there around 11:30 or midnight, and they're not expecting us."

"We could call." Matt wrapped her hand around the gold on

her opposite forearm. Here was her hotline to Ginny. Should she open it up? "I could sleep on one of those couches in the living room. They sure looked comfortable. Or stay in the car."

"We can all stay in the car if we have to. I don't know if Abby will want to see us again so soon, or at all," Edmund said. "Could you find out?"

"Sure." Matt put her fingertips against the deeper gold of her arm band. —Ginny? Ginny, can you hear me?—

"We can all stay in the car?" Suki said. "We don't have to stay in the car. For heaven's sake, I have credit cards. We can stay in hotels."

"The car's more comfortable than a hotel," Edmund said.

"Does the car have a shower?"

"Hmmm. Good point," Edmund was saying, when the gold tingled under Matt's fingers and Ginny's voice came to her.

—Matt? You okay?—

—We found Edmund's friend and now we're headed north again. We got her with us. How are you all doing?—

—It's been pretty exciting here.— Matt felt Ginny's mental smile. —Abby and Tony yell a lot, but not like they're really mad. They're already forgetting what I am. They think I'm the nanny now.—

—I guess that's good, huh?— Matt wondered.

—It's okay with me,— Ginny thought. —Can't think of anything I'd like better at the moment. They're still arguing about Gold, though.—

—Huh.— Matt wondered if she should ask what kind of arguments they were having, then decided it was none of her business, unless somebody told her she should do something about it. —Did the other kids get pets?—

—Yeah. Keith has a cat and Iris has a dog. I think Tony would rather they had real animals. These ones are never going to be normal. Awful cute, though.—

Matt smiled and wondered if Ginny could tell. —Hey, Edmund wants me to ask you if we can come back now. Would that be too weird?—

—I think . . .— Matt sensed confusion in Ginny's whirl-wind thoughts. —They're adjusting to a lot of things at once.—

—Better if we don't come, huh?—

—I don't know for sure. But I have that impression. Huh?— Matt felt Ginny startle, turn away from the link.

—We'll be fine,— Matt thought. She pressed closer to Ginny's mind, got an image of Tony tapping Ginny's shoulder, trying to find out why Ginny had gone silent. —Talk to you later.—

—Good.— The touchtalk vanished.

"What was that?" Suki asked.

"What that?"

"Who's Ginny?" Suki gripped her banded wrist. "Who's Tony? Who's Keith? Who's Iris?"

"Yow! Did you hear us?" Matt tried to review everything she had said. Lots of things about Suki bothered her. Had she told Ginny any of that? It was so odd to have a friend who had appeared out of nowhere and yet seemed like the best friend a person could have: Ginny, Matt's reflection. Matt had the impulse to tell Ginny everything and anything. Lucky the contact was so short. Matt didn't think she'd said anything particularly upsetting about Suki.

"Sort of dim at first, but it got louder," Suki said.

"Your gold came from my gold." Matt touched one of her wristbands. "Guess you must of got part of Ginny's gold too."

"Who's Ginny? Who are all those people? The only name I recognize is Abby," said Suki.

Matt opened her mouth to try to answer, but Edmund interrupted. "What did Ginny say, Matt?"

"She thinks they're trying to adjust to too many things already, so maybe it's better if we stay away for now," Matt relayed.

"Okay. So we need some direction pretty soon, I guess. Do we have a goal? Keep going north? Head over to the valley and I-5? Or what?"

Nobody answered for a couple minutes.

"Maybe it's time to ask for help again," Matt said.

"Ask for help?" Suki stared back at Matt between the front seats.

"Edmund does this thing where he talks to spirit and it helps him pick a direction. That's how we found you."

"Hmm." Suki glanced at Edmund. "Sounds pretty nebulous."

"I'm open to suggestions," Edmund said.

Suki thought about it for a while, then shrugged. "This is your quest, right?"

"Oh," said Edmund slowly. "I guess it is. So I'll ask."

Matt explored the grocery sack again and came up with a bag of red delicious apples. She took three out and polished them on her shirt, then handed two forward.

Edmund said, "Hold the wheel, please." He sank his teeth into his apple and held it in his mouth, then let go of the steering wheel and shoved his hands into his pants pockets.

Suki gave a startled yelp and grabbed for the steering wheel before she realized that it was holding steady on its own. "Autocar?" she asked.

"Mm." Edmund brought out the lead weight on its fishline. He set the apple on the dashboard, kissed the sinker, then held it between both hands and murmured to it. After a moment he looped it over the rearview mirror and grabbed the steering wheel again.

The sinker swayed slightly forward.

"Good," said Edmund. "We can do a better seek when we find a good place to pull over, but these city exits make me nervous. I never know if you can get back on again." They passed lighted billboard advertisements for Las Vegas hotels and nightclub acts and recent blockbuster movie releases. To their left, the taller buildings of true downtown San Francisco stood.

At the interchange where Highway 101 went north into the city and Highway 80 went east across the bay, the sinker pulled to the right. They headed east across the Bay Bridge.

After a lingering look at the light-glittering city receding behind them, Matt lay down. She hadn't been in a city this big in a while. She listened to see if the city was talking. And it was, in a million nighttime voices. The bridge stood with its toes deep in the bedrock below the bay, stitching from the San Francisco shore to Yerba Buena Island to the Oakland shore with a tunnel in between, water hugging its supports and wind singing through its suspension cables. The road talked about the tastes of all the different tires that rode it and exhausts that breathed on it, the sizes and weights of different vehicles and how they massaged its back in strips, how the wind shifted it, how sometimes the Earth moved beneath it, how fog caressed it and sunlight heated it. The cables sang of constant tension and constant countering strength. Other cars whispered past them, dreaming of garages and gas stations, with the occasional image of gravel road scoring an undercarriage, an occasional flicker of a remembered collision or a screeching halt, sometimes a deep identification with the human inside and sometimes a total machine mind.

She lay quiet, listening to the city singing, for the moment not wanting anything more or less than this, to be traveling through the night in a car that comforted her, connected to whatever the car touched and whatever touched what was connected to the car, an encompassing, spreading awareness of Things telling their concerns, stresses, joys, and moments.

She hadn't slipped under a surface like this in a long time. She had done it much more when she was alone, especially when she first came to a new place and hadn't made human friends there yet.

The city sang her toward sleep and steel and concrete dreams, but Suki pulled her out of it by shaking her shoulder. "What are you doing?" Suki asked.

"Mmm," said Matt, drowsily.

"Please. This weird noise you're making is giving me a headache."

"Noise? What noise? Get out of my head."

"Your head?"

"Stop listening. It's rude," Matt mumbled.

"But I—" Suki turned away. "Edmund?"

"Matt's not making any noise," he said. "She's only tuning."

"What?"

Matt yawned, then grasped each wrist with her opposite hand. —Gold?—

—Yes.—

—Please stop talking to the gold on Suki, okay? I don't want to talk to her unless I plan it myself.—

—Very well.—

Matt felt something click in her head. Alone again? —Let's stay apart. Seesstroosstraass.—

"Tuning?" asked Suki. "Ouch." She gripped her head. "What was that?"

Matt sighed. "Your gold is yours now. Do whatever you want with it. I just don't want it listening to mine anymore."

"Okay," said Suki. Her voice came out a little wobbly, and a minute later she held her hand up and the scarf thing dropped down around her head. So, she had another bad mood; only this time Matt couldn't tell what it was. The mood eater did its work and turned back into a bracelet.

It occurred to Matt that the listening had gone both ways, even before Suki had taken the gold from Matt. Matt had known more about Suki's moods and thoughts than she should have, all through their discussion at Caroline's house and on till the first time the gold scarf came down and ate Suki's mood.

It had helped Matt to be able to speak to what Suki meant instead of what she said. It was almost like talking to a building or a car: somehow she had known more than she could remember knowing before about what was happening behind another person's face. People often didn't talk straight. Matt couldn't always figure out what they meant without looking at them with dream-eyes. This time had been different, even though Suki had talked pretty crooked.

How did that work?

Her wristbands flexed under her sleeves.

—You were doing that?— Matt thought.

—Translating. Aiding in it, anyway,— said Gold.

—Why?—

—I sensed your need and your desire.—

In most situations, Matt knew more than the other people around her, but she wasn't sure she wanted to add this kind of personal information. If she didn't like it when Suki listened in on her, how would Suki feel about it going the other direction?

Matt sat up and leaned forward. "Hey, Suki, does it bother you when I listen in to your head?"

"In a way," Suki said. She sounded self-possessed again. She peered back at Matt. Pale light glinted in the crescent of her eye.

"I didn't know I was doing it. Gold did it for me, and I didn't even know. I'm not doing it now."

"Okay," Suki said. She sat quiet for a minute, then said, "It bothered me in a way, and in a way I liked it, because nobody else has done that in a long time, really paid attention to me. I have a wall up. Usually it works. Nobody looks past it, so I never have a real conversation. That keeps me safe. It keeps me totally alone too."

"Oh," said Matt.

"But I think I've dropped the wall for now. It doesn't work with you guys anyway."

The bridge swooped over the last bit of bay, touched down, and split in two. Edmund consulted the sinker and took the left lane to stay on I-80.

Suki finally ate her apple. Matt sat back, hugging her legs, resting her chin on her knees and pondering the practice of meddling. She had told Suki she loved Edmund and Nathan, but she didn't know how Edmund felt back, or what to do with feelings like this. She knew Nathan loved her. Was that enough? Not if she never saw him again.

Suki said, "What's tuning?"

"Tuning?" asked Matt. Image of fiddling with radio dials.

"Matt tunes in to things," Edmund said.

"Oh. The talking listening. Paris tickets. Auto-car." Suki set her purse next to the Fritos on the emergency brake and said, "Are the tickets still excited?"

Matt listened for a minute. "No." She put her hand on the soft brown leather of Suki's purse. The purse itself was contented, secure in its mission to hold Suki's things safe and travel with her wherever she went. Different things inside had different feelings. "The tickets are sad now. Pointless. They know they're not going across the sea."

"Why would tickets care about a thing like that? Do they have eyes? How can they even tell when they change countries?"

"It's what they're for. They know what they're for."

Suki opened her purse and took out a key ring. "How about these?"

Matt held out her hand. She could talk to things without touching them, but touch helped sharpen the focus. Suki handed her the keys.

Most of Suki's keys worked in her apartment door, but there was a car key here too, and a set of office keys, and a small key that worked in a bike lock. The bike lock key was sleepy with long disuse. The office keys gave Matt an image of where Suki worked: some place with hardly any windows and lots of people and computers and dead air. The door keys and the car key longed to be used: they only felt alive when they were in their locks. "They're sad too. They know they're not going to be used again soon." Matt held the keys out.

Suki accepted the keys, cradled them in her hands. "Poor things. All these sad things around me. Wish I could make you happy."

The gold around her wrist snaked across her palm and clumped around the business ends of the keys.

"Wah," said Matt. The keys' mood had changed, definitely. Matt wasn't sure what gold was doing to them, but they were now deliriously happy. "Your wish is granted."

"Hey." Suki lifted the lump in her hand, studied it from below and above. "Wishes," she whispered. "Gotta watch that. Gold?" She ran her finger across the lump, and it flowed back into a bracelet. The keys jingled as they dropped to her palm. "Are they still happy?"

"More kind of sleepy," Matt said, touching the keys. "Everything's got a mood all the time. You can't always fix it. Or, I guess you could try, but you'd wear yourself out, and as soon as you stopped, the moods might come back."

Suki patted the keys and stowed them in her purse. "Moods," she said. "What were you doing when you were making that noise in your head?"

"Just listening to the city. Not trying to change its moods, just listening to everything talk. I like doing that."

They drove on in silence, to places where there were gaps between small pieces of city, stretches of darkness without light; hills and fields drawing away from them. They crossed another short piece of bay and paid a toll. Matt lay back and fell asleep as more road slipped by beneath them.

• • •

"Matt?" Gentle shake of her shoulder. She opened her eyes to darkness and quiet: the car had stopped.

A small globe of gray light appeared, grew slightly brighter, lighting Edmund's hand from the inside. Edmund reached up and tapped it against the roof of the car, where it clung. Matt looked up at Edmund's face. He was leaning in the open side door.

"Sorry to wake you, but we have to rearrange some stuff back here so everybody has a place to lie down."

"Mm. Sure," she said, pushing herself up. "Where are we?"

"The middle of nowhere," said Suki, still sitting in the front seat. She sounded grumpy. "Someplace without bathrooms, even. I never thought you were serious about sleeping in the car."

Matt peered over Edmund's shoulder. It was very dark, but she could smell pine trees and water, and hear wind through grass and branches, and a stream running. No civilized sounds at all.

"Will things bite us if we go in the bushes?" she asked. It always made her nervous to be away from things she could talk to. She liked looking at trees and lakes and mountains, but they seemed entirely alien.

"It's winter. Too cold for mosquitoes and snakes." Edmund glanced behind him, though. Tonight was not very cold at all.

Matt felt gold moving on her arms. It spread under her clothes until it covered her completely from toes to chin. "Oh," she said. She felt safe from any biting thing, including bears and cougars, now. Magic would protect her. —Thanks.—

She grabbed her shoes, which she had removed after they drove away from the airport, and jumped out of the car.

"Careful," Edmund said. "There are rocks."

Gold shielded her feet. —Can you help me see in the dark?— she thought, and gold slid up past her ears to form spectacles over her eyes. The night lightened. Strange, pale, sourceless light was everywhere, outlining the edges of things, changing the way shadows worked, sharpening different details and softening others. The car glowed foxfire green, and the road it had arrived on, little more than two faint ruts through grassy undergrowth, had orange-red tire tracks on its pale surface. Nearby lay a lake, its surface illuminated by dancing turquoise mist, surrounded by a pine forest, each tree haloed with pale fire. The car stood in a fragment of clearing. A murmuring stream not far off ran into the lake. Pine needles half-carpeted the ground, with fist-sized sharp rocks beneath them.

The rocks were singing.

Matt knelt and placed her hand on them. Gold bared her palm. —Hello?— she thought.

—Greetings, man-thing. Thing like those that chopped us and split us and carried us and buried us, looking for seams and nuggets and ore. Greetings, thing that stripped us from our parent and brought us to a new place. Greetings, thing that left us shattered here an age ago.—

—Uh, greetings,— Matt thought. None of these events sounded very positive, but the rocks didn't seem too angry about them. On the other hand, all the rocks had sharp edges. Matt was very glad she had gold on the soles of her feet.

And on her butt. Matt sat down on the rocks and pulled on her shoes. "Suki? Want to come with me? I gotta go."

"Sure," Suki said. "Better than going off alone, I guess. And it's a girl thing, isn't it, going off in a group?" She sounded resigned.

Edmund handed Matt a roll of toilet paper. Matt went around the car. "You got your shoes on?" she asked Suki. "There's sharp rocks all over. Hey, get your magic to make you night glasses, huh? It's cool."

"Is that what you did? I can't see a thing."

Matt reached across and touched Suki's bracelet with her gilded fingertips. "Mine will tell yours what to do," she said, "if that's okay with you."

"Sure, great."

Matt's gold talked to Suki's gold. Suki held her hand up to her face, and her bracelet turned into glasses. "Oh! Oh, man. This is amazing." Suki looked up at the sky.

Matt looked up too. The stars were pinwheels and fireworks of brilliance against a soft green backdrop. "Wow," she muttered.

—Thanks again!—

—My pleasure.—

Matt and Suki walked off through the glowing woods. They didn't have to go far, or even away at all, Matt thought; she didn't think there were any other humans for miles. The only sign of people were those singing rocks and the little overgrown road. The rocks, Matt figured, were left over from the gold rush a hundred and fifty years earlier. Still, she and Suki kept wandering, putting trees between them and the car.

Matt picked up a stick to dig a hole with. "You ever done this in the woods before?"

"No." Suki sat on a fallen log.

"It's not one of my favorite things," Matt said, "but you do a lot of stuff like this when you're homeless."

"Are you homeless?"

"Pretty much. It's not hard for me now that I can talk to so many things. In fact, it's been real nice for the last few years." She scraped out a hole in the ground. "If we were near any buildings, I wouldn't have to do this, but we aren't. So here's what you do."

A few minutes later they wandered back through the woods toward the lake. They came out somewhere they didn't recognize, but Matt talked to gold and it told her which direction to head. They found the car in five minutes.

Edmund had moved all the food and luggage into the front seats, clearing the futon for sleeping. He had laid a blanket on the car's roof. "I'll sleep on top," he said, "and you guys can have the inside."

"Edmund, what are we doing here?" Suki asked.

"This is where the trail led."

"I don't understand. Why couldn't we have stayed at one of those hotels on the way? I hate this."

He was quiet for a long time. He climbed up on top of the car and sat looking at the stars. Finally he turned to her. "I'm sorry. This is where I need to be right now. I didn't ask where you need to be. I need to be somewhere where I can face . . . a lot of fire. I hoped you'd be with me. I could really use your help. But I didn't mean to force you into anything. If you need me to, we can drive back out of the mountains and I'll drop you off anywhere you like."

"I came to help you."

He reached down and took her hand. "Please," he whispered.

"Do we do it now?" Matt asked.

"What are we doing?" said Suki.

"Looking at the past." Edmund released her hand and straightened. "How tired are you?"

Suki paced away and came back. "I'm nervous and anxious

and wired. I shouldn't have had that cappuccino back in Vacaville. I'm more ready to do something than to try to sleep, but I'm—I'm really scared. Huh. I said that out loud. Huh."

"Matt?"

"I just had a nap. I'm wide awake now. Vacaville? We stopped in Vacaville?"

"You didn't seem to want to wake up," Suki said. "I shook your shoulder a couple of times, but you never opened your eyes. I thought maybe you needed to sleep. Edmund and I went grocery shopping. We got some doughnuts. He said you'd like them."

"Huh," said Matt. It bothered her that they had gone without her, but at least Suki had tried to wake her. "How tired are you, Edmund?"

"I'm not tired. I'm just waiting."

"Let's start," Matt said.

Suki asked, "How?"

Matt took a deep breath and let it out. She leaned against the car, her palms flat on its hood. —Can we sit on you and do this? I don't know how dangerous it's going to get. There's fire.— She glanced over her shoulder, wondering if Edmund's memories were strong enough to set the forest blazing. But he wouldn't hurt trees, would he?

—It would take a lot of fire to hurt me,— thought the car. —I am strengthened in strange ways. Please use me any way you can. I wish I had been there for the earlier part of this.—

Whoa! Matt hadn't known the car felt left out. But it made sense: Edmund's longtime trusted companion had made Matt welcome, and then Matt took Edmund away and changed him.

—We didn't know it was going to happen before it did,— she thought.

—Of course you didn't. Many things happen without me. And I heard some of your dreams about this one, so I didn't miss it entirely. I'm pleased to be here now.—

"Matt?" Suki said.

"We can sit on the car," Matt said. She climbed up on the hood, crossed it, and settled on the roof next to Edmund.

"How do I get up there?" asked Suki. She glanced at the rear bumper, then back up at them. "I'm not much of a scrambler."

Edmund leaned forward. "Take my hand," he said.

She gripped it, and then she floated upward. "Omigod," she said. Edmund tugged her gently, and she drifted down to sit at his other side. "Oh, God. I'll be able to do that for myself when I get this gold stuff figured out, won't I?"

Matt laughed, surprising herself. Edmund took her hand. "How do we do this, Matt?"

Matt collected her thoughts. "Know how strong you are now. Hang onto that. Remember you're with friends and we want to help you. Spirit. Spirit can help you too. Remember that it's now and you can look back safely. Just look. Just see. Just understand. Know that it's not happening now. And remember that it's okay to stop whenever you need to."

"What do you need me to do?" Suki asked.

"Maybe we need you to start telling us what happened," Matt said. "Edmund remembered the séance, and helping you pack. He remembered that your father came home early. He got that far, and then he blanked on it. Do you remember what happened next?"

"You're trembling," Edmund said to Suki.

"Oh, God," she said in a drowned voice.

He put his arm around her and she leaned against him. "I'm not going to cry," she muttered, "I'm not going to cry. I *am* going to cry. I knew this would happen. I'm falling apart."

Matt leaned across Edmund and gripped Suki's hand. "I can watch it in your thoughts and tell it. You don't have to say any of it out loud if you don't want to."

"Wait," said Suki. She sniffled. She pulled her hand free and touched her night glasses, and gold dropped over her face. It blazed with pinprick lights, so many her head looked like it was drowning in glitter. It took a long time for the gold to revert, and there was a lot more of it when it had finished: Suki had her night glasses back, but she had a new heavy gold collar too. "Oh," she said, startled.

"Are you okay?" Matt asked.

"Wow. The wall's down. And I can see." Her voice sounded calm.

"Is it okay if I look too?"

"Yes," said Suki in a flattened voice. "So strange. Dirty laundry. Never tell. Lock it up. Just between us. This is one of our special secrets, too special to share with anyone else. You know what'll happen to your mother if you talk. This could just kill her." Suki shuddered and shook and yelled, "No! It can't! She's dead already, so shut up!"

Gold masked her face, ablaze.

The phrases echoed strangely in Matt's mind. She remembered special secrets of her own. She hadn't had gold to wash them away with, but she had spoken them to walls and roads and rooms, stamped them out, shared them, killed their power.

"I'm ready," Suki said, calm again.

Matt opened dream-eyes.

They were in a boat, a fairy-tale boat with timbered sides and plank deck. Silver sails bellied out with night breeze, and golden ropes tied it all together. Matt had her hand on the tiller. Edmund and Suki sat beside her. Sea spread out in all directions, calm. A full moon trail led across the water to the east, where the moon was just coming up. Stars sparkled in the sky.

—Whose dream is this?— Matt wondered.

—Mine— said the car. —I'll carry you safe through it.—

—Wow! Thanks. I don't know anything about sailing, though.—

—It's all right. I'm the ship and the wind and the sea.—

Matt smiled. She shifted focus. She saw Suki's bedroom again.

Here was the painfully pink and white room, the canopied bed with a suitcase open on its white lace spread, spindle-legged, gilt-edged furniture, a shelf of dolls, a shelf of glass horses Matt didn't remember from last time, and a porcelain ballerina on the desk by a stack of homework books.

Here next to the open-drawered dresser stood Susan, not quite as confectionary as she had looked last time: dust on the hem of her blue dress, one of her white socks sagging. She held the same armload of clothes. And this time Edmund's image was clearer, a tall, thin, serious boy in a black pullover sweater and blue jeans, also clutching an armload of clothes.

"Hang on," said Matt. She shifted focus with the dream-eyes again, trying to see what present-day Edmund was looking at. Trees. Trees whose edges were outlined with flickering red.

—Gold?— Matt gripped her wristbands with opposite hands. —I have a wish now.—

—Tell me.—

—Can you see what I see?—

—If you wish it.—

—Can you show what I see?—

—If you wish it.—

She thought for a minute. —Did I ever shape you not to hurt anybody?—

—No.—

—Except the gold I gave you,— said Ginny's voice, suddenly.

—I think this is going to hurt. I think it's going to teach and heal, but it'll hurt first. Can we do it?—

Dark gold flowed up her arms and banded around her biceps, leaving the lighter gold in her grip. —Wish when you are ready,— said the light gold.

Matt looked into Suki's dream again, concentrating on the placement of everything. —Please start,— Matt told gold.

On the cleared ground beside the car, Susan's bedroom flickered into sight, all its furniture and objects in place, just the way they were in Suki's memory; and Edmund and Susan stood there holding their armfuls of clothes, vivid in detail—Suki was much better at remembering color and shape than Edmund had been, and much more aware of how she had looked—and frozen in time. Those sitting on the car looked down on the bedroom from somewhere near the ceiling. Matt wondered how Suki could have a viewpoint like that, and then remembered how sometimes, when life was totally unbearable, she too had left her body and floated nearby, within sight, but not in range of feeling.

"Oh!" Suki cried, and Edmund straightened.

"You can both see this?" Matt said.

"How are you doing that?" asked Edmund.

"Gold."

"Matt," he said. He gripped her shoulder.

"Ready?"

"All right," said Edmund.

"Suki, what happens next?"

The bedroom door slammed open. A tall, pale-haired man stood there. This time he looked much bigger, his muscles bulging beneath his suit, and he was outlined in heavy black lines. His mouth opened wide and scream lines came out.

—Can we hear this?— Matt asked gold.

Voice boomed into being.

"What's going on here? Who is this hooligan? Oh, it's the young Reynolds boy, isn't it? Your father designed the community center. What do you think you're doing in my house with my daughter?" A torrent of more words, hard-edged, some blunt, some sharp, all battering. No room left for replies or responses. As the man spoke he grew larger and darker, filling the doorway, his dark aura entering the room, spreading toward Edmund and Susan.

". . . and if you think for one minute you're ever going to be alone with my daughter again, or that she's ever going any-where but downstairs, you have another think coming. You haven't seen strings pulled until you've seen my technique, boy. I can get your father fired. I can get his license pulled. I can make sure he never works in this state again. I could arrange for some accident to happen in the community center and trash his reputation in all fifty states, how would you like that? If I find out you've laid one finger on my daughter's body, boy . . ."

Image Edmund turned toward Image Susan, who looked

back. Her arms lowered to her sides. The clothes she held drooped and then dropped to the floor. Her face paled. All the hope drained out of it.

"Hell, forget your father. How about you? You look like a boy who might knife another. I pull the right strings and you'll be in jail for life. I could even set it up so they fry you. I can call six cops at the drop of a hat. Plant evidence, get your fingerprints on it, build you an airtight case out of nothing. I'll wrap your life up so tight you'll have no future, boy. I'll make you wish you were dead—"

Susan crumpled slowly to the floor, her hands covering her ears.

"Stop it," Image Edmund said, his voice a clash of cymbals.

"Wha-a-a-a-at?"

"Shut up." Two kettle drum thumps.

"Don't you take that tone with me, young man!"

"Listen," Image Edmund said, clear as flutes. His hands glowed red. "I have something to give you." Red flames licked up from his hands. "Here. Here's what I think of what you do. Here's how I feel about what you've done. Here's how it hurts to think of how you've hurt people." He held out his hands toward the dark man and heat and light poured from his palms, streaming across the small space between them, scarlet flames bathing and then battering the man's head.

The man screamed. It started like a growl, then the lower registers dropped out and it soared up into a shriek. It turned into a howl so horrible Matt couldn't listen anymore.

—Stop,— she thought, and gold let go of the vision and the sound. A haze of light still flickered in the air where the images had been.

Matt collapsed across the roof of the car, drowning in fatigue. Her bones felt like chalk and her muscles like mush. All the gold around her wrists had vanished except for one thin line, narrow as a pencil mark.

"Matt!" Present-day Edmund's voice came out harsh and hot. She looked up at him and saw that his eyes glowed red, and flames flickered off the ends of his curls. He shone like a torch against the night sky.

The red boy. Finally. Matt's eyes fell shut.

The car cradled her. —Open,— it whispered.

—Open what?— She was so tired she couldn't think.

—Open to me.—

She remembered other times she'd heard words like that. Most of them were threats, promises of pain. But the car? Not this car. She closed her eyes and laid her palms flat on the car. Warmth flowed into her, faint and slow, comforting.

"Matt," Edmund said, and this time his voice sounded gentle. "Are you okay?"

"Are you?" she asked faintly. She didn't have the energy to sort through what she had seen, but she knew it was staggering. She had thought Edmund was going to discover how someone had hurt him terribly, and that wasn't what she had seen. "Is Suki?" She felt as though she might be able to move sometime in the foreseeable future.

"I'm fine," said Suki in a surprised voice. She leaned over Matt from the other side. Confused, Matt rolled her head, saw Suki was kneeling on the car hood and leaning near her. Suki wore a gold blouse now, or maybe it was armor: it went from her neck down her arms and across her chest, reaching almost to her waist. It glowed pale gold in the dark. "I looked at that, I watched it, I remembered it, and every time I got scared or upset, the gold ate it. What happened to you?"

"I used most of my gold to color in your memory so Edmund could see it." She raised her forearms. Still weak, but not so watery. The car pulsed beneath her, its heartbeat drumming with hers, its slow strength and comfort seeping into her.

The pencil streak of gold around her left wrist was now surrounded by a narrow band of dark gold. Dark gold banded her right wrist too. —You okay, Matt?— Ginny's voice asked, so faint Matt wasn't sure she heard it.

"I'm so tired," Matt mumbled. She closed her eyes again.

Cool hands clasped her wrists, and she felt shifting and rustling along the skin of her forearms. "I don't need all this stuff," Suki said. "Have some back. Take it all, if it'll help."

—Mattmattmatt,— the new gold thought as it crept up her arms. Its mental voice felt different, edged with smoke and vinegar and salt. Tasty, but uncomfortable. Suki's recycled moods?

"Go back," Matt told it.

—In a minute.— It wove around her, tracing spirals on her skin, moving up and down and all over. Matt's skin tingled and fizzed, and she felt strange. Then Suki's gold zipped away.

"Whoa!" said Suki. "What happened? You don't want it?"

Matt rubbed her eyes and sat up, energized. "What did it do? I feel okay now. Sort of. That was weird."

Edmund set a gray light globe on the car's roof in front of her and handed her a bottle of water. She drank half of it. "Oh, yeah. That helps." —Thanks, car. Thanks, Suki's gold. What did you do?—

—Washed out the tired,— the gold told her.

—Cool. Neat trick.—

—Thanks. It was her wish.—

"Thanks, Suki," Matt said.

"But you didn't want it," said Suki. Gold cloaked her upper body. "I've got way more of this than I can use. Are you *sure* you don't want some?"

"Not right now." She touched the thin line of pale gold at her wrist. —Thanks to you, too, for giving me my wish. It's what I wanted.—

—It's what I'm for,— gold whispered.

Matt glanced at Edmund. "Are you okay? I didn't mean to have a problem while we're working on yours."

After a moment, he said, "I'm not okay." He bent his head and covered his face with his hands.

Matt put her hand on his shoulder. "It wasn't what I thought."

"No," Edmund whispered. He looked up. His face was pale in the gray light, his eyes dark and haunted. "I did it. I did that evil thing, and he lost his mind. I destroyed him."

"If you hadn't stopped him, I would never have been able to get away," Suki said. "You saved my life, Edmund."

"That was important. That was a good thing. I'm glad I did that much. But the rest of it—" Edmund shook his head. "I was just getting used to having power at all, but I didn't know I had *that* kind of power. I wanted to hurt him so much. And I did. I didn't look for the right way, or the gentle way. I did it *his* way. Bludgeoned him with my feelings until he collapsed. I never wanted to let him up again. And he didn't get up. For all I know, he's still trapped in his head while my ideals and ethics and his actions battle each other." He stared down at his fists.

"That . . . I couldn't get that . . . what I really needed to do was just get you out of there and keep you safe. I could have done that by making him fall asleep. I knew I could make people fall asleep. I tested it on Mr. James in science class one time when he gave us a pop quiz. Why didn't I just do that to your father?"

Suki said, "But then as soon as he woke up, he would have done all those things he threatened you with. Ruined your father's career, sent you to jail for years and years. He really did things like that to people. And he would have come after me. He would never let me go."

"How far could he get if he kept falling asleep?" Edmund opened one fist, then the other. His brow furrowed. He studied his palms. "I don't curse people, but I could have cursed him: a little curse so that every time he planned anything that might hurt you, he'd fall asleep, unless it would put him in danger. I bet that would've worked."

"How could you think of something that complicated in the middle of all that yelling?" Matt asked.

"I could have slept him right away and figured out the curse later. It doesn't matter. I should've done something else."

"You couldn't do anything else," said Matt.

"I could have slept him. I could have changed him into something else long enough for us to get out of the house. Except I didn't have much practice transforming things. Might have messed up bigtime. Maybe I could have just used my voice on him, made him turn around and lock himself in his office while we left, told him not to come out for six hours."

"You couldn't do anything else," Matt repeated.

"What do you mean?"

"You did what you could. You did the only thing you could. Because that's what happened."

"What are you saying?" Edmund asked. "Are you saying that Susan's father did the only thing he could when he beat her mother to death, when he made Susan suffer? Are you saying your father did the only thing he could?"

Matt took a deep breath, held it, let it out. "That's right. I'm not saying any of us did the *right* thing. But we did the only thing we could at the time. Maybe my dad tortures himself thinking he should of been different to me and Pam. Well, I know he does. I saw it. Not in his waking life, but underneath. But he did what he did. He did the only thing he could, because that's what happened. The only place we can change anything is right now."

Edmund stared at Matt, his brows lowered.

"You can't go back and change anything you did, or anything anybody else did," Matt said. Then she looked at the gold on her wrists. "Well, I'm not sure *what* you can do, since there's magic. But even if you could go back and change something, how could you be sure it would come out better? At least this way you know what happened. Now what you have to do is figure out what you want to happen next."

Edmund sat hunched over for a long while, staring into the night-dark forest, his hands gripping each other.

Matt tucked her hands into her armpits and waited. Now that she didn't have gold, she noticed the night's chill. Her army jacket was inside the car, not six feet from her, but she didn't want to disturb Edmund's concentration by going for it.

After a few minutes slipped away, Edmund said, "What I want to do next is find him and help him."

Chapter Ten

· · · · ·

"WHAT?" Suki pressed both her hands on her sternum. Her breath came out in gasps.

"You don't have to come with me, but this is what I need to do, Suki. I need to find your father and try to make amends. I'll take you wherever you want first."

"Amends," she whispered.

"I know he did horrible things," Edmund said slowly. He paused for a minute. "It doesn't excuse me for doing a horrible thing to him. I have to live with myself. Wait, that's not quite right. I've been not living with myself until now, but now I'm home, and I need to do what I can to repair this harm. When I hurt him, I hurt myself, and I want to see what I can do about healing that wound."

"What if he—if he turns back into himself, he—he can make all our lives hell."

"No," Edmund said.

"But you don't—he—"

"He's a terrifying person," Edmund said. "But we're not helpless kids anymore, Suki. We've both learned how to take care of ourselves, more or less, and he has no authority over either of us. But you don't have to come with me. I could take you to Mexico if you want. Or the East Coast, or Canada, anyplace we can get by car."

"I—I don't know what I want. I want him dead and gone."

"I can't do that for you," Edmund said gently.

Suki turned her back and hunched in on herself. "I want him to stay dead." Her voice was flat and harsh.

"It might turn out that way," Edmund said. "I don't even know if he's still alive. Do you?"

"Aunt Caro kept tabs on him, but I told her not to tell me what she found out. I did have to sign some sort of document setting up a trust fund to take care of him. I couldn't even look at it. Uncle Henry got a lawyer to fix it. I couldn't get myself to listen to them when they were talking about it."

"Mrs. Danvers in Guthrie thought he was in a nursing home in Salem. That's all we've got to go on."

"That and the sinker," Matt said.

Suki shook her head. "I so want you to not do this. Why can't we just leave things alone? At least this way they're tolerable."

Edmund turned away. "I don't want to live like this." His voice sounded anguished. "As long as I was separated from what happened, I could go on living and be fairly content, but now I'm connected to it again, and it hurts."

Suki reached across Matt's lap to touch Edmund's hand. "I'm sorry," she whispered.

Matt felt a twisting in her guts. She had never wanted to hurt him. It sounded like this hurt a lot, and she had helped it happen.

She couldn't change the past, but she could try to fix it now. "You could forget what happened again," she said.

"No, Matt. I want this, even though it hurts. I need to know that I have this possibility in me—I need to live with that. I want a chance to fix what I did."

Matt remembered looking at Ginny before she was Ginny, when she was Young Mattie. It had hurt, but it was a pain she wanted to go through. Maybe if she looked at her untouched self long enough, she could remember what that had been like. Darkness had smeared her world for a long time, and now she was out the other side of that; but her vision now was different from the vision she had had as a child. She wasn't sure why that felt important, but something in her longed to explore it.

"Let's not go anywhere else tonight," Matt said. "Except to sleep."

Suki straightened. "I need to brush my teeth. How'm I going to brush my teeth without a sink and a cup?" Her voice was young, unsure, strange.

They left all the car doors open to the night. The car was wide enough that Matt and Suki could lie side by side without touching. Each had her own blanket and pillow. Matt wore her giant T-shirt, long johns, and socks, and she laid her army jacket over her blanket for extra warmth. She missed gold's protective presence.

"Do you think he's comfortable up there?" Suki whispered, staring up at the car's roof. Edmund lay on top of it, perfectly still.

"Are you comfortable in here?"

"Yeah. It's weird. I thought you guys were crazy when you

said the car would be comfortable, but this mattress is so soft, and . . ." Suki smoothed a gold-sheathed arm across her covers. "And this stuff," she muttered, staring at the faint golden glow outlining her arm. "It's comfortable too."

"Edmund'll be fine on the roof. The car makes itself comfortable. It's a great car."

"What? Oh." Suki turned on her side, resettled her head on the pillow several times. "I feel so strange," she murmured. "This morning I had a life, a whole life. Scouted, mapped, laid out, known. And now . . ."

"Your apartment's still there, huh? And your aunt. It's not like you walked off the edge of the Earth."

"You're right." Suki sighed, but it sounded more neutral than sad. "But . . . finding Daddy . . . that *is* like jumping off the edge of the Earth. Oh, God. I can't think about this now."

Matt sensed more conversation hovering. She waited and it went away. Suki's breathing stretched into sleep rhythm.

Matt lay on her back, stared up at the dark roof above her, and wondered about her own past and future. Now that she was traveling with Edmund, she had a home—the car. She had a direction—wherever he was going next. Did she still want this home and this direction, now that she had seen into his past? What would Edmund be like with the red boy awake inside him?

More than anything else, she wanted to find out.

She loved the parts of him she had already met, and she understood the person who had cast the spell on Suki's father. She had wanted to punch the guy's face in herself.

She had seen Edmund at his worst: she had seen the part of him he had hidden from himself. She had seen the way he dealt with finding that part again. Better than she would, maybe.

She thought about waking up on top of Edmund, his warmth, his shape, his smell. How he had carried her more than once, and put his arms around her more than once. How she had leaned against him knowing it was safe, clung to him when she was scared. They had touched a lot right after they first met, but not so much since.

Was the pulling away on her side or his? Was it because they had hesitations about going further? Matt knew she had hesitations—she hadn't been intimate with anyone in years, and had preferred to live in a mental state that didn't even recognize the question—and she wasn't sure Edmund had any desire for her sexually anyway. Maybe he was gay. She hadn't seen any definite indicators either way in his mental landscape when she was still looking at it, but that was before they went to the haunted house. Back then he had seemed as asexual as she was. Maybe he was gay, or maybe she just didn't look like the kind of person he was attracted to.

But he hadn't minded touching her before, and he didn't do it much anymore. She had convinced him to take back Young Edmund, and now she knew the red boy was inside him too; she didn't know how this would change things. Was she afraid of the new parts? Did they just not like her? Or was the struggle to work with them going to take up all Edmund's time and energy?

Maybe he didn't touch her because Suki was with them now?

In her talks with the haunted house and Nathan, Matt had learned that Nathan had a lot of feelings for Suki, but she hadn't gotten the impression that Edmund had felt anything special for Suki. Suki was one of the most beautiful women Matt had ever seen: slender but well-built, with that Nordic complexion, thick white-blonde hair and large, clear, deep-blue eyes, her skin clean and pure and golden with peach tints, and her lips lush; if men reacted to a woman's looks, how could they help tumbling into lust or something like it with her? Had Edmund felt the lure, but just never acted on it? Did he feel it now?

What about Suki? Was she interested in Edmund?

Matt thought about opening dream-eyes. She really wanted to know. She decided not to do it, though. It wouldn't be fair. Better if she just asked them.

She sighed and fell asleep.

Something licked her forehead.

She opened her eyes and stared at the neck of a deer. "Yaaah!" she cried, and the deer startled and ran. Thudding hooves sounded outside. Matt tried to sit up and found her fingers tangled with Suki's. What? She disengaged, sat up with a groan, and saw four deer darting into the trees.

Mist lay over the lake, wound between tree trunks. Above, blue sky showed through thin drifts of mist. The sun silvered some of it in the east. Everything smelled damp and piney.

Matt heard the car roof shift. A second later Edmund dropped to the ground just outside the open door. "What happened?"

"It licked me," she said in a small voice. "A wild animal licked me. It kind of startled me. Sorry I woke you up."

"It's okay. This is a good time of day to be awake."

"You people have any coffee?" Suki moaned.

"Sure, we got some instant at that supermarket in Vacaville last night, remember?"

"Oh, right. I'm starving." Suki sat up.

"Supermarket in Vacaville?" asked Matt. "Oh, yeah. You guys went shopping."

"And Suki phoned home and quit her job."

"We bought bananas," said Suki. "Doughnuts. Blueberry muffins. Instant coffee. A coffee pot to boil water in. Eggs and a little skillet. We should probably eat the eggs today, since that cooler isn't very good refrigeration. You can start a fire, right?" She smiled across Matt at Edmund, and he smiled back.

"Yep," he said. "We could even have a smokeless, fuelless fire. Might be best, so we don't disturb the energy too much."

Smokeless? Fuelless? Matt thought of electric burners, then remembered magic.

"Let's make a real fire," Matt said. "It's not like fires never happen in the woods. Lightning, huh? I'll go find some wood." She slipped out from under her blanket.

"What!" Suki said.

Matt looked down at her arms. Whorls and spirals of pale gold patterned her skin. "What are you?" she asked, startled.

—Gold,— it thought. Its mental voice was deeper than the voice her old gold had had. And there was an edge of salt in it, distilled from tears.

She checked her wrists. Her Ginny gold still banded them, with the thin line of her own gold a streak across the left band. —Suki's gold?—

—Your gold now.—

Her fingers had been tangled with Suki's when she woke up. —Did I ask for you? Did I summon you?—

—No. We made a wish, and Suki made a wish. Make another wish if you like. Wish me away.—

Matt stared into Suki's eyes. "I don't remember doing it,"

Suki said. "Maybe I dreamed it. I'll take it back if you want."
—Why don't you want it?— her mental voice asked. —Is there
something wrong with mine?— She put a hand over her face,
and gold blanketed her head for a moment.

"There's nothing wrong with it," Matt said. "I don't know
why I don't want it. I'm not even sure I don't want it. Excuse
me. I have to think about this." She grabbed her boots and jacket,
stomped into her boots and slipped the jacket over her shoulders,
and walked away.

She splashed across the stream without feeling the water's
chill and plunged into the forest on the other side. It didn't take
long for the trees and the mist to surround her. She heard crows
call, and occasionally other birds. She walked a long way and
finally collapsed beside a fallen log, among bracken ferns and
drifts of pine needles and crumbles of rotted wood.

She stared down at her arms and thought about golden
magic.

Magic had helped her a lot already. She had loved the way
her first magic protected her from cold and bugs and some kinds
of fear, and the way it had worked with her to make Suki's
memories visible for Edmund. She remembered how tired Abby
had been after working with her magic, though. Matt had felt
that intense weariness herself after actively using her magic.

Then Suki's magic had washed her fatigue away. And now it
was making paisley patterns on her skin. She lifted her shirt and
checked her stomach. Yep. Paisleys and fingerprints there, too.
She stroked her hand across the golden lace and couldn't tell
where gold ended and skin began; it all felt like part of her.

—How much of you is there?—

—Not very much,— it thought.

—Why do you look like this? Like tattoos?—

—I can look like whatever you want.—

—Come here.— She gripped her wrists.

Gold flowed across her skin. She could see it, but she didn't feel it. It converged at her wrists, edging her Ginny gold with slender bands of light gold. Not much, for sure: half an inch wide, and very thin.

She had gotten used to having magic of her own. Why didn't she want Suki's? She stroked a finger across the band on her left wrist and felt flashes of foreign feelings: terror, anger, totally engulfing sadness—lemon, chili pepper, salt. Pain, the taste of windowglass and iron nails. Ammonia, another flavor of fear. Emotion-fed magic.

—If you're going to be my magic,— Matt thought, —you need to be a different kind of magic.—

—What kind?—

Abby's magic, Gold, had been art magic. Matt had made Ginny from Abby's art magic into some other kind of magic— teach magic. Matt's own gold, though, gift of the first Gold— what kind had that been?

Comfort magic.

Ultimately, useful magic.

—Warmth and protection,— Matt thought. That was all she needed.

She felt the magic changing, releasing all its feelings, shedding them like used skins and settling down into what she wanted. —Thank you,— Matt thought. Her own pencil-mark magic blended with the new gold until her wrists were banded with equal widths of Ginny gold and new gold.

—Welcome.—

Matt leaned back against the log and thought about the rest of it.

After everything that had happened last night, she still felt bothered by the fact that Edmund and Suki had gone shopping together and left her in the car.

So stupid!

She remembered how Edmund had talked in the coffee shop that morning in Guthrie, when he was trying to live with the way the boy felt, having jealous feelings and wishing they would go away. Adolescence! he had said.

Adolescence, she thought. Ballerina Matt, on her way through middle school like a million other kids, peeking at boys from the edges of her eyes, worrying about who to sit with at lunch, trying to find something that would interest her for the rest of her life, zoning out during English and math classes, working hard at ballet class after school without any idea of why. If only George Caruso would *look* at her. But he never did.

Ray was her best friend because they had lived on the same block their whole lives. They both liked bike riding through construction projects after work had stopped for the day. They checked out the skeletal structures of incipient buildings and climbed unfinished stairs to unfinished floors, where they could see through walls like superbeings and look down on their neighborhood. They collected the slugs popped out of electrical outlets. Matt liked wires, both sleeved and unsleeved. She loved the bright braided copper, and she loved the colors wire dressed in, brilliant yellow and green and red and blue, even though it ended up inside walls where no one could see it.

Dust in her pantscuffs, translucent agates she had found in gravel in her pockets. No, that was before she turned into a girl when she was about thirteen. She and Ray had drifted apart around then. Her mom wanted her to wear dresses, learn to use makeup, and stop talking like a boy.

"That was such a long time ago," she said out loud. "And none of it turned out to matter."

None of it had been necessary for survival, and survival was all she had needed for a long time after that. She didn't survive well for a big stretch of that time, but she survived.

She lost a baby. Too much chemistry in her bloodstream, too many distractions. She bled so irregularly she almost didn't notice this particular time. Only, something in her noticed. Something in her stopped. In the midst of that haze, she had screamed and yelled and hit whoever was nearest. She hadn't even known she was pregnant. She had killed something and never known it. Just like her father.

Matt lifted her hand and nudged gold away from her wrist. The scar was very faint now.

So she had killed the person she was, and woke up as someone else, someone who could talk with all kinds of things and see people's dreams. She wasn't going to be the center of her own story anymore. She would listen to everyone else's.

That had worked for a while, until her own story snuck up on her and swept her up again. Now that she could see dreams, she had to see what her father dreamed, had to know if he even knew or cared what he had done to her. So she finally went back to where she had come from and looked at her father's dreams. She discovered that some part of him knew and cared what he had done, but it was asleep and couldn't talk to her directly. She would never be able to make him tell her the incest was his fault. But he knew it somewhere deep inside.

Knowing that released her. She let her own story drift away again, and went back to watching all the other stories out there.

"I forgot about the baby," she said.

"What baby?"

Matt blinked and glanced up. Edmund sat in front of her.

"My baby," she said. "But not a baby, really. A miscarriage."

He didn't say anything, only sat, quiet, studying her. He was wearing green and brown and almost blended into the forest. If she looked away from him, she might not remember he was there.

She gazed down at her hands. "I didn't even know I was pregnant. Then the blood. Too late, I killed it. I felt like a monster. Then I tried to kill myself. And then I woke up and everything was different. I was like I am now. Same way you did it, I guess."

"You have a lot of wisdom," Edmund said.

"Sure. It's easy to see what other people need if you watch people a lot. Harder to figure out what you need for yourself. Sometimes you figure you don't deserve to feel good." She frowned. "I don't feel so bad, though. I did most of my work. I went back to my past and looked at it again with dream-eyes and found more things out about it and figured out he did what he could. He did the only thing he could. Because that's what happened. But I forgot about the baby." Her voice trailed off.

"You did what you could. You did the only thing you could, because that's what happened."

She sniffled and rubbed her eyes. "Yeah," she said after a little. "And now I can think about it some more, now that I finally remember it. That baby deserves some thought."

They sat for a while.

She would have been a horrible mother if the baby had survived. She hadn't cared about anything except trying to escape what was real. She wasn't sure she would have changed even if she had known about the baby. She wasn't sure the baby would have been born undamaged if it had lived to term, because she wasn't taking care of herself, let alone anyone else. Nutrition? Forget it. Stop drinking? At that time, she hadn't been able to.

Would she have had an abortion? She didn't know. Any decision would have been difficult, and she hadn't been able to think very well back then. Even so, she wished she had made a choice.

She hated that she had killed it before she even knew it was alive. —I'm sorry. I'm so sorry. I'm sorry,— she thought to it, wherever it was. She rubbed her hand up and down over her stomach.

—Matt?—

—Ginny?— Matt's hand stilled on her stomach. —Do you know about this too?—

—I do.— And then a rush of reassurance and comfort. Matt closed her eyes and leaned against it, wondering how it was possible, finally just letting it be.

At last she sighed and opened her eyes. Edmund watched her. Presently he said, "Is that why you left the car?"

She shifted thoughts, called back the mind she had had not so long ago. "No. I left because of magic and stupid stuff. I remembered about the baby later."

"Stupid stuff, huh?" He turned away, looked toward the trees. "Is it me? Now that you know what I did, do you hate me?"

"What? No!" She leaned forward and gripped his hands. "So you made a mistake. So what? So it's a bad one. So what! You did what you could, and now you're doing what you can to fix it. I don't hate you. I don't think I'd ever hate you, no matter what you do or did." She remembered how she had gotten him to tell her his stupid stuff, decided she might as well do the same. "I'm jealous of Suki now."

"Because why?"

"Because I don't know how you like me. What if you like her more? Stupid stuff. Came out here to think about it. Fell back into—into the girl. I forgot I *had* a girl, until Ginny showed me. Do you like me the way a boy likes a girl? The way a man likes a woman? I can't tell."

"I do."

"You hardly touch me anymore."

"I don't know what you want. I don't know what might hurt you or scare you. I felt like I knew for a little while, but now that I've got the boy inside, I get all mixed up again. He has urges, and thoughts that aren't thinking. He didn't really get a chance to grow up, and just fusing what I know with what he knows doesn't seem to work. We have to grow up together, I guess. I need to ask you what you want, because I can't figure it out anymore."

"Do you ever think about sex?"

"Never used to. Now I think about it way more than is comfortable."

"Do you ever think about sex with me?"

He sat back, studying her. "Do you think about it with me? Somehow, last I knew, that was all off limits."

"I wasn't thinking about it till last night. I haven't done it in a long time, and when I used to do it, I wasn't paying attention. Now I think . . ." She touched his face with her fingertips. "I feel like I don't know what I'm doing, but I have thoughts. Do you have thoughts about me?"

He put his hand over hers on his face and nodded slowly. "I do. They don't have to go anywhere. I could think forever and not need to do anything about it. I didn't want to scare you."

"Do you have thoughts about Suki?"

"Not on purpose."

She stared at him, saw red rising in his cheek, felt the heat under her hand.

"The boy," he said. "In my mind, she's always been Nathan's girl, anyway. Off limits. But the boy . . ."

"Mmm," Matt said and smiled, thinking about how many times she'd watched men with dream-eyes and seen those thoughts. A pretty woman walked by men, bam! Rippling images here, there, and all over, her naked, her with each of them, different ideas about what would be good, bam! And then gone again. Boy brains. Well, okay, teenage boy brains, no matter how old the men were.

"I forgot what that was like," he said slowly. "Idiotic."

"I wonder if she has thoughts about you."

He took her hand from his cheek and held it. "I can't tell about that, either, but it doesn't matter. I want to be her friend, not her boyfriend."

Matt took a few deep breaths. "Will you be my boyfriend?" she asked.

He smiled and said, "Yes."

She sighed happily. "This is much better than high school. We don't have to wade through all that bullshit."

"We still have a lot to talk over."

"Yeah. I love that part too."

"You looked really cute dressed in magic."

Matt looked down at her arms, simple skin now except for the wristbands. "You liked those gold tattoos? I made it change back."

"You look really cute either way."

She pushed forward onto her knees and leaned into him, hugging him. His arms came around her. For a long time she held him tight and enjoyed his holding her back. Their breathing slowed and synchronized. He smelled so good. She felt a shifting at the base of her spine, a tiny change, the beginning of warmth. Enough for a start. She leaned back and studied his face from up close. Still strange, wild, and beautiful. He returned her regard, his gaze arrested. Stillness spun between them, and Matt thought, now something could happen, but we can do this slow, we can take our time.

He smelled like pine needle smoke, and just a little like fried eggs.

"Breakfast?" she said.

"Oh, yeah. I forgot. That's why I came to find you. Suki was making omelettes."

She kissed his cheek, then stood up. "She said blueberry muffins."

He rose and took her hand. "Let's fly."

"What?" She started laughing as they rose from the ground. "Whoa!" Their ascent was slow as he tried to find a way up between branches to the sky. The mist was dissipating as the sun rose higher, and the day looked as though it was heading toward beautiful. As soon as they reached a level above the trees, they flew quickly.

At first Matt was scared. Out of touch with everything, even unfamiliar ground. What if she fell? The ground was too far away.

Gold rustled at her wrists. —I can carry you,— it whispered.

Magic! She had her own now. She closed her eyes and felt air flow over her face and listened to delight wake inside her.

They passed above a small slice of lake, then dropped to the clearing where the car was.

A fire burned in a ring of stones behind the car. It looked like a real fire, with wood and pine needles in it. A coffeepot perched on a slab of stone across an edge of the fire, and a frying pan lay open-side up outside the circle. A bucket of water stood nearby. Suki sat on the car's tailgate with grocery bags and a few opened cartons and dishes around her. She set down a fat paperback thriller with a dark cover as Matt and Edmund touched down.

"Flying," she said. "You guys fly?"

"Edmund does, anyway." Matt slipped her hand out of his and went to the fire. "Maybe you could too."

Suki glanced at the gold on her arms. The wide gold collar, the chest armor she had worn last night were no longer visible; she was wearing a pink silk short-sleeved shirt. Her arms, though, gleamed with gold from shoulder to mid-forearm. "Hmm," she said. "Maybe I'll experiment. I ate the first omelette, and the second got cold. Thought I better wait to make another one. Didn't know how long you'd be."

"We had stuff to talk about," Matt said.

Suki smiled. "I can tell."

"Cold omelette's my favorite."

"Really?" Suki held out a plastic fork and a paper plate with an omelette on it. "I'm not much of a cook. It's nothing fancy. Cheese and green onions."

"Yum," said Matt, accepting it. "Want some?" She held the plate toward Edmund.

He smiled and shook his head.

"I can make you a fresh one," Suki said.

"I think I'll wait to eat," he said. "Fasting is part of purification."

"Purification?" asked Suki.

"Before I go to face the dragon, I want to do some strengthening exercises. Connect with spirit, purify myself, be sure of my motives, figure out who I am now and how to do this cleanly for the good of everyone, at least as far as I can."

"That's part of being a witch?" asked Suki.

"When you're the kind of witch I am, it is."

Matt took a bite of cold omelette. "Delicious. Thanks, Suki."

"You're welcome. Want some coffee?"

"Sure. Thanks."

Suki handed her a plain white mug with instant coffee in it. "We forgot to get anything to put in it," she said.

"That's okay." Matt finished breakfast and burned her plate. "Thanks. Thanks a lot! Now what?"

"I need to go away from you guys," Edmund said.

"Want us to drive away?" Suki said. "We could try to find a town—seems like we went through a couple on our way up here. I sure could use a shower."

"I don't, actually, want you to leave. I just need a little distance for a little while—maybe three hours. Then we can talk about what you'd like to do next, Suki."

"There's a whole lot of water right there," Matt said, pointing to the lake.

Suki hunched her shoulders. "Thing one, it's cold. Thing

two, isn't it all full of bacteria and parasites and horrible things like that? Or pollution? Thing three, I'd like to use soap. We're not supposed to use soap in wild water, are we? Doesn't it kill stuff?"

"Most soap is biodegradable now," said Edmund.

"Your gold could probably protect you from bad stuff in the water," Matt said.

Suki stared at the gold on her arms. "Really? Amazing. So okay, I'll check the soap package, but what about thing one?"

"Edmund, could you ask the water if there's any hot springs around here?" Matt said.

He smiled at her and went to the lake, plunged his hand into it. He closed his eyes and listened. Matt felt calm just watching him.

A couple minutes later he stood and turned to them. "Nowhere nearby," he said. "Sorry."

"If we wait a little bit, the day will get warmer," Matt said. "We can go swimming."

"I didn't pack a suit."

"We're all alone up here. We don't need suits."

Suki hugged herself and looked doubtful.

"You come with me," Matt said. "I'll protect you. Okay?"

"All right," Suki muttered.

Edmund searched one of the grocery bags until he found a salt shaker. "Okay. You'll be okay? If not, Matt, use gold to call me."

She checked the gold bands at her wrists. —We could do that,— gold told her. "All right," she said. "See ya."

He smiled at both of them and loped off into the woods.

"I've never done anything like this before," Suki said. "Never spent a night outside, never went to the bathroom in the woods, never took a bath in a lake."

"It's kind of spooky, isn't it? I feel much better in cities. I don't know how to talk to all these things out here. They just seem strange and maybe dangerous. But pretty."

"I don't know how to deal with dirt."

Matt remembered Edmund's dream, of night swimming and a campfire by a lake, and how Suki had been there, but Edmund knew it was a dream, because Suki wasn't allowed to get wet or dirty. "Dirt I can handle. And bugs and stuff. It's just being out here in nature. I don't know what it cares about or wants. It's so big, and it doesn't talk." Except for the singing rocks, whose intentions Matt didn't know. "I think we'll be okay. Some animal licked my head this morning, though. Why would it do that?"

Suki laughed and said, "Salt, maybe?"

Matt felt her forehead. She was willing to admit to dried sweat. "I thought wild animals were scared of people. Well, let's have an adventure. You got soap?"

"I picked up some bar soap at the market last night, and I have shampoo in my toiletries kit."

"I got a couple towels. If one's dirty, we can steal Edmund's."

"I want to change my clothes after we wash. I slept in these."

"Let's get our stuff."

Suki took the bucket of water by the fire and poured it over the flames and coals. Hissing and smoke rose up.

Matt grabbed a blanket as well as towels. They both took a change of clothes. Suki packed her toiletries bag with soap and some other things, then looked doubtfully at the car. "My purse," she said. "My laptop. All my clothes. Car, will you take care of them for me? I'd hate to lose them. I'm scared to leave my wallet, and I'm scared to take it with me. How far away are we going?"

"I saw a beach across the stream. Not too far." And the direction opposite of the way Edmund had gone. Matt laid her palm on the car for a moment, and it closed and locked all its doors. "Look," she said, pointing at the front windows. Suki peered through one and gasped.

"What happened to our stuff?" It looked as if the car had empty seats and floormats.

"Car did a spell for you. Invisible luggage. Pretty cool, huh?"

"It's great." Suki leaned over and kissed the car. "Thank you."

—You're welcome,— the car said. Matt heard it and wondered if she should translate for Suki, but then she noticed Suki's eyes widen.

"Did you hear it?"

"Almost." Suki stroked her hand along the car's roof. "Like when I was little. Used to hear things."

"Keep listening."

Suki smiled at her and grabbed the bag and clothes. "Lead on."

Matt and Suki walked up the stream a ways until there was a place where they could cross on stones without wetting their feet. Matt wondered if they should look for a swimming hole in the creek itself, but she touched the water with her bare hand and decided it must come from snow—way too cold, and as far as she could see, too shallow.

Sun sent occasional shafts of light to the forest floor. Matt recognized nothing from her earlier run, but she had seen a beach somewhere, she knew it; so they traveled along the lakeshore for a ways and finally found a small cove with a sandy beach and sun on the water.

Matt shucked off her boots, socks, long johns, underwear, and T-shirt, thinking a bath would feel good. Her head itched, and the rest of her felt grimy. The morning air was cool against her bare belly and breasts. How strange to stand somewhere totally naked. Well, naked except for magic. She never did this. Communal showers in a shelter, that she had done. But prancing around out in nature—well, she'd done that too, admit it, way back when she couldn't get into buildings and really wanted a bath. She had gone in a river a time or three. When she was a kid, she'd gone skinny dipping a few times with Ray and his sister Emily.

She glanced down at her breasts. Not that big, but bigger than she liked. Before she joined Edmund, she had bound them so they wouldn't show, but now she felt relaxed about them. They were okay. And it was nice not to have to wrap them.

She shivered in the breeze and thought she must be crazy to contemplate going into even colder water. Her head did itch, though. It had been a long time since that hot shower at Abby and Tony's house.

Suki sat on a log next to their spare clothes, towels, and the blanket. She slowly unbuttoned her shirt. Matt walked over to wait for her. "Don't look at me," Suki said. "Please."

"Oh. Okay." Matt strode down to the water and dipped a toe in. "Yow!" The water was freezing. It would take forever to get used to if she went in an inch at a time, so she walked right out till it was up to her thighs and dropped under. Her skin screamed in surprise. A moment later she jumped up and took a big breath.

"Whoa. What a thing," she said, rubbing her eyes. "Can I use your soap and shampoo?"

Suki, wrapped in a big towel, stood at the water's edge, her head and long beautiful legs visible, everything between hidden. "Soap? Shampoo? I forgot." She went back to the log, picked up her toiletries bag, and brought it down to the water. She pulled out a big bar of white soap and a small bottle of Pert Plus. "Here you go." She tossed them. Matt caught them.

"Thanks," Matt said. She turned her back and soaped her head, giving Suki space. "The water's freezing, but kind of refreshing. This feels good." She looked across the lake as she spoke. Trees touched toes to their shadows on the other side; the sky above burned blue, reflected in wavering shimmers on the surface of the water.

Suki screeched and splashed in, bellyflopping beside Matt. "You must be crazy! How can you stand this?" she yelled.

"Wait a few seconds, you'll be all right."

"I hate this!"

"Good. Good. Tell it like it is." Matt capped the shampoo and kept her face away from Suki so she wouldn't embarrass her. She rubbed soap in her armpits.

"Shut up!"

"Okay, aye aye, shutting up, sir."

"This is awful. I want a shower. A *hot* shower."

Matt held the shampoo out in Suki's general direction. Presently Suki took it from her. Matt ducked down and washed the shampoo out of her hair, hoping it wouldn't hurt anything. With her hair so short, it only took a little bit. She finished running the soap over her skin and held that out in Suki's direction until Suki took it, too, then rinsed herself.

"I'm going to swim out," Matt said, "and I won't look back till you tell me it's okay."

"Oh, shut up," Suki said again. "Why should I care if you see me? Anyway, most of me is underwater. You can look."

"Okay. Thanks." Matt glanced over just as Suki ducked her head under the surface.

She jumped back up to her full height and screamed, "Cold! Cold, cold, cold!" Her body was model-perfect and bouncy. The gold had retreated to a heavy collar at her neck and a wide belt at her waist. "This is TORTURE!" Suki yelled, startling birds out of a tree. She poured shampoo in her hand and scrubbed it through her hair. "I'm going to get clean out of it if it's the last thing I do," she muttered.

Matt swam out into the lake, away from Suki's splashing and grumbling. She hadn't swum in years, either, but she remembered how. Away from the shore, she turned over and floated on her back, staring up into blue infinity.

Edmund was off purifying himself, and Matt had just purified herself with Pert Plus and Ivory. She smiled at the sky and thought about the future. She wanted to be with Edmund when he went to find Suki's father. No way to know how that was going to turn out, but it had to happen.

But what about Suki? Well, if she wanted to go to Mexico or Canada the way Edmund had suggested, Matt guessed they'd be visiting Mexico or Canada. Wouldn't Suki be better off at the haunted house? Nathan could finally take care of her the way he wanted to.

Was this the Suki of his dreams, though? Prickly and inhibited and distant and frightened. Maybe she was.

Sun warmed Matt and water moved around her and below

her, cells of cold rising up against her back, the thin layer of slightly sun-warmed water flowing across her belly. She lay for a long time, watching rose-colored sunlight through her eyelids, and let thoughts sink to nothing.

Something nibbled her leg. She whipped around, searching for piranha. It was only some fish checking out a hair on her leg, though. Maybe lying still as a log wasn't the best idea she ever had. But she had scared the fish away when she moved.

She glanced toward the shore and realized she had drifted. She couldn't see the beach anymore.

—Suki okay?— she asked gold.

It thrummed for a moment, then said, —She is out of the water and dressed.—

—Thanks.— Matt turned over and dog-paddled toward the shore, edging along it in search of the little beach. It took a while to find it again. She walked out of the water, splashed it with one hand to say thank you, and looked around for Suki.

Suki sat on the log, fully dressed, wrapped in the blanket, and shivering. "Where have you been? How can you stand it?" she demanded. "I need a fire. There's nothing to plug my blow-dryer into, and I'm really cold."

"I'm sorry," Matt said. She toweled off and dressed. The day felt warm to her now, but Suki's distress seemed real. "Is it okay if I touch you?" Matt asked Suki.

"Touch me? Why?"

"Just here," Matt said. She reached out, pushed down the edge of Suki's sweater so she could touch Suki's gold collar.

Suki shrugged.

Matt touched gold. —She's cold. You could warm her, couldn't you?—

—Could I?— It sounded surprised. All its spices lingered, Suki's unbearable moods, drunk on themselves, unable to think past their trance.

Matt pressed her gold to Suki's gold. She felt them talking to each other, but couldn't hear what they said. Suki's gold collar flushed, shifted toward red gold. Then it flowed. Matt lifted her hand away as a red-gold skin enveloped Suki, even coated her hair, turned her into a metal statue for a moment. Then gold retreated back into its collar shape.

Suki breathed out. Her cheeks glowed. Her hair was dry now. "What—what was that?"

"Magic."

"Magic," Suki repeated, touching the collar. "It could do that all along? I'm so stupid."

"No, you're not. Jeeze. You've had this stuff less than a day. No way could you know how it works. I only met it a couple days ago, and I don't know what it can do either. I have a few more ideas than you do, but I've seen it do a lot more things."

Suki sighed.

"So, I'm sorry you were uncomfortable," Matt said.

"I'm sorry I'm being so whiny. I don't usually say any of this stuff. Hell, I don't usually feel any of this stuff." She ran a hand through her hair. "I don't know what's the matter with me. Usually I don't feel cold. Nothing bothers me. I could stick a knife through my hand and not notice. I never complain about anything, and here I am yelling about nothing. Yelling. I never yell either."

Matt cocked her head and studied Suki. So in a way she had never met Suki, because ever since they started talking, Suki had been acting different from her usual self? Or the usual self was the unreal one? Or something else entirely? No. Gold had told Matt who Suki really was, back when it was still skimming her thoughts. But yes: Suki was a person who hadn't felt much. Flashes of shallow rage, and calculation. She was changing now. "We put a lot of pressure on you," Matt said. "We took you away from everything you know."

"But my wall—my wall doesn't care where I am. It always protects me from having to feel anything. Heat, cold, hunger, pain. All this confusion."

"You said your wall was down."

Suki hugged herself.

"And besides, now Edmund wants to talk to your father. Scary, huh?"

"Terrifying."

"Have you decided what you want to do about that yet? Where you want to go?"

"No," said Suki. She stared down at the toes of her shoes. "Talk to my father," she whispered. Her hands gripped each other so tightly the knuckles whitened. "I've felt like my father was dead. All this time, I've felt like my father was dead. And Edmund killed him."

It was like a punch in the stomach. A million ideas blossomed in Matt's head, and her stomach clutched and burned. So Suki had had a terrible father and a dead mother, a terrible father who had *killed* her mother, but sometimes even a terrible father was better than no father, and her friend killed her father, and . . .

Who could she possibly trust? Her mother, who was dead. Her friend, who killed her father and then left. The people she knew destroyed each other, even when she loved them. And then they left.

I used to love my father, Matt thought. *Before he hurt me. And sometimes even after. 'Cause I could remember when he wasn't like that. I remember him pushing me in the swingset. I remember when he taught me how to hammer nails. I remember when he carried me piggyback around the house and we were both laughing. I remember when he helped me say my prayers before I fell asleep. Gosh, that was a long time ago. When our Father Who Art in Heaven had to look like Daddy because he was the Dad, and that was all there was to it. Deliver us from evil.*

I went and looked at him. I saw he knew somewhere inside that he hurt me and Pammy, and that's when I stopped looking. I didn't look to see what ever hurt him. I didn't look for anything good in him. I didn't look to see who else he was.

"Suki," Matt said. Her voice cracked.

Suki turned to her.

"Did you ever love him?"

"What are you talking about? The man was a maniac. He was vile to Mom and horrible to me. Living with him was like being squeezed in a vise."

I didn't look to see who else he was, Matt thought, because it wasn't my job to take care of him. He was the father. He was supposed to take care of me, and he did it terrible. It was my job to take care of me. I took what I needed from that meeting with him, and I left.

I wonder who else he was. I wonder if he's still alive. Sure can't hurt me now. I could maybe find out more.

"Every once in a while," Suki murmured, staring at the lake again, "when I washed every inch of myself just right, and combed my hair just right, and wore the right dress and every crease was just right, and my stockings stayed up and my shoelaces were tied just right, every once in a while, Dad smiled at me and told me what a good girl I was. He called me Fairy. Sometimes that was horrible, but sometimes it made me feel magic."

Matt looked at Suki's hands, which lay on her thighs now, relaxed, not twisted and hurting each other.

"I tried so hard to be perfect," Suki said. "Every once in a while I made it, and then I felt this amazing, huge happiness. I didn't dare smile too wide, because that would jinx it. But I felt it. It tasted like maple syrup."

Matt waited for a while. When she was pretty sure Suki wasn't going to say anything else, she said, "First thing we should do is find out whether your father is still alive. Just so we know."

"I don't—"

Matt looked at her and waited. Suki closed her eyes, took a deep breath, held it, let it out. "Why?" she asked.

"This is so big and confusing," Matt said. "I think it's awful to think your friend killed your father, no matter how awful your father is. I think some little part of you maybe loves your father and hates Edmund for killing him. We need to do something for that little part. Once we know your father's alive, then you can think about talking to him, and maybe you can stop hating Edmund. What do you think?"

"Hating Edmund? I love my dad? Are you crazy? I don't know what I think. There's way too many things swirling around in my brain, and I feel mixed up because of all these stupid feelings. This isn't getting any clearer."

"Let's go back to the car and make lunch," Matt said.

"What?" Suki started laughing.

"Lots happened since breakfast. I think better on a full stomach," Matt said. She grabbed her dirty clothes, towel, and blanket.

Suki rose, gathering her things, and they went back through the woods toward the car.

Halfway back, Suki gripped Matt's arm. Matt stopped and looked where Suki was looking.

A window opened between branches, showing a slice of sky, forest, and lake. Sun struck the pine branches around the opening, making a bright green frame for a small view, contrasting with the darker branches, filtered light, and shaded places around it.

They stood awhile watching. Wind wavered branches, shifting the view. Sunsparks struck up from the water's surface. Calm flowed into Matt.

Presently they both turned and went on.

At the car, Matt snooped through the bags of groceries and the cooler, found two kinds of sliced cheese, mayonnaise, cracked wheat sourdough bread, country Dijon mustard, half a head of lettuce. "You want all this stuff on your sandwich?" she asked Suki.

"Doesn't matter. It all tastes the same to me anyway," Suki said.

"Really?" Matt built two sandwiches on paper plates, handed one to Suki.

Suki bit. She dropped her sandwich and said, "Hah . . . hah . . . hah . . . hot," fanning her mouth. "Ow! What'd you put in this thing?"

"Maybe too much mustard, huh?"

"This is . . ." Suki opened the sandwich and peeked inside. "This is stupid. It *looks* normal."

"Here's a knife. You can scrape the mustard off. I'll give you the squeeze bottle of mayonnaise and you can fix it. Sorry about that."

Suki shook her head at the knife, closed the sandwich, and took another bite. "This is so weird," she said. "This is a taste people like?"

"I do," said Matt.

Suki swallowed and kept eating. Matt gave her a can of kiwi strawberry soda. She gulped some and gasped, spraying soda over her sandwich. "Ouch! What's it doing to my tongue?"

"Haven't you ever had soda pop before?"

"All the time. All we drink at work is Diet Coke. It doesn't do this totally fizzy tongue-burning thing, though."

"Sure it does. Carbonation. We're out of bottled water. Otherwise I would have given you one of those."

Suki glanced at the lake.

"I don't know if it's safe, or how to make it safe," Matt said.

Suki set her sandwich and soda on the car's tailgate, where she'd been sitting. "I hate this. The world tastes terrible. I don't want to be able to taste anything. How can I eat? Why is this happening now? For years and years, nothing tasted like anything. Is this magic, or what?"

Matt found Suki an apple, and said, "Your wall is down."

Suki polished the apple on her sweater. She bit into it. "Oh! This is wonderful!"

"Good," said Matt. She rummaged around some more and found some saltines. "Try these, huh?"

Suki chomped her way through the apple, then accepted

some crackers. "These don't taste good, but they don't taste bad either. I'm so thirsty!" Frowning, she drank some more soda. "Gack!" She checked the coffeepot and found some dregs, poured them into a cup and took a big drink. "Aaaiieee! This is horrible."

"I'm so sorry," Matt said, trying to keep from laughing, and feeling totally mean.

"Go ahead," Suki said.

Matt lay on the ground and laughed. "I'm sorry. I'm sorry!"

"You're just downright evil," said Suki. She set her hand on her head and said, "Magic, take my taste buds. Please."

Instead of draping a gold scarf over her head, though, magic gave her a glass of water. "Oh. Okay! That works! Thanks," Suki said, and drank it before Matt could articulate her hesitations about magic milk, magic water, magic gifts. "Yes. Thank you. Yes."

Edmund came back just as they finished lunch.

"Did it go okay?" Matt asked.

"Want most of a cheese-and-mustard sandwich?" Suki asked at the same time, offering him hers.

"Thanks." He took a big bite. "Good!"

"God, he likes it too," Suki muttered. "You people are crazy."

"It went okay," Edmund said. "I know what to do. Suki's father is still alive, and he's in Salem. I need to go there."

Suki closed her eyes and gripped her elbows. Her face looked skull-like, skin stretched tight over cheekbones and temples and chin. When she opened her eyes, the woman Matt had spent the morning and afternoon with had disappeared. It was as though her spirit had retreated to some far place, leaving a ghost behind. No emotion but resignation showed.

"What do you want to do, Suki?" Edmund asked.

"I'll go with you." Her voice was toneless.

"You don't have to turn into a zombie," Matt said. "Jeeze. We're not there yet."

Suki turned Siamese-cat blue eyes toward her. "I would rather be like this. Everything is too noisy the other way. Too loud, too pungent, too intense. Now I'm safe. Now I can see him."

Chapter Eleven

· · · · ·

"HE'S been with us thirteen years, and he's never had a visitor," said the nurse. "Before that, he was in short-term care at another facility for evaluation and treatment decisions."

"What kind of patient is he?" Suki sounded like she was asking about a stove at a department store. It gave Matt the creeps.

"Nearly catatonic. Almost never initiates movement on his own, but he's perfectly cooperative—allows us to move him, seat him, help him walk, feed him. Doesn't respond to stimuli except touch."

"My father is a vegetable?" Suki asked.

"No," said the nurse. "There's evidence of brain activity. He just doesn't connect to the outside world."

Matt stood facing away from the reception desk of the Riverview Nursing Home in Salem. She could see through an open pair of double doors into a big room.

The activities room at Riverview had a wall of windows that looked out onto a cloudy sky, a lawn green from winter rains, and the tree-hemmed river running beyond. Older people played cards at several of the tables, and a few women worked on quilt squares or knitting projects. A cheery young woman in a pale blue uniform stopped and murmured questions at each occupied table. She went and got a pitcher of something, filled paper cups and handed them around.

Matt watched as another young uniformed woman wheeled an old man into the room and over to a table. The man had only a cowlick of white hair on the back of his pale head, and his crooked hands shook on the arms of his wheelchair. The young woman went and got him a paper cup of something. He looked up to thank her. His light blue eyes met Matt's gaze. After a moment, half his mouth smiled.

Something she couldn't name drew Matt into the room. She heard Suki and the nurse talking on behind her, but she no longer made out the words. She went to the old man's table and sat down, staring into his eyes.

"Had a son once," the man murmured. "Looked a lot like you. He was a scalawag, but I loved him."

Matt opened dream-eyes. A cloudy sky, just beginning to lighten at one edge, a man with a younger man, both of them with fishing poles, standing beside a lake. As the light came up, more and more forms emerged from the darkness: the lake was surrounded by people with poles. "Fishing," Matt said.

"First day of the season," said the old man. "Had to wait for sunup." All the people in the memory tossed their lines into the water. The man and his son laughed as a startled duck flew up from the shallows. "Wasn't that a time, Matthew! Wasn't that a time! Caught your limit, and we had a feast with your mother. Fish coming out our ears." He grinned.

"It was great, wasn't it?" Matt said.

"Our best year." His hand gripped hers. "Best year, but we had a lot of good ones. You should never have gone overseas."

"I'm sorry."

"You had a lot more life to live. Shouldn'ta gone, Matt." Now he was seeing a coffin with an American flag draped over it.

"I'm sorry," she whispered again. "You never know before you leave that that's what's going to happen."

"Too many boys come back in a box. It's not right. Children shouldn't die before their parents. It's not right."

Edmund touched her shoulder and she looked up.

The old man said, "That another angel, Matt? Guess you can't stay. I'm glad to see you again, boy. Come any time."

"Thanks, Dad. You take care now." The voice that came out of her mouth wasn't entirely her own. She could feel him there, the other Matt, but whether he was visiting from his father's memory or from somewhere else she didn't know. She gripped the man's hand, released it, and stood up.

Edmund took her hand as they walked back to the entrance hall, where Suki stood straight and splendid and icicle cool, perfectly groomed, wearing a dark blue dress that covered her from neck to wrists and ankles, hiding her gold entirely. It was the sort of dress Matt imagined women wore to fancy concerts at expensive performing arts centers. Suki had golden freshwater pearls in her ears and a string of the same pearls around her neck. She looked formidable and glacial.

Matt, in a black turtleneck sweater, blue jeans, and combat boots, felt out of place. She had left her army jacket in the car. As armor, she had bound her breasts again. Only her hands and head were bare.

Edmund wore a moss-green sweater and black jeans and his navy peacoat with the devotions kit in the pocket. They had spent the night in a motel in southern Oregon, and Suki had insisted on getting another motel room once they reached Salem so she could dress up before they did the final seek to find this place. All three of them were squeaky clean, which made Matt feel like a kid going to a grandparent's house for a holiday meal.

The nurse said, "Please follow me. I'll take you to him."

She led them along a spacious, carpeted hallway. Most of the doors that opened onto it bore personalized computer-generated signs in a bewildering array of colored fonts: SALLY'S SOLARIUM; ANNA'S ATTIC; OSCAR'S OBSERVATORY; ELEANOR'S EYRIE. Some doors stood open, showing large rooms with big windows. Some rooms had French windows that opened out onto fenced patios, where plants grew in redwood tubs. Each room was individually furnished, though those with hospital beds had some similarities. Windowsills bore bottle collections, crockery cats, houseplants, dolls with crocheted dresses, family photos. Walls sported artwork, art plate collections, more photos, an occasional weaving. Some rooms had big overstuffed recliners; some had desks and chairs. Each displayed personality. Some inhabitants were home; some waved; some watched TV or talked on the phone.

Smells of antiseptic cleansers, incontinence, air freshener.

They came to room 118. RICHARD'S RETREAT. The nurse knocked on the half-open door and said, "Mr. Backstrom? Mr. Backstrom, you have visitors." She pushed the door wide.

The man in the chair did not move or speak.

The walls were papered with picture postcards showing exotic places: too bright blue skies, lurid sunsets, monuments to unknown dead or unknown deeds, pale beaches edging down into too blue water, finger-fringed palm leaves, some views brand-new, some small hand-tinted windows onto past times. A yarn-sprigged quilt lay on the bed, and a braided rag rug covered half the floor. Against one wall stood a large television console, its picture on but its sound off. From the fraught expressions of the people onscreen, Matt guessed an afternoon soap opera was playing.

Richard Backstrom sat static in a light blue recliner, his eyes fixed on a spot on the wall where no postcard was. He looked gaunt, but still startlingly handsome, the same blonde good looks Suki had, the same intense blue eyes.

"Who did the decorating?" Suki asked in a distant, amused voice.

"Tess. She's a volunteer here—spends time with patients nobody else visits. She comes and talks to Mr. Backstrom at least once a week. We're so lucky to have her. She's unfailingly cheerful, and that can be a big help in some cases."

The nurse went to the man in the chair and touched his shoulder, leaned over to speak directly to him. "Mr. Backstrom? Your daughter and some friends are here."

The man did not respond. Suki, Edmund, and Matt stood just outside the threshold of the room. Matt felt a strange apprehension that if they crossed into the room, they would lose themselves.

Edmund stepped across the line. Suki followed, and then Matt.

"Well, I'll leave you to visit, then," the nurse said. "The nurse call button's here. Let us know if you need anything."

"Thanks," Suki said, still in that faint voice. Matt suddenly realized its breathlessness came from terror.

"Matt," Edmund said. His voice was full of music. She looked up at him. Flame burned in his eyes. "Will you look for me?"

The red boy. He was here: Edmund was armed. This was not an Edmund Matt had spent any time with, but at least this time he knew who she was.

Matt nodded to him, walked past and sat on the floor, staring up into Suki's father's face. He looked relaxed, with a statue's placid beauty. Seeds of so much sadness and trouble lay somewhere behind his face, she thought, and opened dream-eyes.

For an instant, she saw a small blonde baby wrapped up in ropes, dangling in the midst of a huge open space, suspended like a fly in a spider's web, strings leading from him in all directions. His mouth was open in a soundless cry, and his eyes looked hollow.

That image flickered and vanished. She saw a red wilderness, coiled trees with blood-red branches, whip-swift crimson bamboo stalks, gashing plum-red grasses, slicing scarlet leaves. Two figures fought against the slashing vines and rains of thorns: a paper-white boy and a shadow-black boy, clubbed and beaten by everything around them, punching back, snapping off giant leaves and trying to make them into shields, only to have them shredded.

Matt shut dream-eyes, closed her other eyes, sat and shook.

"What did you see?" Edmund asked. He and Suki stood out of range of Suki's father's fixed gaze.

Matt said, "It's awful. First a baby trapped in a web like a fly.

Then two little boys trying to fight a red forest. They can't beat it. It just keeps hitting and cutting, and they just keep fighting."

Edmund frowned at the floor for a moment, then glanced at her. "Will you watch what happens when I move into his field of view?"

Matt scrubbed her face and said, "Okay." She opened dream-eyes again. Black boy, white boy, fighting. They weren't side by side, but they weren't far from each other.

Edmund stood in front of Mr. Backstrom. He stared into the man's eyes.

The white boy turned around, looked up.

Paper-white, curly headed, features sketchy black lines. The white boy's mouth opened in soundless surprise. Matt recognized him.

The lance of a red branch plunged through his back, thrust from his chest. He screamed without noise and wilted. The branch danced in victory with his spitted body on it. After a little while he woke again, reached down, broke off the branch protruding from his chest. He pulled himself off the branch and sank to the ground. In a little while he got back to his feet. His wound, which had been gaping and red, had disappeared. He was solid white again. He took one last look up, it seemed to Matt directly at Edmund, and then he turned back to fight the forest again.

"It's you," Matt said, her voice scratchy as it left her throat. "The white boy is you. You surprised the white boy, and he looked up, and the forest killed him, but after a while he came back to life."

Suki came to stand beside Edmund. She stared down into her father's unblinking eyes. Her hand gripped Edmund's. Matt saw that Suki was shaking, but she didn't look away or even summon her gold.

The black boy turned this time, his features sketched in white, and Matt realized it was an image of Suki's father. He stared up at Suki and leaves sliced him to pieces. With a soundless scream, he fell apart. It took longer for these pieces to collect themselves and revive. Meanwhile the white boy had to fight harder, and was killed again. The forest quivered, coiled, waved tendrils, but left the boys alone until they were strong enough to fight.

"The black boy is your father," Matt said. "When you stepped in front of him, the black boy looked up. The red trees killed him and the white boy again. It took them a while, but they came back to life. Then they kept fighting. I can't watch this anymore." She closed dream-eyes.

Edmund tugged Suki to the side, away from her father's gaze. Suki's father blinked. Suki sat on the bed, hunched her shoulders.

Edmund knelt below the man's line of vision and touched Matt's hand. "I didn't know what to expect, but it looks like I could really use your help."

Matt looked away. "What if that's all that's been going on in his head for years and years?" she whispered.

"That's what I'm afraid of. That's what I want to try to fix. Will you help?"

She rubbed her eyes. She squared her shoulders. "I came to help you. What do you want me to do?"

"What happens when you step into his field of view? He's seen me and Suki before, but he's never seen you."

Matt opened dream-eyes. She was looking in Edmund's

direction. She saw his clearing again, the waterfall, the trees, lush plants, the slope of a mountain. Leaning against a tree was the red boy, and sitting beneath another tree was Young Edmund. They looked at her, their faces calm.

Matt scrambled to her feet and, dreading it, turned to meet Suki's father's eyes.

The red forest and the black and white boys had disappeared. Now she saw blue water, its surface wrinkled with ripples leading off in all directions. Its edges stretched to the horizon, where it met and melted into blue sky. Gradually an image of Matt's face lay reflected on the water, which calmed.

Where had the war gone?

"Mr. Backstrom?" Matt said.

A ripple raced across the water.

"Are you awake in there?"

Her image fragmented. A small wave rolled across the water. She waited, and everything stilled again.

"He sees me, but . . . I don't think he knows how to talk back, or if he wants to. At least the war went away."

"The war went away?"

"Now it's just water. I wish I had Nathan," Matt said. Gold flexed at her wrists.

"What? Why?" asked Suki. She sat on her father's bed, her hands quiet in her lap.

"If Nathan was here, he could help me make you see this stuff too." She pushed her sleeves up and studied her narrow wristbands. She had used most of her gold for visions last night. And now the last of her light gold had disappeared, leaving only the narrow bands of her Ginny gold. How could she show Suki and Edmund what was happening with the little bit of gold she had left? Would Ginny's gold work to make visions visible? It hadn't last night. "Suki—" She reached toward Suki's neckline, knowing the gold was just beneath the edge of her dress. "Is it okay if I—"

Someone knocked on the door and came in. "Oh!"

They all looked, saw a pretty mid-fifties woman with long, wild, crinkly black hair barely restrained by an orange silk scarf at the nape of her neck. She wore a bright yellow flower-dotted knit dress whose skirt fell around her legs in soft folds. "I'm so sorry. I didn't know Richard had visitors. He never did before." Confusion hovered around her in a pink cloud.

"Are you Tess?" Matt asked.

"Why, yes. How did you know?"

"The nurse told us you put up the postcards. Nice."

"May I come in? I just want to say hello." Tess swept into the room, twinkling. She joined Matt in front of Suki's father and looked into his eyes. "Hello, Richard. Hey! People came to see you. Imagine that!"

Matt watched Mr. Backstrom's dreamscape. Land drifted up from below, pushed through the surface of the water. An expanse of bare sand. A single footprint appeared.

"You look nice today," Tess said, patting his shoulder.

A second footprint, and then feet, ankles, calves, knees, thighs—legs—just a shadow of them at first, then a gradual filling in. The process continued upward until Tess's whole form stood on the beach. Her dress had no detail, but her face and arms looked like her.

"He sees her," Matt said.

"What?" Tess turned to her.

Matt startled. She had forgotten she was speaking out loud. "Uh. He sees you," she repeated.

"What makes you say that?" Tess turned to Mr. Backstrom, leaned closer. "Richard, do you know I'm here? I always hoped you would."

Something prickled over Matt's skin. Cold shot through her, chilled her to her bones, then shifted to warmth. —What?— said a new voice.

—What?— Matt shook her head. —Who's thinking in my head?—

—What? Matt? Where are we?—

—Nathan?—

Matt's head rose and she looked around the room, taking in the man in the chair, the woman in front of him, Edmund beyond. Her gaze stopped at Suki, sitting on the bed.

—Oh, wow.—

To Matt, Suki looked frozen, her face expressionless, her eyes distant. Her hands trembled in her lap. To Nathan, she just looked amazing. Grown up, more beautiful than ever, heart-touching.

—You found her! She's alive! She grew up! Oh, thank God.—

—Nathan, what are you doing here?—

—I don't know. Where are we?— He turned her head again and looked into the unseeing eyes of Suki's father. —Him! That's him?— Matt's hands fisted. Her shoulders tensed. —I'll kill him!—

—Stop that right now,— she said, straightening her fingers with effort. —You just wait. There's a lot you don't know.—

For a moment he resisted. Then he said, —I'm sorry.— She

felt him settle, release her muscles back to her control. —Please explain. How did I get here? Did you summon me? It's not like any summoning I've felt before.—

"Richard?" Tess said again. She laid her hand on Mr. Backstrom's cheek. "Please let me know you know I'm here. Just one little sign." His face remained frozen, and Tess turned to Matt. "What makes you think he has any idea I'm here?"

—I wished for you,— Matt said.

—You wished for me,— Nathan repeated with a rising tone.

—Suki's father doesn't speak or move or anything. Edmund and Suki need to talk to him, though. I thought if you and I worked together, we could show them what he's thinking.—

—Suki? Susan changed her name to Suki? You wished for me and I came? But we didn't even talk about this, Matt.—

—I know. I'm sorry. I didn't know it would work. I wasn't thinking.—

—Hey, don't apologize. I'm glad I'm here, even if I don't know how. What's going on?—

"Miss?" Tess said.

—Look,— Matt said, and looked at Mr. Backstrom's mental landscape. It still showed the island in the middle of endless blue water and sky, and Tess still stood on the island, firm-footed. —Can you make that visible?—

—Hmm.— Matt felt herself frown. Nathan said, —Do I still have powers this far from home? What? What's this on our wrists? Matt! What on Earth are we wearing?— His voice in her head laughed.

—Gold. It's magic. That's how you came, I guess. I wished you were here, and it heard me.—

—Oh! Magic. I've never seen this kind of magic before, but

if it works like other kinds . . .— He thought something at her gold, and Matt felt it respond, the faintest tingle, like the touch of a tip of a feather.

Blue water hovered above Mr. Backstrom's head. A sand bar, with a woman standing on it, blue sky above her.

Matt closed dream-eyes and the picture was still there. —Thanks!— she thought, and glanced at Edmund to see if he could see it. He stared at her, wide-eyed. She remembered: the red boy could hear her and Nathan when they talked silently, and Edmund had brought the red boy with him to this meeting.

Tess gasped. "What?" She took three steps back. Above Mr. Backstrom's head, her image shrank.

"He sees you," Matt said.

"What are you doing? What *is* this? What are you?"

"This is a picture of what he's thinking."

—That's all he's thinking?— Nathan asked.

—It was horrible before. This is much better.—

"This is some kind of trick, isn't it? Who are you people, anyway?" Tess returned to stand right in front of Mr. Backstrom, and her image enlarged. "Richard?"

He blinked. A shutter dropped over the image of Tess, lifted.

"What *is* this?" Tess wailed, backing away, out of Mr. Backstrom's line of vision. Her image shrank and disappeared, and the land dropped below the surface of the water. "What are you people doing here? Is this black magic?"

—Uh oh,— Nathan thought, and spoke to gold again. The image vanished.

Matt glanced down at her wrists. She still had Ginny's gold, or most of it. Nathan knew some kind of image magic that worked much more efficiently than what she had done last night.

—Last night?— he thought.

Matt thought through a little of what she had done last night.

—Oh, Matt,— he thought. —You made them solid. Not just visible. Solid. That takes lots and lots of power.—

Solid!

—Here,— he thought, and showed her how to use magic with light particles to make visions visible. It took much less magic than she had used the night before.

Suki stood. "Tess. Whoever you are," she said, and her voice was firm and powerful. "This man is my father. I thank you for your care and concern for him. I need to talk to him, and I understood that direct methods might not work, so I asked my—my psychic friends for help. There's nothing bad about this kind of psychic power."

Nathan wanted to drink Suki's image, record her words. Matt wanted to check on Mr. Backstrom. For a moment she was caught between imperatives, and then Nathan apologized and stopped resisting Matt's desire to turn her own head.

The war had returned, small black and white boys fighting vicious red monster plants, being scored, cut, killed, rising to fight again. "God!" Nathan said aloud, sickened. "What is that?"

Matt clapped her hand over her mouth.

—Sorry. Sorry! Oh, Matt, I'm sorry I'm not a better guest, but this . . .—

—Don't worry about it, it's done,— Matt thought. —See what I mean? Why hurt him when he's living with this? It's terrible!—

"Na—" Suki said. Matt looked at her. Color drained from

Suki's face and she sat down on the bed again, her composure lost.

"You're Richard's daughter?" Tess said. "Why did it take you so long to come to him?" Anger edged her voice. "He's been here for years, all alone. Don't you even care?"

Suki touched the hidden gold collar at her neck. Before the golden veil could cover her face, Edmund stood, his eyes flickering red. "Tess," he said, music burnishing his voice. "You're obviously a good person, but you don't know their family history. How could you? Please accept that this is a matter beyond your ability to judge right now. We need time alone with him. Excuse us."

"What? Leave you alone with him? Who's going to protect him from you?"

"Leave," he said, with trumpets in it. Matt felt herself wanting to rise and go.

Tess walked out, pulling the door shut behind her. The lock clicked.

"Matt," Edmund said, a question chorded on a harp.

Matt sighed. "I wished Nathan was here, and my gold heard me." Then Nathan said, "But look, Edmund. It's awful."

The war winked into sight above Mr. Backstrom's head.

Edmund and Suki stared as the forest tortured the boys. "Oh, God," Suki moaned after a moment.

Matt covered her eyes. "Mr. Backstrom," she said, "why don't you let them work together?" She peeked between her fingers.

For a little while nothing happened. The black boy died. The white boy died. They gathered themselves and fought on.

Then they edged closer to each other.

"Yeah," whispered Matt.

Finally they stood back to back, punching out the forest. At least no branches stabbed them from behind.

"But they can't win," Edmund murmured. "They have no weapons, and it's endless."

"They can't win, but the forest can't win either," Nathan said.

"Nathan!"

"Susan." He turned Matt's head, and she let him.

—Want out of me?— Matt asked.

—I don't know. What if I leave you, lose touch, and the house calls me back? It can do that. I'm not supposed to leave the house during the day, except when certain conditions are met, and I'm not sure this counts. I'd like to stay and help.—

—Maybe gold can help you,— Matt thought, but she looked at her wrists. Was she imagining it or were the bands growing even thinner?

—If it's okay with you, I'll stay here. Okay if I talk?— Nathan asked.

—Go ahead.—

"Are you all right?" Nathan asked Suki.

"You *are* here? *How* are you here?"

"Matt summoned me to help her with this. I know more about making images visible than she does at the moment. In the abstract, I wanted to kill him for everything he's done to you. But look what he's living with. He's in hell already." He looked at the war. Back to back, the black boy and the white boy fought the red jungle. It skewered, stabbed, sliced them. They fought and died, revived, fought, died.

"I did that," Edmund said, his eyes still lit from within with flame.

"What?" asked Nathan.

"That's what I couldn't remember. I cursed him, and this is what happened." His face looked haggard. "I didn't know what I was doing. I cursed him. I gave my sister a wish. I didn't know what happened to either of them." He turned and stared into Matt's eyes. "Until Matt." Then he smiled. It was a strange smile, not warm or welcoming; a pain smile.

Matt felt a chill. She remembered telling him that nothing he could do would make her hate him. He hadn't made her the same promise. She had brought him knowledge that hurt.

She met his gaze and held out her hand, and he took it. "Is it better to know?" she asked in a small voice.

He drew in breath, let it out. "Yes," he said. "How do we fix this?"

Everyone watched the war.

"Does it change at all?" asked Matt.

"Every time Suki speaks, the trees slow down," Edmund said.

"They do?" Suki said. "Father? Can you hear me?"

The trees slowed. The black and white boys had breathing room. They looked up and all around, but Mr. Backstrom's head didn't turn; his eyes didn't shift. Suki was out of range. After a moment, the trees whipped back into frenzied kill mode, and the boys fought and died.

"I don't know how to fix it," Matt said. "I only know how to watch it. You have to figure out what you want to happen next."

Edmund said, "Maybe if we could stop it, at least he'd be able to wake up. How did it change from the war into the water before?"

Someone knocked on the door. "Excuse me, Ms. Backstrom, what's going on in there?" asked the nurse's voice.

Nathan switched the visible war off. Edmund rose and opened the door wide. The nurse stood there, with Tess behind her. "We're just talking," Edmund said, "trying to bring him out of it."

"Tess said something about—rituals?"

"Sure," said Edmund. "We might burn a little incense, see if it helps. Other things have been tried, haven't they?"

The nurse glanced at Tess. Tess's face looked stormy.

Suki crossed her arms over her chest and stood. "I understand you care for my father," she said to Tess.

Mr. Backstrom turned his head and looked at Suki.

The nurse said, "Oh!"

Matt checked the war. All the trees had stopped moving. The boys, back to back, looked up.

"Keep talking," Matt said. "He's listening."

"We didn't come here to hurt him," Suki said. She stared into her father's eyes. "Or maybe I did, Father. I don't know. I wanted to beat you senseless. I wanted to kill you." Her eyes narrowed, and her cheeks flushed. Threads of gold spun up her neck. "No," she said, putting her hand on them to halt them before they ate her mood. "I'll feel this." The gold retreated. She stared at her father for a long moment. "This. Mustard. Carbonated. Rage." A vein pulsed in her pale forehead. "You kept me in a cage," she said in a harsh low voice, almost a whisper.

The war vanished from Richard Backstrom's thoughtscape, replaced by the image of the blonde baby suspended in midair, threads leading out to everywhere, his arms tied tight to his sides, his legs roped together, his scream without sound.

"And I got away, and put myself in another cage," Suki said. She stared into his eyes for a long moment. "Well," she said at last, "no more." One thread of gold shot up her neck and formed a perfect spiral across her cheek. The hand she held at her throat turned gold. She held her golden hand out and clenched it into a fist.

The sound of breaking glass shattered and shivered through the air. The nurse and Tess looked around. Matt did too. Such a vivid noise, but no glass on the floor, and the windows were still intact.

"You can't hurt me," Suki said in a cold, clear voice. "You can't touch me anymore."

The red jungle returned, but the plants were frozen in place. The boys stared into Suki's face. The black boy took a step toward her. "You don't understand, Fairy," Mr. Backstrom said in a rusty voice. "It's a jungle out there."

Tess and the nurse gasped.

"The jungle is in your head, Father. Not out here."

"The jungle is everywhere. If you don't fight it every minute, it grows over you and buries you. Turn your back, and it knocks you flat and burns you. Forget to listen for it, and it eats you alive. You never did understand, Fairy. I only wanted to keep you out of the jungle."

"What's the jungle doing now?" Suki asked.

The black boy looked behind him. The trees stood motionless. "It's waiting," Mr. Backstrom rumbled.

"Trees don't really want to hurt you," Edmund said gently. "Remember?"

Mr. Backstrom turned to look at him. "Trees kill me," he said in a flat voice. "No matter how hard I fight them. The forces of evil lie in wait. Hold still for a minute and they wrap you up and you can't move, and then they can do things to you and you can't stop them. You have to keep fighting or you lose control of everything."

Edmund went to him and placed two fingers on his forehead. "Please. Please let me help you now."

Sunlight shone down on the white boy. He grew taller. He grew up, turned into a man who looked like Edmund did now. The white man touched the black boy's shoulder, and the black boy turned.

"Will you let me help you? You've been fighting such a long time. Do you want to stop now?" Edmund asked, and the white man said the words with him.

"I want to stop. I want to rest."

"Take my hand."

Mr. Backstrom reached up and took Edmund's hand. The white man and the black boy gripped each other's hands. Sparkling light shone down on them. They stared into each other's eyes and leaned closer and closer together.

Then they melted into each other.

A gray man faced the forest, and it struck him down. He lay peacefully as the plants sliced him up. "I surrender," Edmund whispered. Mr. Backstrom breathed loud and hard, and then he relaxed. The gray man lay quiet as plant roots grew into and over him, and he bled green blood.

The red trees and bushes stained green, and bloomed, huge, lush vivid flowers, everywhere. Lavender, scarlet, orange, blue, passionflowers, hibiscus, orchids, geraniums. A stream came from the forest, dug itself a bed, flowed strong and fast.

A small blonde boy walked out of the woods and squatted

beside the stream. He stared into the water. A silver-blue fish leaped.

Mr. Backstrom cried out and slumped in the chair.

The day was cold and threatened rain. Matt retrieved her army jacket from the car and Suki got a jacket too before they went for a walk on the nursing home grounds, leaving Edmund and Tess to watch Mr. Backstrom sleep.

They sat on a concrete bench facing the river. Matt reached down into an outside pocket of her jacket and fished out a crumpled white bag with doughnut crumbs in it. She tossed the crumbs onto the asphalt path, and birds flew down immediately. Probably people fed them from this bench every day.

Suki, beside her, wore an elegant London Fog raincoat, shimmering gray with navy undertones. She slipped her stockinged feet out of her high-heeled shoes and wiggled her toes. "Is my boyfriend still inside you?" she asked presently.

Matt leaned back in her own head and left the body to Nathan. "I can't be your boyfriend, Susan, no matter how much I love you."

"Why not?" Suki looked toward the river instead of at Matt. Matt could see the side of her smile, though.

"I'm too young for you. I'm too old for you. I'm too short. I'm dead. I don't get out much. You need somebody you can grow old with, somebody you can touch. Somebody who can leave the house."

"Why?" she said.

He hesitated, then said, "Are you laughing at me?"

Suki turned and stared into Matt's eyes. "No."

"What is it you really want?" Nathan asked.

She watched the river for a couple minutes, then glanced back. "You know what mustard tastes like?"

"It's been a long time. I can't remember."

"Yesterday I tasted it. I've probably been eating it for years, but I never tasted it before. Yesterday . . . yesterday I got cold, and mad, and I whined about things, and I felt terrified, and irritated, and jealous. I've never really done those things before." She frowned and studied the river. "Maybe you love me because I don't do things like that. I'm not sure why you feel the way you feel about me."

"You accepted and understood me more than any of the others, and faster. Kinship."

"Neither of us could taste mustard," Suki said.

He thought about that. "You're growing away from me? Isn't that what I said to you?"

Suki gripped Matt's hand. "You say you love me now. Will you hate me if I change?"

"No."

"You promise?"

"I do."

She looked away. "Because you're the only one I trust to do what you say. You love me, and you don't try to control me, or make me be someone else, or feel some way I don't. You're old enough to know your own mind and whether it will change. *I'm* changing. I've been frozen a long time, but I started thawing yesterday, and it surprises me. Not all of it's pleasant. I feel *so* angry." She stared down at her hand. A gold spiral lay on her palm. She smiled down at it. "I can make those feelings go away with this gold stuff that Matt gave me," she said, showing him her hand, "but I think I need to find out what happens when I don't."

He touched her palm. Matt glanced at her own wrists. The last threads of her Ginny gold glinted in the clouded light. Not much left.

"You were amazing," Nathan said.

She smiled. "I felt amazing." She lost her smile. "I don't know if I can keep that up, though. Not without practice, anyway. Can I come see you?"

"Yes, oh yes. Any time. I've missed you."

"I've missed you," Suki whispered.

"Come soon," said Nathan.

Matt's last bit of gold vanished, and she felt Nathan leave her. She sighed.

Suki looked closely at her. "He's gone?"

Matt nodded and stared at her bare wrists. She had gotten used to having gold, to knowing she could reach out to Ginny if she needed to. She had liked owning the possibility of doing amazing things.

—You're not alone,— thought the bench they were sitting on.

Matt patted the bench and smiled.

Hands linked, they walked toward the nursing home a little later. "I don't know what Father will be like when he wakes up," Suki said. "I'm still scared."

"He can't hurt you now," Matt said.

"It's hard for me to believe that."

"We won't leave you alone with him."

—Matt?— said the path they were walking on.

—What?— She knelt and touched the ground.

—Better come now.— It was Edmund's voice in the concrete.

Matt rose and gripped Suki's hand. "We have to go back," she said. They ran; they were panting by the time they made it to the room.

Suki stroked her hand over her hair, straightened it so it fell back into perfect place before she knocked on the door of Room 118.

Tess opened the door. "He just this moment opened his eyes."

Mr. Backstrom lay on the bed under the yarn-sprigged quilt. Edmund sat in a folding metal chair beside the bed.

Suki squeezed Matt's hand, let go, and walked to the bed, leaving Matt and Tess to follow. She stared down at her father, and he rolled his head so that his eyes met hers. "You've grown," he said, his voice still creaky.

"You've been gone a long time."

He closed his eyes. "A moment. An endless nightmare moment."

Presently he lifted his eyelids again. "I seem to understand a lot of things I didn't know before." He glanced at Edmund. "You knocked me down."

"Yes."

"Put a curse on me."

Tess gasped.

"Yes."

"Took it off again."

"Yes."

"And I understand why. I understand why you did what you

did then, and why you did what you did now." He shook his head. "I don't ever want to make you mad at me again."

"I will never do that again."

"Listen, son," said Mr. Backstrom. "You don't want to tell a man like me a thing like that. You need me to stay scared."

"Do I?"

They stared into each other's eyes for a long moment, and finally Mr. Backstrom smiled. Then he laughed. Then he groaned. He put his hand on his forehead and said, "I am so confused."

Suki said, "Father?"

"Fairy."

"Do you know where you are?"

He dropped his hand and stared at the ceiling, thought for a moment, then recited, "I am in the Riverview Nursing Home in Salem, Oregon." He paused, then said in a different voice, "I'm in a nursing home? Oh, yes, I suppose that makes sense. Catatonic schizophrenia. Why not a mental hospital? Not a danger to self or others. Expensive place. Skilled care. Who arranged for this?" He glanced at Suki.

"I think Uncle Henry did."

"Ah. Given the circumstances, I imagine I have much to be grateful for."

"Richard," said Tess.

He looked at her.

"Do you know me?" she whispered.

"Tess," he said, and frowned. He gazed around the room, pausing at the postcards. "Tess. You gave me the moments that weren't nightmares. Thank you."

She gripped his hand. He frowned, but he didn't pull away

from her. After a moment his face smoothed. He glanced at Suki. "I need to sleep now," he said. "When I wake up, will you still be here?"

"No."

"Will you tell me where to find you?"

"No."

"If I leave a clear trail when I leave this place, will you someday come and find me again?"

She hesitated. At last she said, "Maybe. It depends on who you are now and who I might turn into. Maybe not. I don't know if I can forgive you."

"It's strange, but I understand that too." He stared at Edmund for a long, intense moment. "You. Keep in touch," he said.

"I will," Edmund said.

"Hi, House. I'm home!" Matt yelled as she crossed the threshold into the haunted house. If this were a fifties sitcom, a wife would come out and say supper was on the table, and maybe give her a kiss.

But that wasn't about to happen. Still, this time they had shopped before they came; Matt and Edmund had armloads of groceries. This time they'd be able to eat while they stayed here.

"Hi, Matt," said the house. "Welcome, Susan, Edmund."

Suki, carrying suitcase, laptop, and purse, said, "Hi, House. I'm home too."

"We've missed you."

Suki pressed a gold-plated palm to the wall, and all the furniture returned. She sighed and smiled. "I've missed you too." Then she looked around. "I wonder where Julio and Dee are. Do you know?" she asked Edmund.

"I haven't seen them since I left, and I left right after you left," he said.

"We're going to find them next," Matt said. She glanced at Edmund, and he looked surprised, but then he nodded. "Where's the kitchen? That's something I didn't see last time."

"This door." Nathan stood down the hall, half in shadow.

Suki dropped her luggage and walked to him. She held out her hand. Gold lifted from her palm and reached for him.

"Hey!" he cried, as gold turned to mist and flowed into his shape. "What are you—what is this—I feel strange!"

"Solid," Suki said. "Matt said gold could do solid." She leaned forward and hugged him.

After a moment, he hugged her back.

TELL THE WORLD THIS BOOK WAS

GOOD	BAD	SO-SO
✗ Great!		